RANGER'S APPRENTICE

BOOK FIVE: THE SORCERER OF THE NORTH

RANGER'S APPRENTICE

BOOK FIVE: THE SORCERER OF THE NORTH

JOHN FLANAGAN

PHILOMEL BOOKS

Copyright © 2008 by John Flanagan.
Published in Australia by Random House Australia Children's Books.
First American Edition published 2008 by
PHILOMEL BOOKS
A division of Penguin Young Readers Group. Published by The Penguin Group.
Penguin Group (USA) Inc., 375 Hudson Street, New York, NY 10014, U.S.A.
Penguin Group (Canada), 90 Eglinton Avenue East, Suite 700, Toronto, Ontario M4P 2Y3, Canada
(a division of Pearson Penguin Canada Inc.).
Penguin Books Ltd, 80 Strand, London WC2R 0RL, England.
Penguin Ireland, 25 St. Stephen's Green, Dublin 2, Ireland (a division of Penguin Books Ltd).
Penguin Group (Australia), 250 Camberwell Road, Camberwell, Victoria 3124, Australia
(a division of Pearson Australia Group Pty Ltd).
Penguin Books India Pvt Ltd, 11 Community Centre, Panchsheel Park, New Delhi - 110 017, India.
Penguin Group (NZ), 67 Apollo Drive, Rosedale, North Shore 0632, Auckland, New Zealand
(a division of Pearson New Zealand Ltd.)
Penguin Books (South Africa) (Pty) Ltd, 24 Sturdee Avenue, Rosebank, Johannesburg 2196, South Africa.
Penguin Books Ltd, Registered Offices: 80 Strand, London WC2R 0RL, England.

Published simultaneously in Canada. Printed in the United States of America.
Design by Marikka Tamura.
Text set in Adobe Jenson.
Library of Congress Cataloging-in-Publication Data is available upon request.
ISBN 978-0-399-25032-3
1 3 5 7 9 10 8 6 4 2

To Lyn Smith,
for your years of support
and encouragement.

1

IN THE NORTH, HE KNEW, THE EARLY WINTER GALES, DRIVING THE rain before them, would send the sea crashing against the shore, causing white clouds of spray to burst high into the air.

Here, in the southeastern corner of the kingdom, the only signs of approaching winter were the gentle puffs of steam that marked the breath of his two horses. The sky was clear blue, almost painfully so, and the sun was warm on his shoulders. He could have dozed off in the saddle, leaving Tug to pick his way along the road, but the years he had spent training and conditioning in a hard and unforgiving discipline would never allow such an indulgence.

Will's eyes moved constantly, searching left to right, right to left, close in and far ahead. An observer might never notice this constant movement—his head remained still. Again, that was his training: to see without being seen; to notice without being noticed. He knew this part of the kingdom was relatively untroubled. That was why he had been assigned to the Fief of Seacliff. After all, a brand-new, just-commissioned Ranger was hardly going to be handed one of the kingdom's trouble spots. He smiled idly at the thought. The prospect of taking up his first solo posting was daunting enough without having to worry about invasion or insurrection. He would be content to find his feet here in this peaceful backwater.

The smile died on Will's lips as his keen eyes saw something in the middle distance, almost concealed by the long grass beside the road.

His outward bearing gave no sign that he had noticed anything out of the ordinary. He didn't stiffen in his seat or rise in the stirrups to look more closely, as the majority of people might have done. On the contrary, he appeared to slouch a little more in the saddle as he rode—seemingly disinterested in the world around him. But his eyes, hidden in the deep shadow under the hood of his cloak, probed urgently. Something had moved, he was sure. And now, in the long grass to one side of the road, he thought he could see a trace of black and white—colors that were totally out of place in the fading greens and new russets of autumn.

Nor was he the only one to sense something out of place. Tug's ears twitched once and he tossed his head, shaking his mane and letting loose a rumbling neigh that Will felt in the barrel-like chest as much as heard.

"I see it," he said quietly, letting the horse know that the warning was registered. Reassured by Will's low voice, Tug quieted, though his ears were still pricked and alert. The packhorse, ambling contentedly beside and behind them, showed no interest. But it was a transport animal pure and simple, not a Ranger-trained horse like Tug.

The long grass shivered once more. It was only a faint movement but there was no wind to cause it—as the hanging clouds of steam from the horses' breath clearly showed. Will shrugged his shoulders slightly, ensuring that his quiver was clear. His massive longbow lay across his knees, ready strung. Rangers didn't travel with their bows slung across their shoulders. They carried them ready for instant use. Always.

His heart was beating slightly faster than normal. The movement in the grass was barely thirty meters away by now. He recalled Halt's teaching: *Don't concentrate on the obvious. They may want you to miss something else.*

He realized that his total attention had become focused on the long grass beside the road. Quickly, his eyes scanned left and right again, reaching out to the tree line some forty meters back from the road on either side. Perhaps there were men hiding in the shadows, ready to charge out while his attention was distracted by whatever it was that was lying in the grass at the road's edge. Robbers, outlaws, mercenaries, who knew?

But he could see no sign of men in the trees. He touched Tug with his knee and the horse stopped, the packhorse continuing a few paces before it followed suit. His right hand went unerringly to the quiver, selected an arrow and laid it on the bowstring in less than a second. He shrugged back the hood so that his head was bare. The longbow, the small shaggy horse and the distinctive gray and green mottled cloak would identify him as a Ranger to any observer, he knew.

"Who's there?" he called, raising the bow slightly, the arrow nocked and ready. He didn't draw back yet. If there was anyone skulking in the grass, they'd know that a Ranger could draw, fire and hit his mark before they had gone two paces.

No answer. Tug stood still, trained to be rock steady in case his master had to shoot.

"Show yourself," Will called. "You in the black and white. Show yourself."

The stray thought crossed his mind that only a few moments ago he had been daydreaming about this being a peaceful backwater. Now he was facing a possible ambush by an unknown enemy.

"Last chance," he called. "Show yourself or I'll send an arrow in your direction."

And then he heard it, possibly in response to his voice. A low whimpering sound: the sound of a dog in pain. Tug heard it too. His ears flicked back and forth and he snorted uncertainly.

A dog? Will thought. A wild dog, perhaps, lying in wait to attack? He discarded the idea almost as soon as it formed in his mind. A wild dog wouldn't have made any sound to warn him. Besides, the sound he had heard had been one of pain, not a snarl or a warning growl of anger. It had been a whimper. He came to a decision.

In one fluid movement, he removed his left foot from the stirrup, crossed his right leg over the saddle pommel and dropped lightly to the ground. Dismounting in that fashion, he remained at all times facing the direction of possible danger, with both hands free to shoot. Had the need arisen, he could have loosed his first shot as soon as his feet touched the ground.

Tug snorted again. In moments of uncertainty like this, Tug preferred to have Will safely in the saddle, where the little horse's quick reflexes and nimble feet could take him quickly out of danger.

"It's all right," Will told the horse briefly, and walked quietly forward, bow at the ready.

Ten meters. Eight. Five . . . he could see the black and white clearly now through the dry grass. And now, as he was closer, he saw something else in the black and white: the matted brown of dried blood and the rich red of fresh blood. The whimper came again and finally Will saw clearly what it was that had stopped them.

He turned and gave the "safe" hand signal to Tug, and the horse responded by trotting forward to join him. Then, setting the bow aside, Will knelt beside the wounded dog lying in the grass.

"What is it, boy?" he said gently. The dog turned its head at the sound of the voice, then whimpered again as Will touched it gently, his eyes running over the long, bleeding gash in its side, stretching from behind the right shoulder back to the rear haunch. As the animal moved, more fresh blood welled out of the wound. Will could see one eye as the dog lay, apparently exhausted, on its side. It was filled with pain.

It was a border shepherd, he realized, one of the sheepdogs bred in the northern border region, and known for their intelligence and loyalty. The body was black, with a pure white ruff at the throat and chest and a white tip to the bushy tail. The legs were white and the black fur repeated again at the dog's head, as if a cowl had been placed over it, so that the ears were black, while a white blaze ran up the muzzle and between the eyes.

The gash in the dog's side didn't appear to be too deep and the chances were that the ribcage had protected the dog's vital organs. But it was fearfully long and the wide-gaping edges were even, as if they had been cut by a blade. And it had bled a lot. That, he realized, would be the biggest problem. The dog was weak. It had lost a lot of blood. Perhaps too much.

Will rose and moved to his saddlebags, untying the medical kit that all Rangers carried. Tug eyed him curiously, satisfied now that the dog represented no threat. Will shrugged and gestured to the medical kit.

"It works for people," he said. "It should be all right for a dog."

He returned to the injured animal, touching its head softly. The dog tried to raise its head but he gently held it down, crooning encouraging words to it as he opened the medical pack with his free hand.

"Now let's take a look at what they've done to you, boy," he said.

The fur around the wound was matted with blood and he cleaned it as best he could with water from his canteen. Then he opened a small container and carefully smeared the paste it contained along the edges of the gash. The salve was a painkiller that would numb the wound so that he could clean it and bandage it without causing more pain to the dog.

He allowed a few minutes for the salve to take effect, then began applying an herbal preparation that would prevent infection from setting in and help the wound heal. The painkiller was working well and his ministrations seemed to be causing no problem for the dog, so he used it liberally. As he worked, he saw that he had misnamed the dog by calling it "boy." It was a female.

The border shepherd, sensing that Will was helping, lay still. Occasionally, she whimpered again. But not in pain. The sound was more a sound of gratitude. Will sat back on his haunches, head to one side as he surveyed the now cleaned injury. Fresh blood still seeped from the gash and he knew he would have to close it. Bandaging was hardly practical, however, with the thick fur of the dog and the awkward position of the gash. He shrugged, realizing that he would have to stitch it.

"Might as well get on with it while the salve's still working," he told the animal. She lay with her head on the ground, but one eye swiveled around to watch him as he worked.

The shepherd obviously felt the sensation of the needle as he quickly put in a dozen stitches of fine silk thread and drew the lips of the wound together. But there seemed to be no pain and, after an initial flinching reaction, she lay still and allowed him to continue.

Finished, Will rested one hand gently on the black-and-white head, feeling the softness of the thick fur. He had done his job well but it was obvious that the dog would be unable to walk.

"Stay here," he said softly. "Stay."

The dog lay obediently as he moved to the packhorse and began rearranging its load.

There were two long satchels, holding books and personal effects, on either side of the packsaddle. They left a depression between them and he found a spare cloak and several blankets to line the space until he had a soft, comfortable nest in which the dog could lie—with enough space for her to move a little, but snug enough to hold her securely in place.

Crossing back to where she lay, he slid his arms under the warm body and gently lifted her, talking all the time in a low crooning voice. The salve was effective but it didn't last long and he knew she would be hurting again soon. The dog whimpered once, then held her peace as he lifted her into position in the space he had prepared. Again, he fondled her head, scratching the ears gently. She moved her head slightly to lick his hand. The small movement seemed to exhaust her. He noted with interest that her eyes were two different colors. Till this moment, he had seen only the left eye, the brown one, as the dog lay on her side. Now, as he moved her, he could see that the right eye was blue. It gave her a raffish, mischievous look, he thought, even in her current low condition.

"Good girl," he told her. Then, as he turned back to Tug, he realized that the little horse was eyeing him curiously.

"We've got a dog," he said. Tug shook his head and snorted, *Why?*

2

EARLY IN THE AFTERNOON THEY REACHED THE SEA AND WILL
knew he was near the end of his journey. Castle Seacliff was set on
a large, leaf-shaped island, separated from the mainland by a hundred meters of deep water. At low tide a narrow causeway allowed
access to the island, but at high tide, as it was now, a ferry provided
transport across. The difficult access had helped keep Seacliff secure
for many years and was one of the reasons why the fief had become
something of a backwater. In earlier times, of course, the raiding
Skandians in their wolfships had made things quite lively. But it had
been some years now since the sea wolves from the north had raided
the coast of Araluen.

The island was perhaps twelve kilometers in length and eight
across, and Will could not yet see the castle itself. He assumed it
would be set somewhere in the high ground toward the middle—
that was basic strategic thinking. For the moment, however, it was
hidden from sight.

Will had debated stopping for a meal at noon, but now, so close
to the end of his journey, he decided to press on. There would be an
inn of some kind in the village that would huddle close to the castle

walls. Or he might find a meal in the castle kitchens. He tugged the lead rein to bring the packhorse alongside and leaned over to inspect the wounded dog. Her eyes were closed and her nose rested on her front paws. He could see the black sides moving in and out as she breathed. There was a little more blood around the lips of the wound but the main flow had been stanched. Satisfied that she was comfortable, Will touched a heel to Tug's side and they moved on down to the ferry, a large, flat-bottomed punt that was drawn up on the beach.

The operator, a heavily muscled man of about forty, was sprawled on the deck of his craft, sleeping in the warm autumn sunshine. He awoke, however, as some sixth sense registered the slight jingle of harness from the two horses. He sat up, rubbed his eyes, then came quickly to his feet.

"I need to get across to the island," Will told him, and the man saluted clumsily.

"Yes indeed, sir. Of course. At your service, Ranger."

There was a hint of nervousness in his voice. Will sighed inwardly. He was still unused to the thought that people were wary of Rangers—even one as fresh-faced as he was. He was a naturally friendly young man and he often longed for easy companionship with other people. But that was not the Rangers' way. It served their purpose to remain aloof from ordinary people. There was an air of mystery about the Ranger Corps. Their legendary skill with their weapons, their ability to move about unseen and the secretive nature of their organization all added to their mystique.

The boatman heaved on the thick cable that ran from the mainland to the island, passing through large pulleys set at either end of the punt. The punt, afloat at one end, moved easily from the beach until it rested wholly in the water. Will guessed that the pulley arrangements gave the operator a mechanical advantage that allowed him to move the large craft so easily.

There was a tariff board nailed to the railing and the operator saw him study it.

"No charge for a Ranger, sir. Free passage for you."

Will shook his head. Halt had impressed on him the need to pay his way. *Be beholden to no one,* he had said. *Make sure you owe nobody any favors.*

He calculated quickly. Half a royal per person, and the same for each horse. Plus four pennigs for other animals. Close enough to two royals all told. He swung down from the saddle, took a gold three-royal piece from his purse and handed it to the man.

"I'll pay," he said. "Two royals is close enough." The man looked at the coin, then looked at the rider and the two horses, puzzled. Will jerked his head toward the packhorse.

"There's another animal on the packhorse," he explained. The ferry operator nodded, and handed him a silver one-royal piece in change.

"Right enough, sir," he said. He glanced curiously at the packhorse as Will led it onto the punt, taking in the dog in its snug retreat.

"Good-looking dog, that 'un," he said. "He's yours, is he?"

"I found her injured by the road," Will said. "Someone had cut her with a blade of some sort and left her to die."

The boatman rubbed his stubbly chin thoughtfully. "John Buttle has a shepherd like that one. And he'd be the kind to injure a dog and leave it that way. Has a nasty temper, John does, particularly when he's in his drink."

"And what does this John Buttle do?" Will asked.

The boatman shrugged. "He's a herder by trade. But he does

most things. Some say he does his real work at nights along the roads, looking for travelers who are about after dark. But no one's proved it. He's a might too handy with that spear of his for my liking. He's a good man to stay away from."

Will glanced at the packhorse again, thinking of the cruel gash in the dog's side.

"If Buttle's the one who hurt that dog, he'll do well to stay away from me," he said coldly.

The boatman studied him for a moment. The face was young and well-featured. But there was a hard light in the eyes, he saw. He realized that with Rangers, it never did to assume too much. This pleasant-looking lad wouldn't be wearing the Ranger gray and green if he didn't have steel in him. Rangers were deceptive folk and that was a fact. There were even some who held that they were skilled in the black arts of magic and sorcery and the boatman wasn't altogether sure that those people didn't have the right of it. Surreptitiously making a sign to ward off evil, he moved to the front of the punt, glad for an excuse to break off the conversation.

"Best be getting us across then," he said. Will sensed the change in atmosphere. He glanced at Tug and raised his eyebrows. The horse didn't deign to notice.

As the boatman heaved again on the thick hawser, the punt slid across the water toward the island, small waves burbling under the blunt prow and slapping against the low timber sides. Will noticed that the ferry operator's home, a small planked hut with a thatched roof, was on the island side—presumably as a security measure. The prow of the ferry soon grated into the island's coarse sand, the current slewing it sideways a little as the forward progress stopped. The operator unhitched the single rope rail across the front and gestured for Will to disembark. Will swung up astride Tug and the horses' hooves clopped on the planks as they stepped carefully forward.

"Thank you," he said as Tug stepped off onto the beach. The ferry operator saluted again.

"At your service, Ranger," he said. He watched the slim, erect figure as he rode into the trees and was lost from sight.

It took another half hour to reach the castle. The road wound upward toward the center of the island, through well-spaced, wind-swept trees. There was plenty of light, unlike in the thick forests around Castle Redmont, or the dark pine forests of Skandia that Will remembered all too well.

The leaves had turned, but so far most of them remained on the branches. All in all, it was pleasant country. As he rode, Will saw plenty of evidence of game—rabbits, of course, and wild turkey. Once he caught a quick flash of white when a deer showed him its hindquarters as it bounded away. Poaching would probably be rife here, he thought. Will had a basic sympathy for the villagers who sought occasionally to augment their diet with venison or game birds. Fortunately, poaching was a matter of local law and would be policed by the baron's gamekeepers. As a matter of policy, though, Will would need to discover the identities of the local professionals. Poachers could be a prime source of information about goings-on. And information was a Ranger's stock-in-trade.

The trees eventually thinned and he rode out into the sunlight again. The winding uphill road had brought him to a natural plateau, a wide plain perhaps a kilometer across. In the center of the plain stood Castle Seacliff and its dependent village—a huddle of thatched cottages set close to the castle walls.

The castle itself, to one used to the impressive mass of Castle

Redmont or the soaring beauty of the King's Castle Araluen, was something of a disappointment. It was little more than a fort, Will realized, with the surrounding walls barely topping five meters in height. As he looked more closely, he could see that at least one section of the wall was constructed from timber—large tree trunks set vertically into the ground and bound together with iron brackets. It was an effective enough barrier, he thought, but it lacked the dramatic impact of Redmont's massive ironstone walls. Yet there were solidly buttressed towers at each corner and a central keep, which would provide a haven of last resort in the event of an attack. Over the keep, he could see the stag's head banner of Baron Ergell as it stirred on the light afternoon sea breeze.

"We're here," he told Tug, and the horse shook its mane as it heard his voice.

He had reined in at the first sight of the castle. Now he touched Tug's side with his heels and they started forward again. As ever, the packhorse moved off a little more slowly, dragging momentarily on the lead rope as they made their way through the open farm fields toward the castle. There was a smell of smoke in the air. The corn stooks had been bundled up and burned after the harvest was brought in and they were still smoldering. In a week or two the farmers would plow the ashes back into the fields and the sequence would begin once more. The smell of smoke, the bare fields and the low-angled autumn afternoon sunlight all evoked memories in Will. Memories of growing up. Of harvests and harvest festivals. Of hazy summers, smoky autumns and snow-covered winters. And, in the last six years, of the deep affection that had grown between him and his mentor, the deceptively grim-faced Ranger called Halt.

There were a few workers in the fields and they stopped to stare at the cloaked figure as he rode toward the castle. He nodded to one or two of those who were closest to him and they nodded back, cautiously, raising their hands in salute. Simple farm people didn't understand Rangers and as a result, they didn't wholly trust them either. Of course, Will knew, in times of war or danger, they would look to the Rangers for help and protection and leadership. But now, with no threatening danger, they would keep their distance from him.

The occupants of the castle would be a different matter. Baron Ergell and his Battlemaster—Will searched for the name for a few seconds, then recalled it was Norris—understood the role of the Ranger Corps and the value that its members brought to the kingdom's fifty fiefs. They didn't fear Rangers, but that didn't mean he would enjoy a close relationship with them either. Theirs would be a working partnership.

Remember, Halt had told him, *our task is to assist the barons but our first loyalty is to the King. We are the direct representatives of the King's will and sometimes that may not exactly coincide with local interests. We cooperate with the barons and we advise them. But we maintain our independence from them. Don't allow yourself to become indebted to your baron, or to become too close to the people of the castle.*

Of course, in a fief like Redmont, where Will had done his training, things were slightly different. Baron Arald, the Lord of Redmont, was a member of the King's inner council. That allowed for a closer relationship between the Baron, his officers and Halt, the Ranger assigned to his fief. But in general, a Ranger's life was a solitary one.

There were compensations, of course. Chief among them was the camaraderie that existed between members of the Corps itself. There were fifty Rangers on active service, one for each fief in the kingdom, and they all knew each other by name. Indeed, Will was well acquainted with the man he was replacing at Seacliff. Bartell had been one of his examiners for his annual assessments as an apprentice, and it was his decision to retire that had led to Will's being presented with his Silver Oakleaf, the symbol of a full-fledged Ranger. Bartell, getting on in years and unable to face the rigors of Ranger life—hard riding, sleeping rough and constant vigilance— had traded his own Silver Oakleaf for the gold of retirement. He had been reassigned to the Corps headquarters at Castle Araluen, where he was working in the archives section, compiling the history of the Corps.

Will smiled briefly. He had grown to like Bartell, a well-read and amazingly knowledgeable man, in spite of the fact that their first few meetings had been occasions of distinct discomfort for Will. Bartell had been expert at devising tests for the apprentice that were calculated to make the young man's life miserable. Will had since come to value the tough questions and difficult problems that Bartell had posed for him. They had all helped prepare him for the difficult life of a Ranger.

That life itself was the other chief compensation for the solitary nature of the Ranger's day-to-day existence. There was a deep satisfaction and an irresistible allure to being part of an elite band that knew the inner workings and the political secrets of the whole kingdom. Ranger apprentices were recruited for their physical skills— coordination, nimbleness, speed of hand and eye—but even more so for their natural curiosity. A Ranger sought always to know more, to ask more and to find out more about what went on around him. As a youngster, before Halt had recruited him, that restless curiosity, and the precociousness that stemmed from it, had caused Will more than his share of troubles.

He was entering the small village now and more people were

observing him. Most of them wouldn't make eye contact, and the few who did dropped their gaze when he nodded to them—pleasantly enough, he thought. They saluted, with a clumsy movement of hand to brow, and moved aside to let him pass—quite needlessly, in fact, as there was plenty of room in the broad village street. He made out the symbols for the usual trades that could be found in any village: blacksmith, carpenter, cobbler.

At the end of the single street was a larger building. It was the only two-story structure in the village and it had a wide verandah at the front and the symbol of a tankard hanging above the door. The inn, he realized. It looked clean and well kept, the shutters of the upstairs bedroom windows freshly painted and the mud walls white-washed. As he watched, one of the upstairs windows opened and a girl's head appeared at the opening. She looked to be about nineteen or twenty, with dark, close-cropped hair and wide-set green eyes. She had a clear complexion and was remarkably pretty. What was more, alone among the people of the village, she continued to meet his gaze as he looked at her. In fact, she went so far as to smile at him and, when she did, the face transformed from pretty to breathtaking.

Will, unsettled by the reluctance of people to meet his gaze, was even more unsettled now by the girl's undisguised interest in him. *So you're the new Ranger,* he imagined her thinking. *You look awfully young for the job, don't you?*

As he rode under the window, he realized uncomfortably that as he had raised his head to watch her, his mouth had gaped a little. He snapped it shut and nodded at the girl, stern and unsmiling. Her grin grew wider and it was he who broke the eye contact first.

He had planned to stop for a quick meal at the inn but the dis-concerting presence of the girl made him change his mind. He re-called the written directions he had been given. His own cabin would be some three hundred meters beyond the village, on the road to the castle and sheltered by a small grove of trees. He could see the grove now and he touched his heels to Tug's side, letting the little horse break into a trot as they left the village behind. He could sense twenty or thirty pairs of eyes boring curiously into his back as he rode. He wondered if the green eyes from the upper room of the inn were among them, then shrugged the thought aside.

The cabin was a typical Ranger's house, built of logs with large flat river stones for roofing. There was a small verandah at the front of the house and a stable and saddling yard behind it. It nestled under the trees, and he was surprised to see a curl of smoke from the chimney at one end of the building.

He swung down from Tug's saddle, a little stiff after a day's riding. There was no need to tether Tug but he looped the packhorse's reins around one of the verandah posts. He checked the dog, saw that she was asleep and decided she could stay where she was for a few minutes more.

If there had been any doubts that this was to be his house, they were dispelled by the carved outline of an oakleaf in the lintel over the door. He stood for a moment, scratching Tug's ears as the horse nuzzled gently against him.

"Well, boy," he said, "looks like we're home."

3

WILL PUSHED OPEN THE DOOR AND WENT INSIDE THE CABIN. IT was virtually identical to the one that had been his home for much of the last few years. The room he entered took up about half the interior space and served as a combined sitting and dining area. There was a pine table with four plain chairs to his left, against a window, and two comfortable-looking wooden armchairs and a two-place settle at the opposite end, grouped around the cheerful fire crackling in the grate. He looked around the room, wondering who had laid the fire.

The kitchen was a small room adjoining the dining area. Copper pots and pans, obviously freshly cleaned and polished, hung on the wall beside the small wood-fueled cooking range. There were fresh wildflowers in a small vase under the window—the last of the season, he thought. The homey touch reminded him once more of Halt, and the thought brought a lump of loneliness to Will's throat. The grim-faced Ranger had always contrived to have flowers in his cabin whenever possible.

Will moved to inspect the two small bedrooms—simply furnished and opening off the living area. As he expected, there was nobody in those rooms either. He had exhausted all possibilities in the little cabin—unless the person who had laid the fire and arranged the flowers was hiding in the stables at the back, which he doubted.

The cabin had been cleaned recently, he realized. Bartell had been gone a month or more, yet when he ran his finger along the top of the fireplace mantel there was not a trace of dust. And the stone flagging in front of the grate had been recently swept as well. There was no sign of ash or debris from a fire.

"Obviously we have a friendly spirit living nearby," he said to himself. Then, remembering the animals waiting patiently outside, he moved to the door again. He glanced at the sun's position and estimated there was still over an hour of daylight left. Time to unpack before he made his presence known at the castle.

The dog was awake when he looked at her, her varicolored eyes showing keen interest in the world around her. That was a good thing, he realized. It was an indication of a strong will to live that would stand her in good stead in her current weakened condition. He gently lifted her from her nest on the packhorse and carried her inside the house. She lay relatively contentedly on the flagstones close to the fire, soaking up the warmth into her black coat. Returning to the packhorse, Will dug out an old horse blanket and took it back in to arrange a softer bed for the dog. When he laid it out for her, she rose painfully and limped the few steps to lie on it, settling herself with a grateful sigh. He fetched a bowl of water from the pump that had been built into the kitchen bench—no need to draw water from an outside well here, he realized—and left it beside her. The thick tail thumped softly on the floor once or twice in recognition of his care.

Satisfied, Will went back to the horses. He loosened the girth on Tug's saddle. There was no point unsaddling yet as he still needed to make his official call at the castle. Then he began to unload the small pile of personal belongings that he had brought with him.

That done, he unsaddled the packhorse and led it to the stable, where he rubbed it down and put it in one of the two stalls. He noticed that the manger in the stall was filled with fresh hay and the water bucket was filled too. He inspected the water. No sign of dust on the surface. No trace of green in the bucket. He hefted the bucket from the other stall and took it outside to Tug, letting his horse drink his fill. Tug shook his mane in gratitude.

Will began to organize his belongings in the cabin. There were hanging pegs beside the door for his bow and quiver. He set his bedroll on the bed in the larger of the two bedrooms and hung his spare clothes in the curtained-off closet there as well. His mandola case and a small satchel of books went on a sideboard in the living room.

Will glanced around. In truth, he'd brought little enough with him, but at least now the cabin had a trace of personality to it—as if it belonged to someone. His thoughts were interrupted by a warning neigh from Tug, outside. Simultaneously, the dog by the fire raised her head, turning painfully to look toward the door. Will spoke calmingly to her. Tug's call had not been a danger alert, merely a notification that someone was approaching. A second or so later, Will heard a light footstep on the verandah and a woman's figure was framed in the open doorway. She hesitated and tapped on the door frame.

"Come in," Will said, and she stepped into the room, smiling hesitantly, as if unsure of her welcome. As she moved away from the backlight, he could make her out more clearly. She was around forty years old, obviously one of the women from the village by her dress—a simple woolen garment, without the sort of embellishment favored by the more wealthy inhabitants who would live in the castle, and overlaid by a clean white apron. She was tall and quite well built, with a rounded, motherly figure. The dark hair was close cropped and beginning to show streaks of gray. Her smile was warm and genuine. There was something about her that was familiar, thought Will, but he couldn't quite place what it was.

"Can I help you?" he asked.

She made a perfunctory curtsy. "My name is Edwina, sir. I brought you this."

"This" was a small covered pot, and as she removed the cover Will was conscious of a delicious aroma filling the room—a stew of meat and vegetables. His mouth watered. Yet, mindful of Halt's warnings, he contrived to keep his face stern and uninterested.

"I see," he said noncommittally. Edwina set the pot down on the table and reached into her apron to produce an envelope, which she held out to him.

"This stew will heat up nicely later for your supper, sir," she said. "I suppose you'll be needing to see Baron Ergell first, though?"

"Possibly," Will replied, not sure whether he should discuss his planned movements with this woman. He realized she was holding the envelope out to him and he took it from her. He was surprised to see that the seal was an oakleaf imprint, accompanied by characters from the coded numbering system that were the equivalent to 26—Bartell's number in the Corps, he remembered.

"Ranger Bartell left it for whoever would be sent to replace him," she told him, gesturing for him to open the letter. "I kept the house and did cooking for him while he was here."

Realization dawned on Will as he opened the letter. At the time of writing, Bartell had no idea who would be replacing him, so it was headed simply "Ranger." Briefly, he scanned the message.

Edwina Temple is a thoroughly trustworthy and reliable woman who has worked for me over the past eight years. I can recommend her highly to whoever replaces me. She is discreet, sober and an excellent cook and house-keeper. Edwina and her husband, Clive, run the village inn in Seacliff. You would do me and yourself a favor by retaining her services when you take over. Bartell, Ranger 26.

Will looked up from the letter and smiled at the woman. The prospect of having the cooking and cleaning done for him was a welcome one, he realized. Then he hesitated. There was the question of payment, and he had no idea how much that might be.

"Well, Edwina," he began, "Bartell speaks very highly of you."

The woman made a curtsy again. "We got on well, sir. Ranger Bartell was a true gentleman. Served him for eight years, I did."

"Yes . . . well . . ."

The woman, seeing his obvious youth and guessing that this was his first posting, added carefully, "As to payment, sir, there's no need for you to concern yourself. Payment comes from the castle."

Will frowned. He wasn't sure that he should allow the castle to pay for his upkeep. He had his own stipend from the Ranger Corps. Edwina sensed the reason for his uncertainty and continued quickly.

"It's all right, sir. Ranger Bartell told me that the castle has the responsibility for providing accommodation and provisions to the Ranger on duty. My services are covered by that arrangement."

It was true, he realized. The castle in a fief did have the Ranger's services as one of its expenses and the costs were deducted from the tax assessment made by the crown each year. He smiled at her, finally reaching a decision.

"In that case, I'll be glad to avail myself of your services, Edwina," he said. "I assume you're the one who kept the house clean and lit the fire earlier?"

She nodded. "We've been expecting you this past week, sir," she said. "I've come by each day to keep things tidy—and the fire stops things from getting damp at this time of year."

Will nodded his appreciation. "Well, I'm grateful. My name is Will, by the way."

"Welcome to Seacliff, Ranger Will," she said, smiling at him. "My daughter Delia saw you riding through the town. Very stern you looked, she said. Very much the Ranger."

Will made the connection at that point. He'd felt that the woman was somehow familiar. Now he saw those eyes, green like her daughter's, and the smile, so wide and welcoming. "I think I saw her," he said.

Edwina, the question of her continuing employment settled, was looking with interest at his few belongings. Her eye settled on the mandola on the sideboard.

"You play the lute, then, do you?" she asked. Will shook his head.

"A lute has ten strings," he explained. "This is a mandola—sort of a large mandolin with eight strings, tuned in pairs." He saw the blank look that overcame most people when he tried to explain the difference between a lute and the mandola and gave up. "I play a little," he finished.

The dog, still asleep, chose that moment to let out a long sigh.

Edwina noticed her for the first time and moved over for a closer look. "And you've a dog, I see, as well."

"She's hurt," Will told her. "I found her on the road."

Edwina stooped and laid a gentle hand on the dog's head. The dog's eyes opened and looked at her. The tail stirred slightly.

"Good dogs, these border shepherds," she said, and Will nodded.

"Some say they're the most intelligent of dogs," he said.

"You'll need a good name for a fine dog like her," the woman said, and Will frowned thoughtfully.

"The ferry master told me she might have belonged to a man named Buttle. Do you know him?"

The woman's face darkened instantly at the name. "I know of him," she said. "Most folks know of him around here—and most would rather not. He's a bad man to have around is John Buttle. Were this his dog I'd be in no hurry to hand her back."

Will smiled at her. "I'm not," he said. "But I'm beginning to think I should make this man's acquaintance."

Before she could help herself, Edwina replied, "You'd be best to stay away from that one, sir." Then she covered her mouth in consternation. It was the lad's youth that had led her to say it, awakening her maternal instincts. But she realized she was talking to a Ranger and they were a breed who needed no advice from housekeepers on the subject of who to stay away from. Will, understanding the reasoning, smiled at her.

"I'll be careful," he told her. "But it seems that it's time someone spoke seriously to this person. Now," he said, closing the subject of Buttle, "there are other people I should be talking to first—Baron Ergell chief among them."

He ushered Edwina out, glancing once at the dog to make sure she would be all right in his absence. After taking his bow and quiver from their pegs, he closed the door softly. Edwina watched him as he tightened the saddle girth before remounting Tug. More used to being around Rangers than most people, she liked what she saw in this one. Then, as he swung the gray and green cloak around his shoulders and pulled the cowl over his head, she saw him change from a cheerful, outgoing young man into a grim and anonymous figure. She noted the massive longbow held easily in his left hand as he swung into the saddle, saw the feathered ends of his arrows protruding from the quiver. A Ranger carries the lives of two dozen men with him, the old saying went. Edwina thought then that John Buttle might need to watch his step around this one.

4

BARON ERGELL'S CHAMBERLAIN USHERED WILL INTO THE Baron's study with a gesture that was halfway between a bow and a flourish. "The new Ranger, my lord," he announced, as if he had personally produced him for the Baron's pleasure, "Will Treaty."

Ergell rose from behind the massive desk that was the dominant piece of furniture in the room. He was an exceptionally tall and thin man and for a moment, seeing the long, pale hair and the black clothes, Will had the shocking sensation that he was looking at a reincarnation of the evil Lord Morgarath, who had threatened the peace of the kingdom during Will's youth. Then he realized that the hair was gray, not dead white as Morgarath's had been, and Ergell, although tall, stood nowhere near Morgarath's height. The moment passed and Will realized he was staring at the Baron, who stood waiting with his hand outstretched to greet him. Hastily, Will moved forward.

"Good afternoon, my lord," he said. Ergell pumped his hand eagerly. He was aged around sixty but still moved easily. Will handed him the parchment containing his official orders of appointment. By rights, the guard at the drawbridge should have taken it and had it delivered to Ergell for inspection before allowing Will access to the keep. But the sergeant in charge had simply looked at the Ranger's cloak and longbow and waved him inside. Slack, Will thought. Decidedly slack.

"Welcome to Seacliff, Ranger Treaty," the Baron said. "It's a privilege to have one so distinguished in our service."

Will frowned slightly. Rangers didn't serve the Barons they were attached to and Ergell should know that. Perhaps, he thought, the Baron was trying to assume authority by the simple expedient of implying that it existed.

"We all serve the King, sir," he replied evenly, and the slight shadow that flickered across Ergell's face told him his suspicion was correct. Ergell, seeing a Ranger so young, may well have been trying it on, as Halt would have put it.

"Of course, of course," the Baron replied quickly, then indicated the heavyset man standing to one side of his desk.

"Ranger Treaty, this is Seacliff's Battlemaster, Sir Norris of Rook."

Will put Norris's age at about forty, which was pretty much the average for Battlemasters. Much younger and a man didn't have the necessary experience to lead a fief's troop of knights and men-at-arms into battle. Too many years older and he was beginning to lose the physical strength necessary for the task.

"Sir Norris," he said briefly in greeting. The knight's handshake was firm, which hardly came as a surprise. Men who had spent the greater part of their lives wielding sword or battleax usually ended up with powerful muscles in the hand and arms. He sensed the Battlemaster studying him as they shook hands, saw the quick scrutiny that took in his youth and slight build.

There was something else, Will fancied—a hint of satisfaction at what the knight saw. Perhaps, after years of dealing with the knowledgeable and experienced Bartell, Norris could foresee a slightly easier time with this new, freshly commissioned Ranger. Will felt a slight pang of disappointment at the thought. Halt and Crowley, the Corps Commandant, had warned him that some fiefs saw their relationship with Rangers as antagonistic.

Too many of them see it as an "us and them" situation, Crowley had said when he briefed Will for the posting. *After all, it is part of our task to keep tabs on them, to assess their battle readiness and their level of skill and training. Some Barons and Battlemasters don't like that. They like to believe they're running their own race and they don't care to have Rangers watching over their shoulders.*

That had never been the way at Castle Redmont, Will knew. But then Halt and Arald had an excellent relationship and a deep level of mutual respect. He filed the thought away as he made polite small talk in reply to Norris's and Ergell's questions as to his trip.

Ergell, he realized, was inviting him to dine with them in the castle. Will smiled politely as he offered his apologies. "Perhaps later in the week, my lord. It's not fair for me to disrupt your household. After all, you had no way of knowing that I would arrive today and I'm sure you had already finalized plans for the evening."

"Of course, of course. Later in the week, when you're settled in," the Baron agreed. He was a likeable enough person, Will felt, in spite of his attempt to subtly undercut Will's authority. His smile was warm and welcoming. "Perhaps we can send something from our kitchens for you later on?"

"No need for that, my lord. The woman Edwina has already left me a very creditable beef stew. From the aroma of it, I'll be more than satisfied for the evening."

Ergell smiled in reply. "She's a fine cook, that's the truth," he said. "I've tried to tempt her to work for us here in the castle but to no avail, I'm afraid."

Norris took a seat on one of the long benches that flanked the desk. "You've moved into Bartell's cottage then?"

Will nodded. "Yes, Battlemaster. It seems comfortable enough."

Ergell gave a short bark of laughter. "With Edwina's cooking laid on, I should think so," he agreed. But Norris was shaking his head.

"Far more efficient for you to move in here at the castle," he said. "The Baron can let you have your own suite of rooms—a lot more comfortable than a rickety cabin in the woods. And you'd be closer at hand if we needed you."

Will smiled, recognizing the ploy behind the innocent suggestion. By moving into the castle, he would be taking the first step toward a subtle shift in control. It mightn't happen immediately, but relinquishing his independence would be the thin end of the wedge. Also, the statement that he would be closer to hand *if they needed him* held an unspoken implication that he was at the castle's beck and call. He was aware that Ergell was watching him closely, waiting for his response.

"The cabin is fine, thank you, Battlemaster," he said. "And it is traditional for Rangers to have their quarters apart from the castle."

"Well, yes, traditional," said Norris dismissively. "Sometimes I think we give too much importance to things that are 'traditional.'"

Ergell laughed again, breaking the slightly awkward silence that followed Norris's words. "Come now, Norris, we all know how the Rangers value tradition. Just remember," he added to Will, "the offer stands. If that cabin grows too cold and drafty in the dead of winter, you'll always have a suite of rooms available here in the keep."

His quick glance told the Battlemaster that the subject was not to be pursued further. To his credit, Norris shrugged and complied. Will couldn't really blame them for trying to influence him. He could imagine how galling it might be to have someone quietly standing by, day in, day out, watching over your shoulder as you went about your work, submitting reports to the King on your abilities and activities. Particularly when that someone was as inexperienced as he was. At least, it seemed, he had managed to refuse their advances without causing offense.

"Well then, Ranger Treaty . . ." Ergell began, and Will held up a hand.

"Please, my lord," he said, "I'd be happy if you would simply call me Will."

It was a gracious gesture, particularly as in saying it, Will made it clear that he would continue to use the Baron's title as his method of address. Ergell smiled, with more warmth than Will had seen so far. The gesture had not gone unnoticed.

"Will it is then. As I was about to say, perhaps we could plan for an official welcome dinner two nights from tonight? It will give my Kitchenmaster time to plan something appropriate."

"And we all know how difficult Kitchenmasters can make life if we don't give them that time," said Norris, smiling ruefully. Will grinned in return. It seemed Kitchenmasters were the same the world over, he thought. The atmosphere in the room lightened considerably.

"If there's nothing else then, my lord, I'll take my leave," Will said. Ergell nodded, and Norris rose from the bench again.

"Of course, Will," said the Baron. "If there's anything you need at the cabin, let Gordon know." Gordon was the chamberlain who had shown Will into the office.

Will hesitated, then said quietly, "You have my commission, sir." He indicated the parchment roll on the desktop. Ergell nodded several times.

"Yes, yes. Rest assured I'll look through it shortly." He smiled. "Although I'm sure you're not an impostor." Strictly speaking, Ergell should have broken the seal and read the commission when Will first handed it to him. Things seemed a little bit easygoing in Seacliff Fief, he thought. But perhaps he was just being a stickler for detail.

"Very well, my lord." He glanced at Norris. "Battlemaster," he said, and the knight shook hands with him once more.

"Good to have you with us, Ranger," he said.

"Will," Will reminded him, and the Battlemaster nodded.

"Good to have you with us, Will," he corrected himself. Will gave a slight stiff bow to the Baron, turned and left the room.

Back in the cabin, he found the dog lying where he had left her. She was awake now and her tail thumped the floor two or three times as he entered. There was another bowl on the table and he saw that it contained a meat broth. Underneath the bowl was a small piece of parchment bearing a crude drawing of a dog. Edwina, he thought. The broth was still warm so he placed the bowl on the floor for the dog. She stood carefully and limped a few paces to reach it. Her tongue began a steady lap-lap-lap as she ate. He fondled her ears, checking the wound in her side. The stitches were still holding.

"Lucky she left the drawing, girl," he said. "Or I might have eaten your dinner."

The dog continued to lap at the savory broth. The smell was delicious, he realized, and his empty stomach groaned. Edwina had also left a small loaf of bread with his stew. He carved himself a slice and chewed it eagerly as he waited for the stew to heat on his stove.

5

THE FOLLOWING DAYS SEEMED TO GO BY IN A BLUR AS WILL became familiar with his new surroundings. The welcome dinner that Ergell held for him in the castle dining room was a pleasant enough occasion. As it was an official function, Craftmasters such as the Armorer, Horsemaster and Scribemaster were all in attendance, as well as the knights attached to the castle and their ladies. The faces and names were a blur, but Will knew that over the coming weeks he would begin to remember them, and assign individual traits and characters to each person. For their part, they all seemed curious to meet the new Ranger, and Will was sufficiently pragmatic to realize that a certain reputation preceded him.

As the former apprentice of Halt, one of the greatest and most famous members of the Ranger Corps, Will would always have enjoyed a degree of celebrity. But he was also the one who had discovered and thwarted the secret plans of Morgarath, the evil Lord of Rain and Night, when he had attacked the kingdom little more than five years ago. Then he had served as protector to the Princess Cassandra during her captivity by the Skandian sea wolves. That particular interlude had been rounded off by a major battle with the

Temujai, the fierce cavalry from the Eastern Steppes, and finally, the signing of a non-aggression treaty with the Skandians—a treaty which still held to this day.

In fact, it was his part in securing the Hallasholm Treaty that had given Will the name by which he was known these days—Will Treaty. Raised as an orphan at Castle Redmont, he had known no family name in his childhood.

So perhaps it was natural for people to be surprised at his apparent youth and even, in some cases, to assume that they had mistaken him for some other Ranger—someone who must be older and far bigger in stature. In the years he had spent with Halt, Will had often witnessed the disbelief evident on people's faces when they first met the small, gray-bearded man whose untidy hair looked as if it had been cut with his own saxe knife. People expected their heroes to live up to a romantic ideal. The fact that most Rangers were on the small side, albeit wiry, agile and fast moving, seemed to go against general belief.

So Will faced an air of puzzlement and even mild disappointment as he met his new neighbors—particularly among the ladies of the court. Seacliff was a backwater, as he had surmised, and the arrival of a celebrity—one who had been thanked personally by King Duncan for protecting his daughter—was cause for great anticipation. If the reality was not quite up to people's expectations, that was simply too bad, he thought.

For his part, the more he saw of Seacliff, the more his own sense of disappointment grew. It was a pleasant enough fief, set in a beautiful part of the kingdom. But the years of peace and safety had brought with them a sense of carelessness and neglect in the castle's garrison. And the blame for that neglect could only be sheeted home to the Baron and his Battlemaster. It created an awkward situation for Will, as he felt a genuine liking and respect for both men. But it was undeniable that the readiness and training among the knights and men-at-arms maintained by Ergell was way below the acceptable level.

For days he had considered how he might bring the matter to the Baron's attention without causing offense. He had hinted as broadly as he could that things seemed a little too . . . comfortable. But Ergell and Norris had laughed off the comments, seeming to take them as compliments on the relaxed and enjoyable way of life in Seacliff.

Every baron in the kingdom was required to maintain a force of mounted knights and men-at-arms to ensure the King's peace in the fief. And, in the event of war, each castle would send its men to join the King's army, under the leadership of King Duncan and his inner council. A large fief such as Redmont would maintain a force totaling several hundred mounted warriors and infantry. Seacliff, as one of the smaller fiefs, was required to field half a dozen knights, ten Battleschool warrior apprentices, and an infantry force of twenty-five men-at-arms. An irregular force of fifteen archers was also available if needed, its members drawn from among the villagers and farmers living nearby.

In several weeks at Seacliff, Will was yet to see any formal drilling of the knights and the men-at-arms. There were some weapons drills, held on what seemed to be a haphazard basis, but no real program of training and practice—the sort of constant work that warriors needed to maintain their edge. In addition, the Battleschool apprentices, under the overall guidance of Sir Norris and his two senior knights, were sloppy in their drill and even to Will's young eyes their skill levels seemed to be behind their contemporaries in other Battleschools.

The one area in which Seacliff excelled was in the kitchen. Kitchenmaster Rollo was a true master indeed and his skill rivaled that of Master Chubb at Redmont, long recognized as one of the kingdom's finest. Perhaps that was part of the problem, Will thought. Life at Seacliff was too comfortable, too settled.

Altogether too uneventful.

At the same time, he had traveled to the mainland several times and visited some of the other villages and hamlets within a day's ride of the castle. On several of these occasions, he discarded the symbols of his authority as a Ranger—the gray and green mottled cloak, the longbow and the distinctive double knife scabbard—and took the guise of a traveling peasant. He found that people spoke more freely in front of an anonymous traveler than they would if one of the mysterious Ranger Corps was in their midst. Will sensed that all was not totally well in Seacliff Fief. Life at the castle might be comfortable enough. Life among the outlying hamlets and farms was somewhat less so.

There were rumors of highwaymen and bandits preying on lone travelers. Of strangers being waylaid and even, on some occasions, disappearing altogether. They were rumors only, and Will knew that country folk, with their relatively uneventful day-to-day existence, tended to exaggerate anything out of the ordinary to the point where it assumed massive proportions. But he heard the rumors sufficiently often to sense that they had at least a basis in truth. Several times, as well, he heard the name Buttle spoken—most times with a sense of uncertainty that bordered on fear.

On the positive side, the dog had grown in strength with each day and was virtually recovered from the wound in her side. Now that she could move about more freely, he could see that she was young, probably only half grown. But the reputation that border shepherds held for loyalty and intelligence was no exaggeration. The dog became a constant companion for him and Tug, able to run all day beside the small horse in an effortless lope.

Not so effortless were his attempts to think of a suitable name for the dog. Edwina's comment "a fine dog like that deserves a good name" stuck in his mind. He wanted something special for her, but so far, all his ideas seemed rather pedestrian. For the moment, he referred to her as "the dog" or "girl."

At first Tug seemed merely amused by the presence of the black-and-white newcomer, but as the weeks went on, Tug seemed to welcome her company, as well as the added watchfulness she brought to their night camps as Will explored his new domain. Tug was accustomed to acting as sentinel for Will—all Ranger horses were trained that way. The dog assumed a complementary role in the task and her sense of smell was even keener than Tug's. The two animals, linked by their loyalty to their young master, rapidly developed a mutual liking and a working understanding of each other's skills.

It was three weeks after Will arrived at Seacliff that events contrived to bring matters to a head—at least as far as the unsatisfactory training of the Baron's forces was concerned. Will was leaning on his longbow, watching the Battleschool apprentices practicing sword drills one afternoon. Wrapped in his cloak and cowl, he stood in the shadows of a small grove of trees beside the drill ground, virtually invisible so long as he didn't move. The dog, who had already grown to understand the need for stillness and concealment, lay in the long grass beside him, her nose on her front paws. Her only movements were an occasional twitch of the ears or a flick

of the eyes to check that Will didn't have some visual signal
for her.

He frowned as he watched the apprentices and their swordmas-
ter. Their moves were technically correct. But there was a lack of
urgency, a lack of interest to their work that concerned him. The
drill was a drill and nothing more. They didn't seem to see beyond
it to the reality that it represented. His old friend Horace, now a
knight at the King's court at Araluen, had made all these moves
during countless drill sessions as an apprentice. But he had done
them with passion, and with the understanding that the ability to
produce these moves smoothly, without thought or conscious voli-
tion, could be the difference between life and death in battle.
Horace's instinctive, seamless precision had saved Will's life on at
least one occasion during the battle at Hallasholm.

Will frowned. In just over a week he would have to submit his
first monthly report on the state of affairs at Seacliff to Ranger
headquarters. He could see that it was going to have to be a negative one.

He heard the voice before the man came into view. Then, a few
seconds later, he saw a burly figure break from the trees below the
castle, running and shouting, waving his hand to attract attention.
The words were indistinguishable as yet, but the note of alarm was
obvious in the voice and in the man's body language.

The dog sensed it too. A low growl sounded in her throat and
she rose to a half crouch, instantly alert.

"Still," Will warned her, and she froze obediently. The clash of
practice weapons on the drill field died away as more people became
aware of the shouting, running figure.

And now Will could hear the words he was calling out.

"Sea wolves! Sea wolves!"

It was a word that had chilled the blood of Araluens for centuries past. Sea wolves were the Skandian raiders, who sailed from their snow-covered, pine-forested northern land to raid the pleasant, peaceful coastal centers of Araluen, Gallica and half a dozen other countries. Fearful in their huge, horned helmets and wreaking terrible destruction with their massive battleaxes, the Skandians and their wolfships were the stuff of nightmares.

Yet not here. Not for the past four years, since Erak Starfollower, newly elected as Oberjarl of the Skandians, had put his name to a treaty with Araluen. The strict letter of the treaty had forbidden any organized, massed attack on the Kingdom of Araluen by the Skandians. Yet, effectively, it had put an end to individual raiding as well. While Erak couldn't actually forbid his captains to raid, it was known that he definitely disapproved of it, feeling a debt of honor to the small group of Araluens who had saved his country from the Temujai invasion. And when Erak didn't approve of something, that was usually enough to ensure that it didn't happen.

The shouting man was close to the practice field now, staggering and breathless. By his dress he was a farmer.

"Skandians," he panted. "Sea . . . wolves . . . at Bitteroot Creek . . . Skandians . . ."

Exhausted, he sagged against the drill field fence, his chest and shoulders heaving with exertion. Sir Norris was crossing the field quickly to intercept him.

"What's that?" he asked. "Skandians? Here?"

There was a note of concerned disbelief in his tone. For all the lack of urgency in the training of his men, Will knew Norris was a professional. He may have grown careless and lax in the years of peace that Seacliff had enjoyed, but now, faced with a real threat, he was experienced enough to realize that he was in trouble. His men were not up to the threat posed by a real enemy.

The farmer was pointing back the way he had come, nodding his head to confirm the truth of what he had said.

"Skandians," he repeated. "I saw them where Bitteroot Creek flows into the sea. Hundreds of them!" he added, and this time there was a buzz of concern from the apprentices and knights who had gathered around him.

"Silence!" Norris snapped. Will, approaching unseen, spoke directly to the farmer.

"How many wolfships? Did you see them?"

The farmer turned to face him, a wary look crossing his face as he realized he was talking to a Ranger.

"One," he said. "Huge it was, with a huge wolf's head on the prow! I saw it plain as day."

Again there was a mutter of fear and speculation from those around him. Norris turned angrily and the sound died away. Will met the Battlemaster's eye.

"One ship," he said. "That'll be forty men at most."

Norris nodded agreement. "Closer to thirty if they leave a guard on board," he said.

Not that this made the situation too much better. Thirty Skandians on the loose on Seacliff Island would be a virtually unstoppable force. The ill-trained, unfit men-at-arms and out-of-practice knights who constituted the defense force at Norris's disposal would offer little opposition to the wild pirates, and Norris knew it. The Battlemaster cursed his own laziness, realizing that he was to blame for this situation. It was his responsibility to do something—yet he had another responsibility as well, and that was for the lives of the men he led. Taking them into battle against a hardened, battle-ready band of Skandians would be tantamount to taking them to their deaths.

Yet it was his duty. Will sensed the knight's twin predicaments—practical and moral.

"You're badly outnumbered," he said. The nominal force of men-at-arms was twenty-five. But at short notice, Norris would be lucky to raise twenty—along with three or four of his knights at best. As for the apprentices, Will shuddered at the thought of opposing a force of determined Skandian axmen with the sloppy group he had been watching.

Norris hesitated. He lived a privileged life, as did all noblemen. But the privilege was earned and paid for at times like these. Now, when he was needed, he was unready, unable to protect the people who depended on him.

"There's no point in leading your men to their deaths," Will said quietly, so that only the Battlemaster heard him. Norris's hand clenched and unclenched on the hilt of the sword at his side.

"We must do something . . ." he said uncertainly.

Will interrupted him calmly. "And we shall," he told the older man. "Get the villagers inside the walls, with as much as they can carry. Drive the animals out into the fields. Scatter them so the Skandians have to hunt them down if they want them. Get your men armed and ready. And ask Master Rollo if he could rustle up something quick in the way of a banquet."

Norris wasn't sure if he was hearing correctly. "A banquet?" he asked, totally confused.

Will nodded. "A banquet. Nothing too special. I'm sure he can put something together for us. In the meantime, I'll go and have a word with these Skandians."

The Battlemaster's eyes widened as he looked at the calm young face before him.

"Have a word with them?" he repeated, a little louder than he had intended. "How do you think you can stop them from attacking us by talking to them?"

Will shrugged. "I thought I'd ask them not to," he said. "And then, I'll invite them to dinner."

6

BITTEROOT CREEK RAN INTO THE OCEAN ON THE EASTERN COAST of the island. It was a sheltered spot, with plenty of overhanging trees growing right down to the water's edge to provide concealment—even for a craft as large as a wolfship. The water was deep right up to the bank and it made an ideal landing place for raiders. Will was cantering Tug down the winding path through the forest toward the creek when he heard the sound of galloping hooves behind him.

He turned in his saddle and checked the horse with a touch of his heel as he recognized Sir Norris galloping after him on his battlehorse. The Battlemaster was fully armed and armored now and the steel-shod hooves of his massive gray left a cloud of dust hanging behind them. The dog, who had been loping silently to one side of the track, keeping pace with Tug, dropped on her stomach as the Ranger horse came to a halt, and watched the approaching horse and rider with her head cocked curiously to one side.

Norris reined in beside Will. The battlehorse was at least four hands taller than Tug and horse and rider towered above them. Will inclined his head in greeting.

"Sir Norris," he said. "What brings you here?"

Norris hesitated. Will had a good idea what he was about to say. After a few seconds' hesitation, Norris answered him.

"I can't let you do this on your own, Ranger," he said, the note of bitter self-reproach evident in his voice. "It's my fault that we're unprepared. I've let things go soft and I know it. Now I can't leave it to you to pull my chestnuts out of the fire for me. I'll stand with you."

Will nodded thoughtfully. It had taken courage to say that, and just as much courage to make the decision to accompany him to face the Skandians. He felt a new surge of respect for the Battlemaster. Perhaps if this turned out all right, it might prove to be a blessing, he thought. The arrival of a raiding wolfship had certainly rammed home the lesson that Seacliff Fief was underprepared. And it did so far better than any criticism that Will might have voiced.

"I appreciate your offer," he told the knight. "But it might be better if I did this alone."

He saw the color rising in the other man's face and he quickly held up a hand to calm his anger. "It's not that I doubt your courage or your ability," he added. "Quite the opposite, in fact. But I think I have a better chance of settling this on my own."

"You surely can't plan to fight them alone?" Norris asked.

Will shook his head, a little smile touching his lips. "I don't plan to fight them at all," he said. "But your presence, in full armor and mounted on that huge horse of yours, mightn't give me a choice. Think about it," he went on before Norris could interrupt. "At the first sight of you, obviously ready for battle, the Skandians are likely to attack without further thought."

Norris chewed his bottom lip. What Will was saying made sense. Then the young Ranger continued.

"On the other hand, if they see me alone, they might be willing to talk. We Rangers tend to have an unsettling effect on people. They're never quite sure what we might be up to," he added, the smile widening. Norris had to admit that was true. Yet he was reluctant to leave the young man to face odds of thirty to one, armed only with a bow. Will saw the hesitation and continued, his voice crisper now as he realized that time was running short.

"Besides, if things go wrong, I can always outrun them on Tug here—and pick a few of them off as I go. Please, Sir Norris, it's best my way." He glanced down the track, looking for the first sign of the Skandians, knowing they would be coming this way as there was no other path up from the beach. Abruptly, Norris made his decision. On his light, agile horse, the Ranger could take to the shelter of the forest if need be, or simply outrun the Skandians back to the castle. The sea wolves rarely used bows or other missiles.

"Very well," he said, wheeling his mount. Will nodded his gratitude as the knight set spurs to his horse and began to canter clumsily back the way he had come.

As the hoofbeats faded, Will took stock of the ground around him. At this point, the path ran relatively straight for fifty meters in either direction, the trees were set back and the ground was level, leaving an open space. This would do as well as any other spot to meet the Skandians, he thought. He could keep them at a distance if he needed to and had room to maneuver.

He backed the horse up a dozen paces or so, then stopped in the middle of the path. The dog, belly low to the grass, loped back beside him and dropped flat. Will glanced up at the sun. It was a little behind him, so it would be in the Skandians' eyes. That was all to the good, he thought. He shrugged the deep cowl of the cloak up over his head and settled the longbow comfortably across the saddle bow. His position was ready without being overtly threatening.

Tug's ears twitched and a fraction of a second later the dog let out a low warning growl. Will could see movement in the shadows under the trees at the bend in the path.

"All right," he told his two animals. "Settle down." He eased his seat in the saddle and slouched comfortably, waiting for the Skandians.

Gundar Hardstriker, skipper of the *Wolfcloud*, stepped out into the afternoon sunlight from the shade under the trees. At his back, twenty-seven Skandian warriors marched in double file. His eyes a little dazzled after the dim light of the forest, Gundar stopped in surprise at the sight of a solitary figure on the road ahead of them.

Not a knight or a warrior of any kind, he saw. It was a slightly built figure on a small shaggy horse. There was a longbow held almost casually across his thighs, but no sign of other weapons. No ax, no sword, no mace or club. His men straggled to a halt behind him, fanning out to either side of the path as they moved to see what was causing the delay.

"A Ranger," said Ulf Oakbender, who pulled the bow oar on board *Wolfcloud*, and Gundar realized he was right. The sun's dazzle, almost directly behind the waiting figure, had stopped him from making out the mottled cloak that was the sign of a Ranger. Now, as his eyes adjusted, he could see the strange, irregular patterns that seemed to shimmer and move with a life of their own.

"Good pastnoon," called a clear voice. "What can we do for you?"

It was the surprisingly young voice of the speaker, as well as the fact that he used the traditional Skandian greeting, that caused Gundar to hesitate. Behind him, he heard his men muttering, as puzzled as he was at this sudden appearance. They had expected either resistance or flight from the people they encountered, not a polite inquiry.

Realizing that he had somehow lost the initiative, Gundar called angrily, "Step aside! Step aside, run or fight. We don't care which way. You choose."

He started forward and the figure straightened slightly in the saddle. "No further." The voice had a ring of authority now and no sign of any indecision. Gundar hesitated again. Behind him, he heard Ulf's low voice.

"Be careful, Gundar. These Rangers can shoot like the devil himself."

As if he had heard Ulf's whispered warning, the Ranger continued: "Keep coming and you'll be dead before you take another two steps. Let's just talk a while, shall we?"

Gundar, conscious of the eyes of his men on him, snorted disdainfully and started toward the rider. He saw a brief blur of movement. Recalling the incident later, he had no clear recollection of what the movement was. The strange, shimmering, mottled pattern of the cloak confused the eye and the Ranger moved at lightning speed as well. But he heard the savage *hiss-thud!* and an arrow was quivering in the ground, its head buried directly between his feet. He stepped back rapidly.

"It could have been between your eyes," the voice said calmly, and Gundar realized that it was the truth. He lowered the battleax that had been resting over his shoulder, and leaned on its hilt as its head touched the ground.

"What do you want?" he asked, and the figure shrugged.

"Just a few words between friends. I wasn't aware that the Hallasholm Treaty had been rescinded."

"The treaty doesn't ban individual raiding," Gundar replied. He thought he saw the figure nodding, although it was hard to tell with the cowl of the cloak covering his head.

"Not in so many words, perhaps," he said. "But Erak Starfollower is said to disapprove strongly—particularly where it concerns his friends and their property."

Gundar laughed scornfully. "Friends? The Oberjarl doesn't look for friends among Araluens!" he said, although a worm of doubt was wriggling in his belly as he said the words. There was a pause. The Ranger didn't answer his question directly. Instead, he looked at the sky and the low autumn sun.

"It's late in the raiding season," Will said finally. "I assume you've been raiding the Gallic and Iberic coasts?" It was an easy assumption. There had been no word of any raiding on the south coast of Araluen. Now, watching the group before him, he thought he understood why they had landed here.

"It'll be a long hard pull across the Stormwhite at this time of year," he said, maintaining his easy, friendly tone. "The autumn gales will be starting soon. You'll winter at Skorghijl, I suppose?"

He saw the ripple of surprise go through the Skandians. The leader glanced at his men to silence them.

"Skorghijl? What do you know of Skorghijl?"

"I know it's a black rock, hundreds of kilometers from anywhere. It's wet and freezing and totally devoid of any comfort or even a single blade of grass," Will told him, "but it's still preferable to crossing the Stormwhite in bad weather." He paused for effect, then added casually, "Or at least, it was when I was there in *Wolfwind*."

Now *that* had an effect, thought Will. *Wolfwind* had been Erak's wolfship before he had been elected Oberjarl of the Skandians. Yet there would be very few Araluens who knew the fact—Skandian ships didn't have their names painted on them. He saw the group muttering in low voices, saw the uncertainty in the stance of their leader as they realized that the only way he might have known the name of Erak's ship would be to have known Erak himself.

That was precisely the thought that was going through Gundar's mind. Yet he hadn't made the obvious connection. Ulf had. He grabbed his leader's arm.

"It's him!" he said urgently. "The one who helped defeat the eastern riders!"

Gundar peered at the figure on the horse. He'd heard of the young Ranger apprentice who had fought side by side with the Skandians five years ago, but he'd never seen him. Gundar had been upcountry during the brief, bloody war with the Temujai. Not so Ulf. He'd taken his place in the shield wall during the final confrontation. Now, as Will tossed back the cowl of his cloak and the shock of unruly hair was visible, he recognized him.

"It's him, Gundar!" he told his captain, then added, with a grim laugh, "As well you stopped when you did. I saw him empty five Temujai saddles in as many seconds during the battle."

That wasn't all, Ulf knew. If this were the legendary apprentice he was thinking of, then he was a close friend of the Oberjarl—and raiding in his territory might not be the best career move a wolfship skirl could make. Erak was renowned for his loyalty to friends—and his short temper with those who offended them.

Gundar, not the quickest of thinkers, had reached the same conclusion a few seconds after his deputy. He hesitated, not sure what to say or do next. He and his men had an urgent need that had influenced their decision to raid Seacliff. They needed provisions to see them through the long, bitter winter months on Skorghijl. The bare island provided a safe harbor for wolfships but little in the way of food, and *Wolfcloud*'s cruise had been anything but successful when it came to capturing supplies. If they sailed to Skorghijl as they were, they would quite possibly starve to death. At best they would go very hungry. Gundar and his men needed to raid. They needed meat and flour and grain to see them through the winter. And wine, if they could get it, he thought, his tongue unconsciously licking his dry lips as the thought crossed his mind. Friend or not, he thought, the Oberjarl could hardly blame him for looking after the well-being of his crew.

"Ride away, Ranger," he called, making a decision. "I'd prefer not to raise my weapon against a friend of Skandia, so I'll give you this last chance."

He hefted the massive ax again as he spoke. He was a little disconcerted to see a smile touch the young man's face.

"How very kind of you," Will said pleasantly. "And if I do 'ride away,' what do you propose to do?"

Gundar pointed in the direction of the castle and the attendant village that he knew lay some way beyond the trees.

"What we came here to do," he declared. "We'll take what we want and go."

"You won't get much with only ten men," Will said, in a reasonable tone of voice. Gundar snorted angrily.

"Ten? I've got twenty-seven men behind me!" There was an angry growl of assent from his men—although Ulf didn't join in, Gundar noticed.

This time, when the Ranger spoke, there was no trace of the pleasant, reasonable tone. Instead, the voice was hard and cold.

"You haven't reached the castle yet," Will said. "I've got twenty-three arrows in my quiver still, and a further dozen in my packsaddle. And you've got several kilometers to go—all within bowshot of the trees there. Bad shot as I am, I should be able to account for more than half your men. Then you'll be facing the garrison with just ten men."

Involuntarily, Gundar's eyes swung to the tree line. He realized that the Ranger was right. He could fade into the forest and keep a constant fire on them as they tried to reach the castle.

"Try to come after me and you'll just make it easier," Will added, and Gundar swore explosively under his breath. Mounted as he was, and with a Ranger's skill at avoiding detection in the trees, Will could evade pursuit easily while he cut the small force of Skandians to ribbons. The wolfship skirl felt rage boiling up inside him. He was trapped here, with no options left to him. On the one hand, if he didn't raid the village, he and his men would starve. On the other, if they tried, a lot of them would certainly die. Will watched him carefully, waiting for the right moment, just before the rage boiled over into frustrated action.

"Alternatively," Will said calmly, "we might be able to come to some arrangement."

7

"THEY'RE COMING!" THE LOOKOUT'S CRY ECHOED DOWN FROM the highest tower on Castle Seacliff. Baron Ergell squinted up, his eyes narrowed against the glare, then followed the direction the man's arm was pointing.

A group of Skandian warriors was emerging from the trees into the cleared ground around the castle. A mounted figure rode beside the man who led them. There was also, he made out, a black-and-white dog trotting ahead of the group.

"He talked to them, you say?" Ergell asked, and Norris nodded, standing at the battlements beside his leader. When he had left Will on the path, he had gone no farther than the next bend. He had watched the Ranger meet the Skandians, ready to go to his aid if necessary.

"That's right. He simply barred the way and talked to them. I saw him fire one arrow as a warning—actually, I didn't see it," he added, correcting himself. "It just sort of . . . happened. They're uncanny, those Rangers."

"And he said something about a banquet?"

This time Norris shrugged. He'd already passed that instruction to Rollo, mystified as he was by it. "A banquet, my lord. Although what he has in mind I can't tell you."

As they had been talking, Ergell had been counting the Skandian force approaching the castle. Nearly thirty of them, he saw. More than they could afford to engage. They'd have to face up to the fact that the village would be plundered and burned to the ground. The villagers themselves would be safe enough inside the castle walls and the livestock had been scattered as Will had ordered. But his people, his dependents, would lose their homes and their belongings, and the Baron knew it was his fault.

The Skandians had stopped now, some two hundred meters from the castle. He saw the Ranger lean down from his saddle to talk to their leader, a massive man wearing a horned helmet and carrying a double-bladed battleax. Some form of agreement seemed to pass between them and Will turned his horse toward the castle, letting him break into a fast canter. The dog accelerated from a standing start as only a sheepdog could, to keep station ahead of him.

"Perhaps we should go down and see what's in his mind," the Baron said, and he and his Battlemaster headed for the stairs leading to the courtyard below.

They had reached ground level by the time the gatekeepers were letting Will through the small wicket set into the main gate. He nodded to the Baron and to Sir Norris as they approached.

"We have an agreement with the Skandians, my lord," he said. Ergell realized that he had spoken in a carrying voice, and used the word "we" so that those within earshot would assume that he had been acting on the Baron's instructions. It was a tactful thing to do,

Ergell realized. It would have been easy for the Ranger to have undermined his authority in front of his own people, yet he had chosen not to do so.

"I see," he replied gruffly. It wouldn't do to let people know that he didn't have the slightest idea what Will was talking about. The young Ranger stepped closer and lowered his voice so that only Ergell and Norris could hear him.

"They need provisions for the winter," he said quietly. "That's why they're here. I've told them we'll let them have five bullocks and ten sheep, plus a reasonable amount of grain for flour."

"Five bullocks!" Ergell began indignantly, but Will's cold glance stopped him in mid-protest.

"They'll take them anyway," he said, "*and* destroy the village in the bargain. It's a small enough price to pay, my lord."

His steady gaze held the Baron's. Unspoken was the thought that Ergell was in this position because of his own neglect—his and Norris's. In that sense, it was a small price to pay. He saw Norris nodding agreement with Will.

"The bullocks can come from my herd, my lord," he said. Ergell knew his Battlemaster was declaring his share of responsibility for the situation. He sighed.

"Of course," he said. "And the sheep from mine. Give the orders, Norris."

Inwardly, Will heaved a small sigh of relief. He had hoped that the two men would see that this was the best solution. Of course, Will could have made good on his threat to Gundar, but he had no wish to shoot down helpless men. Besides, even ten Skandians could cause a lot of damage and injury, he knew. And frankly, since Ergell and Norris were to blame for the situation, they deserved to pay for it.

"In the meantime, my lord, I've arranged for Gundar and his men to feast with us. I take it Sir Norris mentioned the idea to your Kitchenmaster?"

Ergell was taken aback by that. "Feast with us?" he said. "Skandians? You want me to let them in here?"

He glanced quickly at the thick walls and the stout wooden gate. Will nodded.

"Gundar has given me a helmsman's word that there'll be no trouble, my lord. A Skandian will never break that vow."

"But . . ." Still Ergell hesitated. The idea of letting those wild pirates inside his stronghold was too outlandish. Norris returned at that moment, having dispatched one of the herders to round up the scattered animals. Ergell turned to him helplessly.

"Apparently we're to let these pirates inside the walls—and provide them with a feast!" he said. For a moment, he could see Norris reacting as he had done. Then the knight remembered the sight of the lone, small figure waiting in the road to meet the Skandians and his shoulders dropped.

"Why not?" he said in a resigned tone. "I've never met a Skandian socially before. It should prove interesting."

Will grinned at the two of them. "It should prove noisy," he said, then added a warning, "But don't try to match them drink for drink. You'll never manage it."

8

"Graybeard Halt is a fighting man.
I've heard common talk
that Graybeard Halt he cuts his hair
with a carving knife and fork.
Fare thee well, Graybeard Halt,
fare thee well I say.
Fare thee well, Graybeard Halt,
tomorrow's another day."

Will hit a final chord on the mandola as he finished the last words, letting the notes ring on. Delia clapped and laughed delightedly.

"You're very good!" she said, with a note of surprise in her voice. "You should come over to the tavern and sing sometime."

Will shook his head. "I don't think so," he said. "Your mother wouldn't really appreciate my emptying her bar with my singing and playing."

To tell the truth, he was sure that the idea of singing and playing amusing folk songs in a tavern didn't sit with a Ranger's dignity or air of secretiveness. He wasn't totally sure that he should even be playing to Delia, when he came to think of it. But she was pretty and friendly and he was young and just a little lonely and he'd decided that he could give himself a little leeway in the matter.

They were sitting on the verandah of his cabin. It was late afternoon and the autumn sun was slanting low in the west, the light dappled by the half-bare branches of the trees. In the past week, since the banquet with the Skandian crew, Delia had begun to take her mother's place in delivering his evening meal. This evening, as she'd arrived, he'd been sitting practicing the instrumental break from *Graybeard Halt*, a complex sequence of sixteenth notes, played in a driving rhythm. She'd asked him to play it again, and sing it as well. The song was a traditional one, originally titled *Old Joe Smoke*, and it was about an unwashed, unkempt herder who slept among his goats to stay warm. When Will first began to learn the mandola, he had jokingly retitled it *Graybeard Halt*, as a comment on his mentor's unkempt hair and beard.

"But doesn't Ranger Halt object to you making fun of him like that?" Delia asked, a little wide-eyed. Halt's grim reputation was known throughout the kingdom. The idea of satirizing him seemed a dangerous one to her. Will shrugged.

"Oh, Halt's not as serious as you might think. He actually has quite a sense of humor," he said.

"He was certainly chuckling the time he made you spend all night up a tree for singing that song," came a voice from behind them. It was a familiar voice. Low-pitched, feminine and with a unique cadence that reminded Will of a stream flowing over smooth stones. He recognized it at once and leapt to his feet, turning toward the speaker where she had approached the end of the little porch.

"Alyss!" he said, a delighted grin spreading across his face. He stepped to meet her, his hands out in greeting, and she took them in her own as she stepped onto the verandah.

She was tall and very elegant, dressed in a beautifully cut white gown. It was the official Diplomatic Service uniform and its simple lines belied its stylishness while it set off her slender, long-legged figure to perfection. Her ash blond hair was straight and shoulder length, falling on either side of her face and framing her features. Gray eyes sparkled quietly at a private joke between her and Will. The picture was completed by a straight nose, a firm chin and a full mouth that echoed the hint of amusement and genuine pleasure in her eyes.

They stood wordlessly for a moment, delighted to see one another again. Alyss was one of Will's oldest friends, having been raised, as he was, a ward of Redmont Fief. In fact, when Will had returned to Redmont, heartsore at his parting from the Princess Cassandra, they had gradually become somewhat more than friends. The graceful apprentice diplomat had sensed his need for warmth and feminine company and affection and had been more than glad to supply all three. It hadn't progressed past some tentative embraces and kisses in the moonlight, and perhaps because of that, there was a sense of unfinished business between them.

Delia, seeing their obvious pleasure at each other's company, sensed the relationship and reluctantly surrendered. She was realistic enough to know that she was pretty and vivacious and probably the most attractive girl of her age on the island. But this elegant blonde in the soft white gown was more than pretty. She was poised, graceful and, in a word, beautiful. There was no contest, she thought resignedly—and just as things had been starting to thaw with this interesting and handsome young man.

"What are you doing here?" Will finally found his voice and led Alyss to where he and Delia had been sitting. The village girl noted that he retained his hold on one of Alyss's hands and she made no move to break the contact.

"Oh, just a routine diplomatic pouch from the court," she said, tossing her head to signify that her mission was an unimportant one. "They're going out to half the fiefs. Nothing earth-shattering. I heard you were here at Seacliff, so I traded assignments with another courier so I could come see you."

She glanced meaningfully over his shoulder, raising one exquisite eyebrow to remind him of his manners. Will realized that he had forgotten all about Delia, and now he turned hurriedly, knocking the mandola over where he had leaned it against his chair. There was a moment of confusion as he regathered it. At least, thought Delia, it meant he had to let go of the Perfect Apparition's hand.

"I'm so sorry!" he said in a rush. "Alyss, this is Delia, a friend of mine here. Delia, this is Courier Alyss, one of my oldest and dearest companions."

Delia winced inwardly at the "dearest" but smiled valiantly as she took Alyss's proffered hand. It was smooth and warm, of course, with a surprisingly strong grip.

"Pleased to meet you," she said. Alyss smiled, knowing that Delia was anything but pleased.

"How do you do?" she said. Will looked from one of them to the other, rubbing his hands uncertainly, not sure what to do next. Then his delight in seeing Alyss again took over.

"So are you staying long? Will you have time for me to show you the island?" he asked, and Alyss shook her head regretfully.

"Just tonight and tomorrow," she said. "There's a formal banquet tomorrow, but I'm free tonight and I thought . . . ?" She let the sentence hang and Will seized the opportunity eagerly.

"Well then, dine with me tonight!" He gestured toward the cabin behind them. "I'll ask Edwina if she can cater for another person."

"Edwina?" Alyss repeated, raising an eyebrow. She glanced at the cabin, wondering if Will kept a tribe of women here with him. Delia answered before Will could explain.

"My mother," she said. "We run the local tavern." She smiled over-brightly at Will. "I can tell her if you like. It'll be no trouble for her at all, and it's time I was getting back anyway."

Will hesitated, not sure how to handle this turn of events. "Oh . . . well . . . good." Then, having left it just a shade too long, he added, "Why not join us? We can all have dinner together?"

Delia felt a small thrill of triumph as the smile on Alyss's face faded slightly, and for a moment she was tempted to accept. But she realized almost immediately that this small triumph was likely to be the only one she would enjoy that evening.

"No. I'm sure you have lots to discuss together. You don't want me along."

Alyss, she noticed, made no move to contradict her. Will, a little awkwardly, said: "Well, if you're sure then." He sensed the tension in the air but had no idea what to do about it. Delia was already gathering up the small earthenware pot that she had brought for his evening meal.

"I'll take this back," she said. "It's just a stew, and I'm sure Mother will want to do something special for a dear friend of the Ranger's."

"That's great," Will replied automatically, completely missing the irony in her tone. His eyes were still fastened on Alyss.

Delia waited a second or two, then asked: "What time would you like to dine?"

Alyss answered for him. "I have a meeting with the Baron first," she said. "And I'd like to settle into my quarters and have a bath before that. Perhaps in two hours' time?"

"Two hours it is then," Delia replied. Then she added to Will, "And I saw Mother making one of her special flaky pastry berry pies earlier. Perhaps you'd like some of that for dessert?" Will nodded cheerfully, welcoming the idea.

"That'd be great. Thanks, Delia," he said. She forced a smile, nodded a farewell to Alyss and turned away, walking quickly toward the village.

"Why did you have to offer them pie?" she asked herself softly as she went. It was almost as if she were trying to make matters worse for herself, she thought, adding bitterly, "Perhaps you could come back and light some romantic candles for them as well?"

She glanced back once as she rounded the edge of the grove but Will and Alyss were paying no further attention to her. Sourly, she noted that they were holding hands once more.

"You're making quite a name for yourself," Alyss said, smiling at Will across the dinner table.

"I'm just blundering through," he said. "It's all a little over-whelming, really."

Alyss's steady gaze told him that she saw through his pretense of diffidence.

"Inviting a wolfship crew to a banquet?" she said. "Preventing a pitched battle by handing over a few beasts and a skin or two of wine? I'd say you handled things pretty well."

"Oh, Skandians aren't so difficult to deal with once you know them," Will replied. Then he grinned at her. He was actually quite proud of the way he had handled the potentially ugly situation.

"Besides," he added, "it was worth it to see all those stuffy knights and their ladies sitting down to dine with a crew of bloodthirsty corsairs."

Alyss frowned slightly as she ran her finger around the top of her glass. "Wasn't that a bit risky?" she asked. "After all, anything could have happened with that mix of people."

Will shook his head firmly. "Not once Gundar had given me his word as a helmsman. No Skandian would ever break that oath. And I knew Norris would keep his people under control—it was the least he could do," he added meaningfully. Alyss picked up on the unspoken message and raised her eyebrows in a question. Will hesitated a moment, not wanting to air Seacliff's dirty linen in public. Then he realized that Alyss was a member of the Diplomatic Service, and accustomed to hearing secrets far more important than this one.

"Norris and the Baron had let things become very slack around here. They wouldn't have stood a chance in a battle. Their men were badly trained, badly drilled and out of condition. At least Norris realized the fact and went along with the banquet idea."

"And a good idea it was," Alyss said quietly. Will pursed his lips thoughtfully.

"I suppose it helped that I'd made the crossing of the Stormwhite when I did," he said. "I realized they were short of provisions and they mightn't last the winter without them. By doing things my way, they didn't have to fight for them—and they got to go to a banquet as well." He grinned at the memory once more.

"So they're safely out of the way?" Alyss asked casually. Will shook his head.

"They're still butchering and smoking the meat so it will see them through the winter," he said. "They'll be at Bitteroot Creek for another two or three days, then they'll be on their way."

"Does that mean they're still a danger to the fief?" she asked, but Will hurried to reassure her on that score.

"Gundar's oath still holds," he said. "I trust him totally." He grinned as he added, "Particularly as he knows I'm a personal friend of the Skandian Oberjarl."

"You'll still report on Norris's neglect of his duty, won't you?" Alyss asked. Like the Rangers, the Couriers' main allegiance was to the King. Will nodded.

"I'll have to," he said. "But at least I can report that he's learned his lesson. His men have been drilling nonstop since the morning after the banquet—and that was unpopular timing, I can tell you. In another month or so, he'll have them whipped into shape."

"So things are in good order here?" Alyss said, then added casually, "There'd be no problem if you had to leave for a while?"

Will was reaching for the water pitcher as she said the last few words. His hand froze in midair and he met her eyes. They were serious now, with no hint of the humor and warmth that had been so evident earlier. This, he realized, was business.

"Leave?" he said, and she nodded.

"It's no accident that I'm here, Will. Oh, there were some routine documents to deliver, but Halt and Crowley specifically asked me to take this assignment and give you a message. You're being reassigned."

Will felt a sudden stab of doubt at the words. Perhaps his handling of the Skandian situation hadn't been quite as clever as he thought. Alyss saw the worry written plainly on his face and hastened to reassure him.

"It's no punishment, Will. They were very pleased with the way you handled things—Halt in particular. They have a temporary assignment they need you for."

He felt the weight of doubt lift at her words. "What sort of assignment?"

Alyss shrugged. "I don't know the full details myself yet. It's all highly confidential," she said. "As I said, they wanted me to deliver the message because I was an old friend. That way, people won't begin wondering why you should suddenly disappear after a visit from a Courier. They'll just put it down to the normal Ranger liking for secrecy. Hopefully, they'll think my visit was purely social— particularly with your girlfriend Delia to stoke the fires of gossip."

Will colored slightly. "She's just a friend!" he protested awkwardly.

But Alyss didn't answer. She was pointing at the dog, which had been lying contentedly on the warm stones beside the fire. Now she was awake, her ears flattened against the side of her head, her teeth bared. A low, rumbling growl sounded in her chest. Her gaze was fixed on the door of the cabin.

"There's someone outside," Will said softly.

9

MOTIONING FOR ALYSS TO REMAIN WHERE SHE WAS, WILL ROSE and moved silently to the door. The latch was moving, a fraction at a time, as the person outside tested it to see if it was locked. As the wooden tongue rose from the socket that held it in place, Will took a position on the latch side of the door, flattened against the wall.

He nodded to Alyss, and the girl, quick-witted as always, began talking again, rambling on about Halt and Crowley and how they had sent their greetings to him. She began to describe a meal she had enjoyed with them, going into great detail over the preparation and the skill of the cook, Master Chubb of Redmont.

The door had stopped moving as their conversation had paused. Now, as Alyss began talking once more, it began to inch open, infinitely slowly, the well-oiled hinges making no noise. Will made a mental note to stop oiling the hinges. Halt had always allowed a patina of rust to build up on the hinges to his front door. *Nobody can take you by surprise that way*, he was fond of saying.

Will frowned. The only person about to be surprised was the intruder outside, he thought. For a moment, he wondered if it might not be Delia, come back to eavesdrop on his conversation with

Alyss. Then he abandoned the idea. The dog would never have be-
haved as she did if that were the case. The door was open about
fifteen centimeters now and he could see the hand on the outer
latch. A man's left hand, he recognized. And he knew that the right
hand would probably hold a weapon of some kind. Alyss let out a
rising peal of laughter, presumably to convince the intruder that
they were totally preoccupied with her fake conversation. The ruse
seemed to work, as the door opened wider and more of the man's
arm was visible in the gap.

Will moved quickly, grabbing the man by the wrist with his
right hand and pivoting to jerk him forward into the room. At the
same time, he let the pivot movement throw his left leg out across
the doorway as a barrier, so the outsider was jerked forward and
tripped over the outstretched leg.

With a shout of surprise, the man stumbled into the room, pro-
pelled by the totally unexpected jerk on his arm, and tumbled over
Will's leg, crashing to the floor and knocking a chair flying into one
corner as he did so.

But he was fast to recover and he rolled quickly, bounding to his
feet to face the Ranger. As Will had expected, there was a weapon
in his right hand—a heavy-headed war spear on an ash shaft. He
extended it now toward Will in a two-handed grip, the razor-sharp
head weaving slightly as if to mesmerize his enemy.

Will didn't move. He stood, balanced on the balls of his feet,
ready for instant action. His hands were empty of weapons. Alyss,
he noticed with interest, had come to her feet, a long and dangerous-
looking dagger in her hand. She held it loosely, looking as if she
knew how to use it.

The dog, excited by the sudden flurry of movement, was barking furiously. Without taking his eyes from the intruder, Will called

sharply for her to be still. She subsided, growling threateningly while he took stock of the spearman.

He was big and heavy-shouldered, with unkempt black hair and a black beard. The eyes were dark and burning with anger under heavy brows and the large nose had been broken at some time and badly reset so that it had a distinct crook in it. He wore dark clothing, a jerkin and woolen trousers, and a dark brown cowled cloak. Will had never seen him before, but he knew who he was.

"John Buttle," he said calmly. "What do you want here?"

An unpleasant smirk touched the man's mouth as he answered. The voice was deep and throaty and his accent and manner of speech marked him as a commoner.

"Know me, do you? Ain't that a prize."

"I know *of* you," Will replied evenly. "You have a reputation around this fief."

Buttle sneered. "Reputation! Nothing's ever been proved against me. Nothing ever will be."

"That could be because there are never any witnesses left alive when you do your dirty work." Then Will added briskly, "Now get on with it! What are you doing sneaking around my home in the middle of the night?"

For a moment, a puzzled look flicked across Buttle's face. Will's peremptory tone took him by surprise. After all, he was the one who was armed. The small Ranger, who he now saw looked to be still a boy, had no weapons. Oh, he did have what appeared to be an oversized knife at his hip, but Buttle would have him spitted on the spear before he could get that unsheathed. As for the blond girl, her dagger held no fears for him.

"I've come for my dog," he said, at length. "Heard you'd stolen her and I want her back."

He glanced at the dog as he spoke and she flattened her belly to the floor, the growling intensifying as she did so.

"Shut up, you!" he shouted at her, but the dog only snarled more, baring her teeth at him.

"You certainly have a way with her," Will said. He made a quick hand gesture and she quieted instantly.

"Very clever!" Buttle sneered, now thoroughly angry. "I'll teach her manners, like I taught her last time. Little bitch tried to bite me, so I taught her."

"With that great big spear, I suppose?" Alyss asked. "How incredibly brave of you." She leaned nonchalantly against the back of the chair she'd been sitting in, assessing the bearded man coolly. Will smiled quietly to himself at her absolute composure. Buttle, on the other hand, seemed to be enraged by it.

"Don't come the high and mighty with me, girl!" he shouted. "Not you with your little knife and your secret Courier doings!" He lowered his voice and continued, "Got a secret assignment for our Ranger, have we? I'll bet there'll be those who'll pay to know about that."

Will and Alyss exchanged quick glances. Buttle saw the exchange and continued, with growing confidence.

"Oh yes, I heard you and your plotting. Rangers and Couriers, always sneaking around with secrets, aren't you? Learn to keep your voices down when John Buttle's around, you should."

He was in control of the situation now and pleased to see that he had shattered their air of unconcern. He realized now that he had overheard something important when he had been outside the door and his criminal brain was working to see how he could profit by it. Long experience told him that when there was something that somebody wanted to keep secret, there was inevitably another some-body who would pay to know about it.

"Oh dear," said Alyss to Will. "He seems to have overheard our conversation."

Buttle laughed at her. "Overheard you, all right. And there's nothing you can do about it."

Alyss seemed to consider his words for a moment, thinking them over. Then, in a very matter-of-fact way, she replied, "It seems not. Short of killing you."

As she said the words, she flipped the long dagger, catching it by its point and taking her arm back in a smooth, flowing motion. Buttle swung instantly toward her, dropping into a defensive crouch, the spear ready to thrust . . .

. . . and heard a strange *hiss-clunk!* followed by a jarring sensation in both hands as Will's saxe knife seemed to leap from its fleece-lined scabbard. Without pause, it swung in a chopping arc to strike his spear just behind the steel head.

Heavy as an ax, sharp as a razor, the specially tempered blade of the saxe cut through the hard ash wood as if it were cheese. The heavy head dropped to the cabin floor with a ringing thud and Buttle stared in amazement at the spear, suddenly headless and seemingly weightless in his hands. He had a half second or so to register the fact before Will, stepping toward him and pivoting again, brought the brass pommel of the saxe thudding into his temple.

At which point John Buttle lost further interest in proceedings and sagged to the floor like a sack of potatoes.

"Very neat," Alyss said, impressed in spite of herself by the speed of Will's reactions. She reversed the dagger again and replaced it in the sheath concealed by a specially cut fold in her gown.

They smiled at each other. The dog, puzzled, whimpered slightly for attention and Alyss stooped to reassure her, ruffling the fur around her ears.

"I didn't know they trained you to throw those daggers," Will said, and she shrugged.

"They don't. The blades are much too fine to go hurling them all over the place the way you Rangers do. I just wanted to distract our friend here so you could deal with him."

Will crossed to the dresser against the wall of the cabin and rummaged in one of the drawers. He withdrew several pieces of rawhide, then move to the supine figure on the floor, rolling Buttle onto his stomach and placing his hands behind his back. Will looped two small circlets of leather over the man's thumbs, then pulled them tight through a double wooden block to secure them.

Then, using a larger version of the thumb restraints, he fastened Buttle's ankles together as well.

"Very neat," Alyss said once more. He studied his handiwork and nodded.

"One of the Rangers designed them. The loops hold the thumbs and ankles and these wooden deadeyes let you tighten them without having to bother about knots."

Alyss took up her glass and sat sideways on her chair, frowning at the unconscious Buttle. "Of course, there is still a problem. What do we do with him now?"

Will began to answer, then stopped as he realized what she was thinking.

"My assignment," he said. "He knows about it."

Alyss nodded. "Exactly. We went through all this subterfuge so nobody would know you'd been sent on a mission. Now we'll have this moron blurting it out to all and sundry."

Will regarded Buttle, who still hadn't stirred. "I can have the Baron imprison him, of course. He did threaten you, and threatening a Courier is a serious offense." But Alyss shook her head decisively.

"Not good enough. There's still the chance that he'll be in contact with other prisoners, or even his jailers. And we can't risk any word of this getting out. Damn the man! We may have to kill him, Will."

She said it reluctantly, but so calmly that Will was taken aback. He looked at her with new eyes, realizing that his old wardmate had gone through a training process every bit as tough as his own. Then a thought struck him, as memory of their earlier conversation came back to him.

"I don't think it needs to come to that," he said. "I've got an idea. Give me a hand saddling my horses and I'll tell you about it."

Gundar Hardstriker leaned into the smoke and cut a sliver of beef from the joint that was hanging over the coals. He blew carefully on the hot meat, then took a bite, nodding to himself as he tasted it. It was just about right. It was yearling beef, tender and streaked with fat, and with the smoky taste of the fire overlaying the flavor of the beef itself. He looked around the clearing next to where *Wolfcloud* was moored hard up against the shore. His men were busy jointing and smoking the last of the beef. The mutton had already been butchered and salted. In a few more hours, he estimated, they'd be ready. Then there'd be time for a couple of hours' sleep for all hands before full tide let them start on their delayed journey across the Stormwhite.

The flames and smoke of half a dozen fires illuminated the scene and cast weird moving shadows into the trees surrounding the clearing. *Wolfcloud*'s savage figurehead seemed to float unsupported in the smoke, the light of the flames playing on the carved teeth of the wooden wolf's head.

"Gundar!" It was Jon Tarkson, one of his sail handlers, who called from the outer edge of the clearing. The skipper's head swiveled curiously and he made out an indistinct shape emerging from the darkness. He frowned as he realized it was the Ranger. He was mounted, which seemed to be his normal state, and he was leading a second horse, burdened with a large bundle slung crosswise.

Gundar raised his hand in greeting and started forward. He had grown to like the Ranger. He respected the young man's ingenuity in finding a solution to the situation that he had found himself facing and he admired his obvious courage.

"Welcome!" he called and Will returned the greeting, then slid down from the saddle. As Gundar strode closer, picking his way through the fires and the racks of smoking meat, he realized that the bundle slung across the second horse's back was a man—unconscious, and tied hand and foot. He jerked a thumb at the still form.

"Somebody get on your wrong side, Ranger?" he asked.

Will smiled slightly in reply. "You could say that. He's been making a nuisance of himself around here. It occurred to me that he could be useful to you."

Gundar frowned and wiped grease from his chin with the back of his hand. "Useful?" he said. "I've got all the crew I want, thanks. I don't need any untrained southerners on board *Wolfcloud*." He hesitated, then added, "No offense meant."

Will shook his head. "None taken. No, actually I didn't mean to offer him as a crew member. I thought you might like to take him as a slave. You do still have slaves in Skandia, don't you?"

Hardstriker regarded the young man with renewed interest. This one was full of twists and turns and no mistake, he thought. It had been a meager voyage for *Wolfcloud*, as Will had guessed when he first encountered the Skandians. A good healthy slave would be a saleable item when they finally got back to Hallasholm.

"Yes. We still have slaves," he said, stepping closer to the horse and examining the unconscious man more closely. He seized a handful of hair and lifted the man's face to look at it. Aged around thirty. Looked big and strong.

"He healthy?" he asked, and Will nodded.

"Aside from a slight bout of concussion, he's fit as a flea." Will remembered the cruel wound in the dog's side and the rumors that Buttle was responsible for a string of murders in the area. "He'd be good for hours of work on the paddles."

The paddles were a punishment for Skandian slaves. They were large wooden blades that were suspended in the wells during winter. Slaves worked them back and forth and up and down to keep the water moving and stop ice from forming too thickly. In the process, they were invariably splashed until they were soaked to the skin with the freezing cold water. In his time as a Skandian slave, Will had been assigned to the paddles. The assignment had nearly killed him before Erak had taken pity on him and helped him to escape.

Gundar was shaking his head. "The Oberjarl did away with the paddles as a punishment," he said. "Besides, a valuable slave like this would be wasted on them." He considered Buttle's still form once more, then came to a decision. "All right," he said. "How much do you want for him?"

Will reached around and tugged at a knot that held Buttle in place across the horse's back.

"Take him as a gift," he said, heaving on the bandit's collar so that he slid off the horse and fell in a heap on the ground. Buttle moaned softly as he did so, then went quiet. Gundar's eyes widened in surprise.

"A gift?"

Will nodded. "He's made a damn nuisance of himself around here and I don't have time to attend to him. Take him and welcome. You can owe me a favor sometime."

The Skandian captain regarded him thoughtfully. "You're one for surprises, all right, Ranger," he said. Then he called to two of his crewmen who had been standing by, interested spectators. "Get this cargo aboard," he told them. "Stow him in the forepeak."

Grinning, they lifted the unconscious man and carried him away. Gundar held out his hand to Will and the Ranger took it, shaking hands firmly.

"Well, you're right, Ranger. I'll owe you a favor for this. Not only have you fed my men for the winter, you've given us a small profit on the trip as well."

Will shrugged. "You're doing me a service by taking him," he said. "I'll be glad to know he's out of Araluen. Fair winds and strong rowers, Gundar Hardstriker," he added, in the traditional Skandian farewell.

"And an easy road to you, Ranger," Gundar replied.

Will swung back up into Tug's saddle. As he rode away, he pictured Buttle's future as a slave in Skandia. Even without the paddles, his life would be a hard one.

10

WILL REINED TUG IN AND LOOKED AROUND THE ALMOST DE-serted Gathering Ground. It was strange to see it so empty, he thought. There was a melancholy feeling to it.

Normally, the lightly wooded meadow would be filled with the small green tents of the fifty active members of the Ranger Corps as they came together for their annual Gathering. There would be cooking fires, the clank and rattle of weapons practice overlaid by the buzz of a dozen or more conversations and sudden bursts of laughter as old friends called greetings to new arrivals riding in.

Today, the campsites between the trees were bare. There were only two tents pitched, at the far end of the field, where the large command tent was normally placed. Halt and Crowley were already here, he realized.

Another week had passed since Alyss's visit to Seacliff Fief. The elegant Courier had given him his final instructions, telling him to wait for two days after her departure, then to leave quietly, without letting anyone know he was going, and to make his way to the Gathering Ground, where Halt and Crowley would explain his assignment. As she was leaving, she placed her hands upon his shoulders and looked deep into his eyes. She was taller than Will by half a head and she had always liked the fact that this didn't bother him. In truth, most people were taller than Will, so it wasn't an issue with him. In his turn, he admired the way Alyss never tried to stoop or conceal her height. She stood proudly, with a firm, straight carriage that gave grace to all her movements.

As their gazes met, he saw the light of sadness in her eyes. Then she leaned forward and her lips touched his—light as a butterfly's wings and amazingly soft to the touch. They remained so for many seconds, then Alyss finally stepped back. She smiled sadly at him, sorry to be leaving so soon after seeing him again.

"Take care, Will," she said. He nodded. There was a huskiness in his throat and he didn't trust himself to speak immediately. Eventually he managed to reply.

"And you."

He had watched her ride away with her two-man escort until the trees hid her from sight. And he had remained watching for some time after that.

Now, here he was, ready to find out more about this assignment—anxious and uncertain, and just a little saddened by the thought of his last moments with Alyss and the sight of the empty Gathering Ground. Then the uncertainty was dispelled and the melancholy lifted as he saw a familiar stocky figure moving near one of the tents.

"Halt!" he cried out gladly, and a slight pressure with his knees set Tug galloping through the deserted Gathering site. The dog, caught by surprise, barked once, then shot in pursuit like an arrow from a bow.

The grim-faced Ranger straightened from the fire at the sound of his former student's voice. He stood, hands on hips and a frown on his face as Will and Tug careered toward him. But inside, there was a lightening of his heart that he never failed to feel when in Will's company. Not for the first time, the realization hit Halt that Will was no longer a mere boy. No one wore the Silver Oakleaf if he hadn't proven himself to be worthy. Despite himself, he felt a surge of pride.

Tug, forelegs braced stiffly, leaning back on his hind legs, slid to a halt beside the Ranger, driving a thick cloud of dust into the air. Then Halt felt himself seized in a bear hug as Will threw himself from the saddle and embraced him gleefully.

"Halt! How are you? What have you been doing? Where's Abelard? How's Crowley? What's this all about?"

"I'm glad to see you rate my horse more important than our Corps Commandant," Halt said, one eyebrow rising in the expression that Will knew so well. Early in their relationship, he had thought it was an expression of displeasure. He had learned years ago that it was, for Halt, the equivalent of a smile.

Will finally released his mentor from his embrace and stepped back to study him. It had only been a few months since he had seen Halt, but he was surprised to see that the gray in the older Ranger's beard and hair was thicker than he remembered.

"Thank goodness we went to all the trouble of keeping this meeting secret so you could ride in here bellowing at the top of your lungs," Halt said. Will grinned at him, totally unabashed.

"There's no one nearby to hear," he said. "I circled the site before I came in. If there's anyone within five kilometers, I'll eat my quiver."

Halt regarded him, eyebrow arched once more. "Anyone?"

"Anyone other than Crowley," Will amended, making a dismissive gesture. "I saw him watching me from that hide he always uses about two kilometers out. I assumed he'd be back in here by now."

Halt cleared his throat loudly. "Oh, you saw him, did you?" he said. "I imagine he'll be overjoyed to hear that." Secretly, he was pleased with his former pupil. In spite of his curiosity and obvious excitement, he hadn't forgotten to take the precautions that had been drilled into him. That augured well for what lay ahead, Halt thought, a sudden grimness settling onto his manner.

Will didn't notice the momentary change of mood. He was loosening Tug's saddle girth. As he spoke, his voice was muffled against the horse's flank. "He's becoming too much a creature of habit," he said. "He's used that hide for the last three Gatherings. It's time he tried something new. Everyone must be onto it by now."

Rangers constantly competed with each other to see before being seen and each year's Gathering was a time of heightened competition. Halt nodded thoughtfully. Crowley had constructed the virtually invisible observation post some four years previously. Alone among the younger Rangers, Will had tumbled to it after one year. Halt had never mentioned to him that he was the only one who knew of Crowley's hide. The concealed post was the Ranger Commandant's pride and joy.

"Well, perhaps not everyone," he said. Will emerged from behind his horse, grinning at the thought of the head of the Ranger Corps thinking he had remained hidden from sight as he watched Will's approach.

"All the same, perhaps he's getting a bit long in the tooth to be skulking around hiding in the bushes, don't you think?" he said cheerfully. Halt considered the question for a moment.

"Long in the tooth? Well, that's one opinion. Mind you, his silent movement skills are still as good as ever," he said meaningfully.

The grin on Will's face slowly faded. He resisted the temptation to look over his shoulder.

"He's standing behind me, isn't he?" he asked Halt. The older Ranger nodded.

"He's been there for a while, hasn't he?" Will continued and Halt nodded once more.

"Is he . . . close enough to have heard what I said?" Will finally managed to ask, fearing the worst. This time, Halt didn't have to answer.

"Oh, good grief no," came a familiar voice from behind him. "He's so old and decrepit these days he's as deaf as a post."

Will's shoulders sagged and he turned to see the sandy-haired Commandant standing a few meters away.

The younger man's eyes dropped.

"Hullo, Crowley," he said, then mumbled, "Ahhh . . . I'm sorry about that."

Crowley glared at the young Ranger for a few more seconds, then he couldn't help the grin breaking out on his face.

"No harm done," he said, adding with a small note of triumph, "It's not often these days I manage to get the better of one of you young ones."

Secretly, he was impressed at the news that Will had spotted his hiding place. Only the sharpest eyes could have picked it. Crowley had been in the business of seeing without being seen for thirty years or more, and despite what Will believed, he was still an absolute master of camouflage and unseen movement. He noticed another movement now—a wagging movement—and he dropped to one knee to consider the dog.

"Hullo," he said softly, "who's this?"

He held out one hand, knuckles slightly flexed and fingers pointing down, and the dog crept forward a few paces, sniffed at the hand, then wagged her tail once more, her ears rising into a pricked-up, alert position. Crowley loved dogs and they sensed it, seeming to single him out as a friend at the first moment of contact.

"What's your name, girl?" the Commandant asked.

"I haven't named her yet. I found her when I was on the way to Seacliff," Will explained. "She'd been hurt and was nearly dead. Her previous owner had tried to kill her."

Crowley's face darkened. The idea of cruelty to animals was abhorrent to him. "I trust you had words with this man?" he said.

Will shifted his feet uncertainly. He wasn't altogether sure how his superiors might view his treatment of John Buttle.

"Well, in a manner of speaking, yes," he said. He noticed Halt's raised eyebrows. His old teacher could always tell when Will hadn't told him the full facts of a story. Crowley, his hand ruffling the fur behind the dog's ears, looked up curiously as well.

"In a manner of speaking?"

Will cleared his throat nervously. "I had to deal with him, but not because of the dog. Well, not directly. I mean, it was because of the dog that he turned up at my cabin that night and overheard what we were saying and then . . . well, I knew I'd have to do something about him because he'd heard too much. And then Alyss said maybe we'd have to . . . you know . . . but I thought that might be a bit drastic. So, in the end, it was the best solution I could think of."

He paused, aware that the two men were staring at him, total incomprehension on both their faces.

"What I mean to say is," he repeated, "it *sort of* involved the dog but not really directly, if you get my meaning."

There was a very long pause, then Halt said slowly, "No, actually, I don't."

Crowley looked at his longtime friend and said: "You had this young man with you for . . . what, six years?"

Halt shrugged. "Near enough," he replied.

"And did you ever understand a word he was saying?"

"Not a lot of the time, no," Halt said.

Crowley shook his head in wonder. "It's just as well he didn't go into the Diplomatic Service. We'd be at war with half a dozen countries by now if he was on the loose." He looked back to Will. "Tell us, in simple words and, if possible, completing every sentence that you start, what the dog and this person and Alyss have to do with each other."

Will drew a deep breath to begin talking. He noticed that both men took an involuntary half step backward and he decided he'd better try to keep it as simple as possible.

When he finished relating the tale, Crowley and Halt sat back, looking at Will with some concern.

"You sold him into slavery?" Crowley asked, eventually. But Will shook his head.

"I didn't sell him. I . . . gave him into slavery. It was either give him to the Skandians or kill him. And I didn't think he deserved to die."

"But you did think he deserved to be . . . given . . . into slavery?" Crowley asked. Will's jaw set a little more firmly before he answered.

"Yes, I do, Crowley. The man has a long history of crimes of violence. He's probably been responsible for more than one murder—not that there's any proof that would stand up in a court of law," he added.

Halt scratched at his beard, looking thoughtful. "After all," he put in mildly, "it is part of our brief to deal with cases where there's insufficient evidence for a conviction." Crowley looked at him sharply.

"That's not formally acknowledged, as you well know," he said. Halt nodded, taking the point, then continued in the same mild tone.

"So the case of Arndor of Crewse wouldn't by any means set a precedent?" he asked, and Crowley shifted his feet uncomfortably. Will looked at the two of them, puzzled by the turn in the conversation.

"Arndor of Crewse?" he asked. "Who was he?"

Halt smiled at him. "He was a giant—over two meters tall. And a bandit. He terrorized the town of Crewse for several months until a young Ranger dealt with him . . . in a relatively unconventional way."

Seeing Will's interest, and Crowley's discomfort, Halt continued, with the barest hint of a grin. "He chained him to a mill wheel in the town and let the people of Crewse use him as a mill pony for a period of five years. Apparently it had a chastening effect on his soul and brought quite a bit of prosperity to the town as well. Crewse flour became well known for the fineness of its grind."

Crowley finally interrupted this tale. "Look, it was a different situation and I . . ." He corrected himself a little too late. "The Ranger concerned . . . couldn't think of any other way of dealing with it. But at least he was making reparation to the people he had wronged. He wasn't just sold as a slave to a foreign power."

"Well," said Halt, "neither was this Buttle character. And actually, as Will pointed out, he wasn't sold. He was given. A good lawyer could probably make a case that with no money changing hands there was nothing done that was against the laws of the country."

Crowley snorted. "A good lawyer?" he said. "There's no such thing. All right, young Will, I suppose you acted for the best and as your *lawyer* here points out, technically speaking, there's no crime involved. Maybe you'd better pitch your tent. We'll talk after supper."

Will nodded, flashing a grin at Halt, who raised that eyebrow again. As he moved off to pitch his small green tent, Crowley stepped a little closer to his old friend, speaking in a lowered tone so that Will couldn't hear.

"You know, it's not a bad way of dealing with awkward cases," he said softly. "Maybe you should contact your friend Erak and see if we could do it on a more regular basis."

Halt looked at him for a long moment in silence.

"Of course. After all, this country only has so many flour mills, doesn't it?"

11

THE THREE RANGERS SAT COMFORTABLY AROUND THE FIRE
Will had built. Their evening meal had been a good one. Crowley
had brought venison steaks with him and they had cooked them,
sizzling and spitting, on flat stones heated in the coals of the fire,
supplementing the meat with boiled potatoes, liberally heaped with
butter and pepper, and greens that had been blanched quickly in a
pot of boiling water. Now, nursing mugs of coffee that Halt had
brewed, they sat in a companionable silence.

Will was eager to know the details of his mission but he knew
that there was no sense in hurrying things. Crowley and Halt would
tell him in their own time, and nothing he did or said would make
them do so any sooner than they planned to. A few years earlier, he
would have been in a fever of anticipation, fidgeting and unable to
relax. But, along with the other skills of a Ranger, he had learned
patience. As he sat and waited for his superiors to broach the subject, he felt Halt's approving eye on him from time to time as his
former teacher assessed this newfound quality. Will looked up once,
caught Halt's eyes on him and allowed a grin to touch his features.
He was pleased that he was able to demonstrate his forbearance.

Finally, Halt shifted his seat on the hard ground and said in an exasperated tone, "Oh, all right, Crowley! Let's get on with it, for God's sake!"

The Corps Commandant smiled delightedly at his friend. "I thought we were testing Will's patience here, not yours," he said. Halt made an annoyed gesture.

"Well, consider his patience tested."

Crowley's smile slowly faded as he gathered his thoughts. Will leaned forward, to hear his new assignment. He'd spent the past few days doing his best to suppress his curiosity and now that the moment was here, he felt he couldn't wait another second. He'd been racking his brain wondering what the assignment might involve and had come up with several possibilities, most of them based on his experiences in Skandia. Crowley's first words, however, instantly dispelled all of them.

"We appear to have a problem with sorcery in the north," he said.

Will sat back in surprise. "Sorcery?" he asked, his voice pitched a little higher than he had meant it to be. Crowley nodded.

"Apparently," he said, laying stress on the word. Will looked from him to Halt. His former teacher's face gave nothing away.

"Do we believe in sorcery?" he asked Halt. The older man gave a small shrug.

"Ninety-five percent of cases that I've seen have been nothing but mumbo jumbo and trickery," he said. "Nothing that couldn't be solved by a well-placed arrow. Then there's perhaps another three percent that involve mind domination and manipulation of a weaker mind by a stronger—the sort of control that Morgarath exercised over his Wargals."

Will nodded slowly. Morgarath, a former baron who had re-

belled against the King, had led an army of bestial warriors who
were totally bound to his will.

"A further one percent comprises the sort of mass hallucinations
that some people are capable of creating," Crowley put in. "It's a
similar case of mind control, but one that causes people to 'see' or
'hear' things that aren't really there."

There was a moment's pause. Again, Will looked from one to
the other. Finally, he said, "That leaves one percent." The two older
men nodded.

"I see your capacity for addition has improved," Halt replied,
but then went on before Will could comment. "Yes, as you say. It
leaves one percent of cases."

"And you're saying they're examples of sorcery?" Will asked, but
Halt shook his head doggedly.

"I'm saying we can't find a logical explanation for them," he said.
Will shifted in his seat impatiently, looking to pin his former teacher
down one way or another.

"Halt," he said, holding the bearded Ranger's gaze steadily with
his own, "do you believe in sorcery?"

Halt hesitated before replying. He was a man who had dealt in
facts all his life. His life's work was dedicated to gathering facts and
information. Uncertainty was anathema to him. Yet, in this
case . . .

"I don't believe in it," he said, choosing his words carefully, "but
I don't disbelieve in it either. In those cases where there seems to be
no cause or logical explanation, I am prepared to keep an open mind
on the subject."

"And I think that's probably the best position we can take,"
Crowley interrupted. "I mean, there is obviously an evil force that
influences our world. We've all seen too many examples of criminal

behavior to doubt it. Who's to say that there isn't the occasional person with the ability to summon that force or channel it to his own use?"

"However," Halt said, "remember that we're talking about one case in a hundred—and even then, we're saying it may or may not be the real thing. If the real thing even exists."

Will shook his head slowly, then took a deep sip of his coffee. "I'm getting confused here," he said at length. Halt nodded.

"Just keep one thing in mind. There's a better than ninety percent chance that the case we're dealing with here isn't sorcery—it just appears to be. Hold on to that thought, and keep an open mind for the rest. All right?"

Will nodded, letting out a deep breath. "Fine," he said. "So what are the details of this case? What do you want me to do?"

Crowley gestured for Halt to go ahead with the briefing. The bond between master and pupil was still strong, he knew, and would facilitate a concise briefing with less chance of misunderstanding or confusion. These two knew each other's minds.

"Very well," Halt began, "in the first place, we're talking about Norgate Fief—"

"Norgate?" Will interrupted, surprise evident in his voice. "Don't we have a Ranger assigned to that fief?"

"Yes, we do," Halt agreed. "But he's known in the area. He's recognized. People are scared and confused and the last person they'll talk to at this stage is a Ranger. Half of them think we're sorcerers ourselves," he added grimly. Will nodded. He knew that to be true.

"But won't they distrust me if I turn up there?" he asked. "After all, they may not know me, but I *am* a Ranger."

"You're not going as a Ranger," Halt told him.

That piece of information succeeded in stopping the barrage of questions Will was about to unleash. To tell the truth, he was a little taken aback by the news.

People were nervous of Rangers, it was true. But there was undeniable prestige that attached to members of the Corps as well. Doors opened for Rangers. Their opinions were sought and respected by the knights and barons of the realm—even, on occasion, by the King himself. Their skill with their chosen weapons was legendary. He wasn't sure if he wanted to put all that aside. He wasn't sure that without the aura of being a Ranger to bolster his confidence, he could actually handle a difficult and dangerous mission—and already, this mission sounded as if it were going to be both of those.

"We're getting ahead of ourselves," Crowley said. "Let's get the big picture out of the way before we start going into details."

"Good idea," Halt said. He gave Will a meaningful look and the younger man nodded. He knew that now was the time to listen without interruption.

"All right. Norgate Fief is rather unique in the kingdom, insofar as, in addition to Castle Norgate, the center of the fief, there is an additional castle in a shire right at the north."

As Halt was speaking, Crowley unfolded a map of the area on the ground between them and Will came onto one knee to study it. He touched the map, where a castle was indicated, virtually on the kingdom's northern border.

"Castle Macindaw," he muttered, and Halt nodded.

"It's more a fortress than a castle," he said. "It's a little low on luxuries and high on strategic position. As you can see . . ." He took one of his black arrows from the quiver beside him and used it to point to the rugged mountains that divided Araluen from its northern neighbor, Picta. "It's placed so that it dominates and controls the Macindaw pass through the mountains."

He paused, watching the younger man as he took in the situation, his eyes intent on the map. Finally, Will nodded and Halt continued.

"Without Castle Macindaw, we'd have constant forays from the Scotti—the wild tribe who control the southern provinces of Picta. They're raiders, thieves and fighters. In fact, without Macindaw, we'd be hard-pressed to keep them out of Norgate Fief entirely. It's a long way north and it's not easy traveling for an army in winter—particularly when the bulk of our troops are from the southern fiefs and not used to the extremes of weather that you find up there."

Nodding to himself, Will sat back from the chart. The picture was imprinted on his memory now. He shifted his gaze back to Halt as the older man continued.

"So you can understand why we get a tad anxious when anything seems to upset the natural balance of things in Norgate Fief," he said.

Will nodded.

"When Lord Syron, the commander at Macindaw, was struck down by a mysterious illness, we were understandably concerned. That concern grew when we started to hear wild rumors of sorcery. Apparently, one of Syron's ancestors, some hundred years back, had a falling-out with a local sorcerer." Halt sensed the question on Will's lips and held up a hand to stop it from being asked.

"We don't know. Could have been mind control. Could have been a charlatan. Or maybe he was the real thing. It all happened over a hundred years ago, as I say, so there's very little hard evidence and a lot of anecdotal hysteria involved. As far as all the accounts of the matter go, he was a genuine dyed-in-the-wool sorcerer who had been feuding with Syron's family over a period of hundreds of years. The most recent appearance was the end of a long line of clashes. Bear in mind, we're dealing with myth and legend here, so don't expect too much sense."

"What happened to the sorcerer?" Will asked, and Halt shrugged.

"Nobody knows. Seems he struck Syron's ancestor down with all manner of mysterious ailments. Naturally, the healers couldn't identify or treat any of them. They never can when they think sorcery's involved," he said with a disparaging note to his voice. "But then a young knight from the household took it upon himself to rid the province of the sorcerer. In accordance with all the conventions of such myths, he was pure of heart and his nobility of character let him overcome the sorcerer and drive him out."

"He didn't kill him?" Will put in, and Halt shook his head.

"No. Unfortunately, they never do. It leaves legends like this room to rise up again over the years, as this has done. The current situation is that Syron, some six weeks ago, was out riding when he was suddenly struck down from his horse. When his men reached him, he was blue in the face, frothing at the mouth and screaming in agony.

"His men got him home and the healers were completely baffled by the condition. All they could do was sedate him to relieve the pain. He hasn't improved since and he's hovering on the brink of death. If they wake him to feed him or give him water, the pain hits him again and he begins screaming and frothing all over. Yet if they leave him sedated, he grows weaker and weaker as time passes."

"Let me guess," Will said, as Halt paused. "These symptoms were identical to the ones his ancestor suffered in the legend?"

Halt pointed a finger at the younger man. "Got it in one," he said. "Which of course gave rise to the rumors that Malkallam was back."

"Malkallam?" Will asked.

"The original sorcerer," Crowley put in. "Nobody knows where the rumors started, but there have been other . . . manifestations as well. Lights in the forest that disappear when anyone approaches, strange figures seen on the road at night, voices heard in the castle and so on. The sort of things calculated to scare the living daylights out of country people. The local Ranger, Meralon, has been trying to get hold of more information, but people have clammed up. He did hear some rumor about a sorcerer living deep in the forest, and the name Malkallam was used. But exactly where he was living he couldn't find out."

"Who's commanding the castle while Syron is out of action?" Will asked. Halt nodded, appreciating Will's ability to get to the heart of the problem.

"Syron's son, Orman, is nominally in charge, but he's not really a soldier. According to Meralon's report, he's something of a scholar—and more interested in studying history than guarding the kingdom's borders. Fortunately, Syron's nephew Keren is also there and he's taken practical command of the garrison. He's more down to earth. He was raised as a warrior and apparently he's a popular leader."

"He can handle things for the time being," Crowley said, "but if Syron should die, then we have the problem of succession, and Orman, a weak, incapable leader, will inherit the position. That could destabilize the whole situation and leave us vulnerable to an attack from the north. That's something we have to avoid at all costs. Macindaw is too important strategically for us to take any risks."

Will tugged thoughtfully at his chin for a few seconds.

"I see," he said finally. "So what do you want me to do?"

"Go up there," Crowley replied. "Get to know the locals. Find out as much as you can. See what you can gather about this Malkallam character. See whether he really exists or whether people are just imagining things. Gain their confidence. Get them talking."

Will frowned. Crowley made it all sound so easy, he thought. "That's easier said than done," he muttered, but Halt replied with just the ghost of a smile.

"It'll be easier for you than for most," he said. "People like to talk to you. You're young. You have a fresh-faced innocent look that disarms them. That's why we chose you. They'll never suspect you're a Ranger."

"So what will they think I am?" Will asked, and now the grin finally broke through on Halt's face.

"They'll think you're a jongleur," he said.

12

"A jongleur?" he repeated. "Me?"

Halt looked at him from under dark eyebrows. "A jongleur. You," he said. Will made a helpless gesture with his hands, for a moment lost for words.

"It's a perfect cover for you," Crowley said. "Jongleurs are constantly traveling. They're welcome everywhere, from castles to the meanest tavern. And in a godforsaken spot like Norgate, you'll be doubly welcome. Best of all, people talk to jongleurs. And they talk in front of them," he added, meaningfully.

Will finally found the words he had been looking for. "Aren't we forgetting one small detail?" he said. "I'm *not* a jongleur. I can't tell jokes. I can't do magic tricks and I can't tumble. I'd break my neck if I tried."

Halt nodded, acknowledging the point. "Aren't *you* forgetting that there are different types of jongleurs?" he said. "Some of them are simple minstrels."

"And you play that lute of yours quite well, Halt tells me," Crowley put in. Will looked at him, the confusion growing.

"It's a mandola," he said. "It has eight strings, tuned in pairs. A lute has ten strings with some of them acting as drones . . ."

He tailed off. Then he felt a small glow of pleasure as he registered what Crowley had said.

"Do you really think I play well enough?" he said to Halt. The older Ranger had always assumed a long-suffering expression whenever Will had practiced the mandola. Will couldn't help feeling a sense of satisfaction to hear that he actually admired his skill. The sense was short-lived, however.

"What would I know?" Halt replied with a shrug. "One cat screeching sounds pretty much like another to me."

"Oh," said Will, more than a little deflated. "Well, perhaps other people are likely to be more discriminating. Can't we find some other disguise for me?" he appealed to Crowley. The Ranger Commandant shrugged in his turn, willing to entertain suggestions.

"Such as?" he asked. Will cast around in his mind before an answer came to him.

"A tinker," he suggested. After all, in the adventures and legends that Murdal, Baron Arald's official storyteller, used to recite at Castle Redmont, heroes often disguised themselves as tinkers. Halt snorted disdainfully.

"A tinker?" Crowley asked.

"Yes," said Will, warming to his theme. "They travel around from place to place. People talk to them and—"

"And they are renowned as petty thieves," Crowley finished for him. "Do you think it's a good idea to assume a disguise that ensures that everyone you meet is immediately suspicious of you? They'd be watching you like hawks, waiting for you to steal the cutlery."

"Thieves?" Will said, crestfallen. "Are they really?"

"They're notorious for it," Halt said. "I've never understood why that boring idiot Murdal used to insist that his characters disguised themselves as tinkers. Couldn't think of a worse idea, myself."

"Oh," said Will, now bereft of ideas. He hesitated, then asked again, "Do you really think my playing's good enough to carry it off?"

"One way to find out," Crowley said. "You've got your lute there. Let's have a tune from it."

"It's not a . . ." Will began, then gave up as he reached behind him for the mandola case, where it lay on top of his saddle and other kit.

"Never mind," he muttered.

He took the instrument from its case and removed the tortoiseshell pick from between the two top strings. He strummed experimentally. As he had expected, the combination of bouncing around on a packsaddle and the effect of the cool night air had affected the tuning. He adjusted the strings, tried another chord and nodded, satisfied. Then he sounded the chord again, decided that the top string was a little sharp and loosened it a fraction. Better, he thought.

"Away you go." Crowley made an encouraging gesture. Will sounded an A chord, then hesitated. He went blank. He couldn't think of a single tune to play. He tried a D chord and then an E minor and a B flat, hoping that the sounds might give him some inspiration.

"Are there words to this tune?" Halt asked, far too politely. Will turned to him.

"I can't think of a song," he said. "My mind's gone blank."

"Could be embarrassing if that happened in a rough tavern," Halt said. Will tried desperately to remember a song. Any song.

"How about *Old Joe Smoke?*" Crowley suggested cheerfully, and Halt whipped around to glare suspiciously at him.

"*Old Joe Smoke?*" Will asked. It was, of course, the song that he had turned into a parody about Halt, and he wondered if Crowley knew that. The Ranger's face was innocent of guile, however. He nodded, smiling encouragement, ignoring the glare from his old friend.

"Always been a favorite," Crowley said. "I used to dance a fine jig to *Old Joe Smoke* when I was a youngster." He made the same go-ahead gesture. Will, unable to think of an alternative, began the introduction on the mandola, his speed and fluency gradually increasing as he became more confident. All he had to do, he told himself, was remember to sing the original words, not the parody version. Throwing caution to the wind, he began to sing:

> "*Old Joe Smoke's a friend of mine.*
> *He lives on Bleaker's Hill.*
> *Old Joe Smoke never took a bath*
> *and they say he never will.*
> *Fare thee well, Old Joe Smoke,*
> *fare thee well I say.*
> *Fare thee well, Old Joe Smoke,*
> *I'll see you on your way.*"

Crowley was slapping his hand on his knee, keeping time, nodding his head and grinning.

"The boy's good!" he said to Halt, and Will continued, emboldened by the praise. He played the intricate pattern of sixteenth notes that made up the interlude, then sang the next verse.

"Old Joe Smoke he lost a bet.
He lost his winter coat.
When winter comes Old Joe stays warm
by sleeping 'mongst the goats.
Fare thee well, Old Joe Smoke,
fare thee well I say.
Fare thee well, Old Joe Smoke,
I'll see you on your way."

He was well into the song now and he played the interlude again, this time trying a more ambitious pattern than before. He fumbled it once on the third bar but covered the mistake artfully, he thought, and launched into the third verse.

"Graybeard Halt he lives with the goats,
that's what I've heard tell.
He hasn't changed his socks for years,
but the goats don't mind the smell.
Fare thee well, Graybeard Halt,
fare thee well I . . ."

And stopped, suddenly, realizing what he had sung.

From sheer force of habit, distracted by his own astonishing skill on the mandola, he had reverted to the parody version. Crowley cocked his head to one side, frowning in mock interest.

"Fascinating lyrics," he said. "Not sure that I've heard that version before."

He covered his mouth with his hand and his shoulders began to shake.

"Very funny, Crowley," Halt said in an exasperated tone of voice as the Ranger Commandant made strange choking sounds behind his hand, his face lowered and his shoulders shaking even harder. Will looked at Halt in horror.

"Halt . . . I'm sorry . . . I didn't mean . . ."

Crowley finally gave up the struggle and burst into peals of uncontrolled laughter. Will made a helpless gesture at Halt. The older Ranger shrugged resignedly, then glared at Crowley. He leaned sideways and dug the Ranger Commandant painfully in the ribs with his elbow.

"It's not *that* funny!" he snarled. Crowley held his bruised rib and pointed at Halt.

"It is! It is! You should have seen your face!" he gasped. Then, to Will, he said: "Go on! Are there more verses?"

Will hesitated. Halt was glaring at Crowley, and Will—even though he was a fully fledged Ranger, a wearer of the Silver Oakleaf and, technically, Halt's equal in rank—knew it would be unwise to continue. Very unwise.

"I think we've heard enough to judge," Halt said. He turned to the three small tents that they had pitched, now just at the edge of the fire's glow, and called in a louder voice, "What do you say, Berrigan?"

There was a rustle of movement behind the tents as a tall figure stood slowly and limped into the firelight. Even before he noticed the six-string *gitarra* that the man was holding in one hand, Will recognized the limping gait. He had seen Berrigan several times before, usually at the Rangers' annual Gathering, when he entertained the assembled Corps. A former wearer of the Oakleaf himself, Berrigan had been forced to resign from active service when he lost his left leg in a pitched battle with raiding Skandians. Since then, he had earned his living as a jongleur, showing a high degree of skill as a musician and singer. Will also suspected that he had from time to time been used to gather intelligence for the Corps.

He realized now that the former Ranger had been listening in for the purpose of judging him. Berrigan smiled at Will as he eased himself down beside the fire, the peg leg he wore making the movement a little difficult as it stuck stiffly out before him.

"Evening, Will," he said. He nodded at the mandola, now laid across the younger man's lap. "Not bad. Not bad at all."

He had a lean face, with high cheekbones and a large, hawk-like nose. But the outstanding features were the bright blue eyes and the wide, friendly smile. He wore his brown hair long, as befitted his calling, and his clothes were those of a typical jongleur—marked in haphazard patterns of bright colors that seemed to shimmer as he moved. Each jongleur, Will knew, had his own distinctive set of colors and patterns. He noticed now that the pattern on Berrigan's cloak was markedly similar to that of the cloaks that all Rangers wore—although more brightly colored than the drab browns, grays and greens of the standard Ranger cloak.

"Berrigan. Good to see you," he said. Then, as a thought struck him, he turned to Crowley. "Crowley, wouldn't it make more sense if Berrigan took this mission? After all, he is a professional jongleur and we all know he still works for the Corps from time to time."

The other three exchanged glances. "Oh, we all know that, do we?" Crowley asked.

Will shrugged diffidently. "Well, we don't *know* it exactly. But he does, doesn't he?"

There was an awkward silence for a few seconds. Then Berrigan broke the tension around the campfire, saying with a lazy grin, "You're right, Will. I still do some work for the Corps when asked. But for this job, I'm a bit short. About a foot or so."

"But you're way taller than me . . ." Will began and then realized that Berrigan was looking meaningfully at the peg leg that stood straight out in front of him. He stopped in embarrassment. "Oh, you mean your . . ." He couldn't say the word. It seemed so crass somehow. But Berrigan's smile widened even further.

"My peg leg, Will. It's perfectly all right. I'm used to the fact by now. No need to pretend it's not there. From what Crowley has told me about this job, it needs someone who's fast on his feet, and I'm afraid that isn't me anymore."

Crowley cleared his throat, glad the awkward moment had passed. "What Berrigan *can* do is tell us if you'll pass muster as a jongleur. What do you say, Berrigan?"

Berrigan cocked his head to one side, thought for a moment, then replied. "He's good enough. It's a pleasant voice and he plays well. Certainly well enough for the sort of remote places and country inns he'll be performing in. I don't know if he's ready for the court at Castle Araluen yet." He smiled at Will to take any sting out of the words. Will grinned in return. He was pleased with the assessment. Then Berrigan went on.

"But the giveaway is his unpreparedness. It always shows up a non-professional."

Crowley frowned. "How do you mean? You say he's good enough singing and playing. What other preparation does he need?"

Berrigan didn't answer directly but turned to Will.

"Let's hear another tune, Will. Any one you like. Quickly now," he said. Will picked up the mandola and . . .

And again his mind went blank.

"There you have it," Berrigan said. "The amateur always dries up when he's asked to perform." He turned back to Will. "Do you know *Lowland Jenny? Spinner's Reel? Cobbington Mill* or *By the Southland Streams?*"

He shot the song titles out in rapid succession and Will nodded glumly to each of them. Berrigan smiled and shrugged.

"Any one of them would have done then," he said. "The trick is not just to know them. It's to remember you know them. But we can work on that."

Will looked at Halt. His former teacher inclined his head to the jongleur.

"Berrigan will travel part of the way with you to coach you," he said. Will smiled at the tall jongleur. He was beginning to feel more comfortable with the idea—and a little less as if he were being thrown into deep water and told to learn to swim.

"And you might as well start now," Crowley said, refilling his coffee mug and leaning back comfortably against a log. "Let's hear a tune from the two of you."

Berrigan glanced a question at Will.

"*The Woods of Far Away*," Will said without hesitation.

Berrigan nodded and smiled. "He learns quickly," he said to Halt, who acknowledged the statement with the barest dip of his head. Then, as the two of them began the introduction to the lovely old song of homecoming, Berrigan stopped and frowned at Will's mandola.

"Your A string is just a little flat," he told him.

"I knew that," Halt said in a superior tone to Crowley.

13

THE FOLLOWING MORNING, WILL UNDERWENT A TRANSFORMA-
tion from Ranger to jongleur. His mottled brown, gray and green
cloak was exchanged for one that was more fitting to his identity as
an entertainer. He was glad that Halt and Crowley hadn't opted for
anything too outlandish in the way of colors, but had chosen a simple black and white motif for him. He swung the cloak, with its deep
cowled hood, around his shoulders. There was something vaguely
familiar about it, he thought. Then it came to him. The irregular
black-and-white pattern woven into the material served the same
purpose as the mottling on his Ranger cloak. It broke up the shape
of the wearer, making the outline indistinct and disguising the hard
edges that would help an observer see him. Halt noticed his interested scrutiny and nodded confirmation.

"Yes, it's a camouflage cloak," he said. "Perhaps not the same as
a Ranger cloak, but where you're going, those colors will be more
useful."

Realization dawned on Will. Norgate Fief in winter would be
covered in thick snow, the colors leached out of the landscape. A
closer inspection showed him that the black sections of the cloak

weren't true black at all, but a dark shade of gray. It would take little effort for a person skilled in the art of unseen movement to blend with the winter countryside. Indoors, of course, the cloak would appear to be nothing more nor less than the sort of random theatrical patterning and dramatic colors that would be expected of a jongleur.

"Very clever," he said, grinning at Halt and Crowley. The two older Rangers nodded agreement. Next, Crowley handed him a sleeveless jerkin made from glove-thin gray leather.

"You can't wear your double scabbard," he said, nodding to the distinctive arrangement that held Will's two knives. "It's too much of a giveaway, seeing how only Rangers use them."

"Oh," said Will uncertainly. He wasn't comfortable at the thought of not having his big saxe knife and the smaller throwing knife close to hand. Crowley quickly reassured him.

"You can keep the saxe," he said. "Plenty of folk carry knives like that. And this jerkin has a scabbard sewn into it for your throwing knife."

He indicated a concealed leather sheath inside the jerkin, below the collar. Will drew his throwing knife and slid it experimentally into the sheath. It fit perfectly. Yet Halt's next words brought his spirits down once more.

"But I'm afraid the longbow will have to stay behind. A jongleur simply wouldn't carry one," he said. He took the massive bow from Will and placed it to one side. In its place, he handed him a small, low-powered hunting bow and a quiver of arrows. Will studied the unimpressive weapon critically, flexing it easily. He doubted that the draw weight could be more than twenty or thirty pounds.

"I might as well not have this," he said. "It would hardly shoot an arrow out of my shadow at midday. Besides," he added, looking more closely at the arrows, "these arrows are far too heavy for the bow." He was definitely uncomfortable with this turn of events. The bow had been his principal weapon since he was apprenticed to Halt so many years ago. He would feel naked and vulnerable without one.

Halt and Crowley exchanged a small smile. "The bow's not for shooting," Crowley said. "It's simply an excuse to carry the arrows. Come this way," he said, beckoning Will to follow.

In the clearing where the horses grazed, he indicated a pack-saddle to Will.

"Your new packsaddle," he said, an expectant tone in his voice. Will frowned.

"There's nothing wrong with my old one," he said, unsure where this was heading. He studied the packsaddle. It seemed perfectly normal, apart from an unusual pommel arrangement. Where Will's packsaddle had two protruding wooden crosspieces in a V shape that could be used as a purchase point to tie items onto the saddle, this one had two curved pieces of flat metal serving the same purpose. They curved inward, then flared away from each other. It was rather ornate, he thought, but no more practical than the simple wooden V.

"We're very proud of this," Crowley said. He reached down and took hold of one of the flat pieces, then pulled it clear of the saddle. Will now saw that it had been held in place in a tight-fitting sheath that was part of the saddle. The metal piece, now that he could see it, was a little more than half a meter long and formed in a shallow S, with the lower curve twice the length of the upper. At the lower end, a slot was cut into the metal. Like the cloak, there was something familiar about it. Crowley grinned at him, then reached for the carrying handle at the rear of the saddle. He twisted it backward and it came clear of the saddle as well. It appeared to be plain, leather-wrapped wood, but there were two milled knobs, one at either end.

As Will watched, fascinated, Crowley slipped the slotted end of the metal arm into a narrow slit in the handpiece. Then he rapidly tightened one of the milled knobs, which Will now saw was the head of a large, threaded bolt, to hold the arm tightly in place.

"My God," said Will quietly, as he understood. He realized now why the flat metal piece had seemed familiar. When he first joined Halt, he had been too small to handle a full-sized longbow, so the older Ranger had given him a recurve bow, where each limb was formed in that shallow S shape. The double curve gave the bow increased power and arrow speed for a lower draw weight. As Crowley quickly bolted the second metal limb in place, Will realized that he was looking at such a recurve bow—one that could be disassembled into its three component parts.

"The armorers made it for us," Halt said quietly. "We've had them working on this for some time now. The steel limbs are amazing. You'll have a draw weight of almost sixty pounds—not as much as a longbow, but quite respectable nevertheless."

Crowley handed the weapon to Will, who turned it over in his hands, feeling the heft and the balance of it. The steelmakers who crafted the Ranger Corps' saxe knives were legendary craftsmen—many a sword had been blunted and notched on a Ranger saxe blade, without leaving a mark in return. Now, obviously, that metalworking skill had been turned to create this spring steel bow. Crowley passed Will a thick, woven cord and gestured for him to string the bow.

He slipped the string over the lower end, seating it in its notch, then stepped his right foot inside the bow and string, bracing the recurve against the ankle of his other foot as he bent the bow and seated the string in the notch. He grunted in surprise at the effort it took. He flexed the bow to test it and nodded contentedly at Halt.

"That's a little more like it," he said. Halt handed him one of the arrows from the quiver.

"Try it," he said, indicating a patch of light bark on a tree some forty meters away. Will nocked the arrow to the string, flexed it once or twice experimentally, then, with his eyes glued to the target, he raised the bow, drew and fired in one smooth movement.

The arrow slammed into the tree trunk, almost ten centimeters above the point he had aimed at. For an archer of his standard, it was a disappointing shot. But Halt made a dismissive gesture.

"Don't be too surprised. It'll shoot flatter than your longbow initially, but then it will begin to lose power and drop more quickly after forty or fifty meters. That's why you shot a little high."

Will nodded thoughtfully. The arrow had struck the tree with quite a respectable force.

"Good for about a hundred meters?" he asked, and his former teacher nodded.

"Maybe a little more. It's not your longbow, but you won't be completely without weapons. And you have your strikers, of course."

Will nodded. Strikers were another piece of Ranger equipment. Carefully weighted brass cylinders, they fitted into the palm of a clenched fist, leaving a rounded knob protruding at either end. A blow to the jaw or base of the skull with a striker was almost certain to incapacitate the strongest opponent. In addition, strikers were balanced for throwing. In the hands of an expert knife thrower— and that meant any Ranger—a striker could stun a man up to six meters away.

"Very well," Crowley said, rubbing his hands together in a businesslike fashion. "That's all we have for you. One other thing: once you're in place at Castle Macindaw, we'll send in a contact agent for you, in case you have to get any messages back."

Will looked up at that piece of news. "Who will that be?" he asked, and the Ranger Commandant shrugged.

"Not decided yet. But we'll make sure it's someone you'll recognize."

Halt dropped a hand on his former apprentice's shoulder. "If you need help while you're there, you can always call on Meralon, of course. But only in an emergency. It wouldn't do to have the two of you seen together. It's vital that you keep your real identity a secret. In fact, he'll be instructed to give you a wide berth. If he's seen to be in the district, people may well clam up completely."

It was going to be a lonely assignment, Will thought.

14

The drinkers in the taproom of the Cracked Flagon looked up as the door opened and an icy draft swirled into the smoky room, bringing with it a flurry of snow.

"Close the door," snarled a heavily built wagoner by the bar, not even bothering to turn and see who had entered. Other drinkers did, however, and there was a stir of mild interest as they saw that the newcomer was a stranger. Such travelers were few once winter put its icy grip on Norgate Fief. The fields and roads were covered with deep snow as often as not and the temperature, driven down by the chill of the constant wind, often dropped below freezing.

The door shut, cutting off the icy blast from outside, and the candles and fire settled down from the mad dance the wind had set them to. The newcomer threw back the deep cowl of his black-and-white patterned cloak and shook a thick powder of snow from his shoulders. He was a young man with a light growth of stubble on his face. He was a little less than average height and slight of build. A black-and-white border shepherd had slipped softly into the room with him, eyes fixed on his face, waiting for a command. He gestured to an empty table near the front of the room and the dog padded silently to it, sliding her forepaws out in front of her till she lay stretched out on her belly by the table. Her eyes continued to roam the taproom, however, belying her relaxed appearance. The young stranger loosened his cloak and spread it over the back of the chair, to dry in the fire's heat.

There was a further murmur of interest as those present saw what the young man had been carrying under his cloak. He placed a hard leather instrument case on the table. If travelers were rare in winter this far north, so was entertainment, and those present saw the prospect of a more interesting night than they had anticipated. Even the previously surly wagoner's face split with a smile.

"Musician, are you?" he asked expectantly, and Will nodded, smiling in return.

"An honest jongleur, my friend, making his way through the bitter cold of your beautiful countryside." It was the kind of easy, joking reply that Berrigan had coached him in over the two weeks they had traveled together, stopping along the way at more than a dozen inns and taverns like this one. Some of the other drinkers moved a little closer.

"So let's have a tune then," the wagoner suggested. There was a murmur of assent from the rest of the room.

Will considered the request, then cocked his head to one side for a moment. Then he raised his hands to his lips and blew on them. Smiling, he replied, "It's a bitter night out there, my friend. My hands are close to frozen."

"You could warm them round this," another voice told him. He glanced up and saw that the tavern keeper had moved from behind the bar to place a steaming tankard of hot, spiced cider on the table in front of him. Will wrapped his hands around the warm container and nodded appreciatively as he sniffed the aromatic steam rising from the tankard.

"Yes. This would certainly seem to do the trick," he replied. The tavern keeper winked at him.

"On the house, of course," he said. Will nodded. It was no more than his due. The presence of a jongleur would ensure that the inn did excellent business that night. The drinkers would stay longer and drink more. Will took a deep sip of the cider, smacked his lips appreciatively, then began to unbuckle the straps fastening the mandola case. The wood on the instrument was cold to his touch as he drew it from its shaped resting place and he spent a few minutes retuning. The sudden change from the icy cold outside to the warmth of the tavern had thrown the strings hopelessly out of tune.

Satisfied, he strummed a chord, made another minor adjustment and looked around the room, meeting the expectant gazes of its occupants with a grin.

"Perhaps a few songs before my supper," he said to no one in particular, then added, "I assume there *is* supper?"

"Yes indeed, my friend," the tavern keeper replied quickly. "A fine lamb casserole that my wife made, with fresh bread and boiled peppered potatoes."

Will nodded. An agreement had been reached. "So it's a few songs, then my supper—then more songs. How does that sound?" he asked. There was a chorus of approval from the room. Before it had died away, he launched into the jaunty introduction to *Sunshine Lady*.

"Sunshine lady,
color of sunshine in your hair.
Happiness is the gown you wear.
I would follow you anywhere,
my sunshine lady."

He looked up, nodding encouragement to the small crowd in the taproom as they joined in on the chorus of the popular country love song, tapping their wine mugs on the tables and singing in rough voices:

"Spread a little light around,
sunshine lady.
Isn't it true?
I love you, la da da daa.
Spread a little love around,
sunshine lady.
You are the one
who lights up the sun."

Then, as he reached the second verse, they fell silent, leaving the singing to him until the chorus again, when their voices joined with his once more. It was a jaunty, bouncing little song—an ideal beginner, as Berrigan described it.

"It won't be the best song in your repertoire," he had said, "but it's bright and lively and well-known, and it's a good one to break the ice with an audience. Remember, you never throw your best song away first. Leave yourself somewhere to go."

Now, as Will reached the final chorus and the room joined with him yet again, he felt a warm flush of pleasure. It grew inside him as he sounded the final chord and the inn patrons broke into a clamor of applause. He had to remind himself, and not for the first time, that this was a role he was playing—that he wasn't really a jongleur and his purpose in life was not really the applause that rang out so freely. Although sometimes, at moments like this, it was difficult to remember.

He did another four songs for them. *Harvest Sunday, Jessie on the Mountain, Remember the Time* and *The Runaway Mare*, a hard-driving song with a galloping rhythm that had fists pounding and feet tapping throughout the room. As he finished the last, he glanced down at the dog, lying with her eyes glued to him, and mouthed the word "Dragon" at her.

Instantly, the dog came to her haunches, threw back her head and barked long and loud—just as he'd taught her to do in the weeks they had been on the road. *Dragon* was their alarm word, the signal for her to bark until he told her to stop. He did so now.

"What's that, Harley?" he asked her. *Harley* was another code-word. It told her that she had done well and now she could stop her barking. Instantly, she fell silent, her tail thumping the boards of the floor twice in recognition that she had played the game properly. Will looked up at the expectant crowd and spread his hands in apology, grinning at them.

"Sorry, my friends. My manager here says it's time for me to eat. We've had a long day in the cold and she gets a tenth of my earnings—and my dinner."

A gust of laughter rang around the room. They were country folk and they knew a well-trained dog when they saw one. They also appreciated Will's gentle way of reminding the tavern keeper that he was owed a dinner.

It wasn't long in coming. One of the serving girls hurried a steaming plate of the lamb casserole to his table. Without his mentioning it further, she also set down a bowl of meat scraps, bones and gravy on the floor. Will smiled his thanks to her and nodded to the man behind the bar. The tavern keeper, busy refilling tankards for people whose throats were dry from singing, smiled widely at him.

"Does your horse need tending, young man?" he called, and Will replied, through a mouthful of stew.

"I took the liberty of putting my horses in your barn, tavern keeper. It's too bitter a night for them to be left outside." The tavern keeper nodded his agreement and Will dug in once more. The lamb casserole was delicious.

The wagoner who had seemed so ill-tempered when he first arrived now made his way to the table where Will sat eating. Will noted with interest that he didn't presume to sit down and intrude on his personal space. He'd already learned that in taverns like this, people afforded jongleurs a certain respect. The big wagoner dropped a silver coin in front of Will.

"Good music, lad," he said. "That's for you there."

Will, his mouth full again, nodded his thanks. Several of the other customers now moved closer, each one dropping a few coins into the open mandola case on the table. He noticed that there were quite a few silver coins among the coppers and felt a flush of satisfaction once more.

"You've a deft hand on that lute of yours, young feller," one of them said.

"It's a mandola," Will replied automatically. "It has eight strings, while a lute . . ." He stopped himself. "Thank you," he said, and they smiled at him.

When he had finished eating, he surreptitiously signaled the dog again, setting her barking.

"Harley? What's that you say?" he said, and the dog instantly fell silent once more. "It's time for me to entertain these folk?" He glanced up at the smiling faces around him, shrugged and grinned at them. "She's a hard taskmaster," he declared, reaching for the mandola.

He played for another hour. Love songs, lively songs. Silly songs. And one in particular that had always been his favorite, *The Green Eyes of Love*. It was a haunting, sad ballad and he sang it well, although to his annoyance, he stumbled slightly on the instrumental line in the middle eight bars. As he finished it, he noticed one or two people wiping their eyes and again felt the pleasure known only to performers when they reach into the hearts of their audience. As he had played, the coins had continued to find their way into the mandola case. With some surprise, he realized that he would not need to delve into the traveling money that Crowley had advanced him. He was more than paying his own way.

The tavern keeper, who had left the bar to one of his serving girls and come to sit close by Will, glanced at the water clock that dripped slowly on a mantle.

"Perhaps one more," he said, and Will nodded easily. Inside, he felt a tightening of his chest. This was the moment he had built to over the night—a chance to get the locals talking about the strange events in Norgate Fief. It was one of the advantages of taking the guise of a jongleur. As Berrigan had told him: "Country people are suspicious of strangers. But sing to them for an hour or so and they'll think they've known you all their lives."

Now he strummed a minor chord sequence and began singing a well-known nonsense song:

"By a muddy ditch a drunken witch
in a voice that was coarser and coarserer
sang like a crow so that people would know
of her love for the cross-eyed sorcerer."

He sensed the change in the room the moment he began singing. People exchanged fearful glances. Eyes were cast down and several actually moved away from him. He began the chorus:

"Oh, the cross-eyed sorcerer was called Wollygelly,
he had breath like a goat and a big fat belly
and a nose that . . ."

He let the song tail away, as if noticing the discomfort among his listeners for the first time.

"I'm sorry," he said, smiling at the room. "Is something wrong?"

Again, glances were exchanged and the people who just a few moments ago were laughing and applauding him were now unwilling to meet his gaze. The big wagoner, obviously troubled, said in an apologetic tone, "It's not the place or time to be making fun of sorcerers, lad."

"You weren't to know, of course," the tavern keeper put in, and there was a chorus of assent. Will allowed the smile to widen, keeping his expression as artless as possible.

"I wasn't to know what?" he said. There was a pause, then the wagoner took the plunge.

"There's strange things happening in this fief these days, is all."

"And these nights," added a woman, and again a chorus of agreement sounded. Behind his innocent, inquiring expression, Will marveled at Berrigan's insight.

"You mean . . . something to do with sorcerers?" he asked in a hushed voice. The room went silent for a moment, people looking fearfully over their shoulders and toward the door, as if expecting to see a sorcerer burst in at any moment. Then the tavern keeper answered.

"It's not for us to say what it is. But there are strange goings-on. Strange sights."

"Particularly in Grimsdell Wood," said a tall farmer and, once more, others agreed. "Strange sights, and sounds—unearthly sounds they are. They'd chill your blood. I've heard them once and that's enough for me."

It seemed that once their initial reluctance was overcome, people wanted to discuss the subject, as if it held a fascination for them that they wanted to share.

"What sort of things do you see?" Will asked.

"Lights, mainly—little balls of colored light that move through the trees. And dark shapes. Shapes that move just outside your vision's range."

A log fell in the fire and Will felt the hairs on his neck prickle. This talk of sounds and shapes was beginning to affect him, he thought. Two hundred kilometers to the south, he could joke about it with Halt and Crowley. But here, on a dark night in the cold, snow-driven land of the north, with these people, it seemed very real and very believable.

"And the Night Warrior," said the wagoner. This time, silence fell over the room. Several people made the sign to ward off evil. The wagoner regarded them all, his face flushed.

"Oh, believe me, I've seen him all right. Only for a second, mind. But he was there."

"What exactly is he?" Will asked.

"Exactly? Nobody knows. But I've seen him. He's huge. A warrior in armor, as tall as two houses. And you can see *through him*. He's there and then he's gone before you're sure you've actually seen him. But I know. I saw him, all right." His gaze swept the room again, challenging the others to tell him he was wrong.

"That's enough of that talk now, Barney," said the tavern keeper. "People have a way to go to reach their homes this night and it's best not to talk about such matters."

From the mumble of agreement, Will sensed that there would be no further discussion this night. He struck a chord on the mandola.

"Well, I agree, this is no time to sing about sorcerers. Perhaps we should finish with one about a drunken king and a staggering dragon?"

Right on cue, the dog barked again and the dark mood in the room receded instantly.

"What's that, Harley? You agree? Well then, we'd better get to it." And he launched into it straightaway:

> "Oh, the drunken king of Angledart
> could blow out candles with a fart.
> But the world never knew
> of the courage in his heart
> till he slayed the Staggering Dragon . . .
> Oh, the Staggering Dragon had four knock-knees
> and he staggered around and knocked down trees
> and he burned his behind every time he sneezed
> with the flames of his dragon breath!"

Laughter swelled up in the room and the black mood was dispelled as Will laid out the tale of the knock-kneed staggering dragon and the king with serious digestive problems. He was accompanied by the dog's enthusiastic barking every time he sang the word "dragon," and that added to the laughter.

It would never do at Castle Araluen, he thought, but it certainly did the trick here in the Cracked Flagon.

15

THE WIND DIED AWAY SOMETIME BEFORE DAWN AS IF, HAVING done its appointed job of clearing the clouds from the sky, it knew it was time to move on. The following day dawned cold and bright, and when Will stirred from the small room the innkeeper had assigned to him, the morning sun glared brightly off the surrounding snowscape and streamed through the windows of the taproom.

Will greeted the tavern keeper over a mug of coffee. The kitchen maid had served him breakfast of toasted bread and slices of cold ham but, as ever, it was the coffee he craved. Apparently the tavern keeper was a kindred spirit. He poured himself a mug and sat opposite Will, taking a sip and sighing appreciatively.

"A good night last night," he said, an unspoken question behind the words. Will nodded.

"Cullum Gelderris is the name, by the way. We never got round to introductions last night."

Will shook the hand. "Will Barton," he said. The tavern keeper nodded several times, as if the name meant something to him.

"Yes, a good night it was," he repeated. Will sipped his coffee, saying nothing. Finally, Gelderris broached the subject that was on his mind.

"Be an even better one tonight. End of the week we usually get a good crowd. Be even bigger than usual if word gets round there's a jongleur in the village." He looked at Will across the top of his coffee cup. "Planning to stay another night, were you?"

Will was expecting this question. Even though he was eager to get on and reach Castle Macindaw, he knew that he had better stay another night at least. The pickings were good in the village, as he'd seen last night. If Gelderris was correct, and there was no reason to assume he wasn't, they'd be better tonight. It might seem suspicious if he passed up the chance to make good money, he realized. Still, a certain amount of bargaining was expected.

"I hadn't really decided," he said. "I suppose I could move on."

"Where to?" Gelderris asked quickly. Will shrugged as if the matter was of no great importance.

"Eventually, to Castle Macindaw. I've heard Lord Syron gives a warm welcome to entertainers. I suppose there's precious little to keep people occupied once the snows come," he added. But Gelderris was shaking his head.

"You'll get no welcome from Syron," he said. "He hasn't spoken a word these past two months or more."

Will frowned slightly, as if not understanding. "Why not? Has he suddenly got religion and taken a vow of silence?" He grinned to make sure Gelderris knew he was joking. But there was no answering smile from the tavern keeper.

"There's little of religion about it," he said darkly. "Just the opposite, in fact."

"Not the Black Art?" Will asked casually, using the county people's term for sorcery. This time, Gelderris glanced quickly around before answering.

"So they say," he said, his voice lowered. "Struck down, he was. Healthy as you or me one minute. The next, he's lying close to death, barely breathing, eyes wide open but seeing nothing, hearing nothing and saying nothing."

"The healers, what do they say?" Will asked. Gelderris snorted in scorn.

"What do they ever know? They can't explain his condition. Nor can they do anything to ease it. Occasionally, he rouses himself enough to take a little food, but he's barely conscious even then. And then he's gone again, back into his trance."

Will set his empty coffee mug down, thought about another cup, then reluctantly dismissed the idea. Since he'd been living by himself, he had become a coffee hound and it was time to moderate his behavior.

"Is this anything to do with that business last night?" he asked. "That mysterious warrior person and such?"

Again, Gelderris hesitated before answering. But it seemed easier to discuss these matters in the bright light of morning.

"If you ask me, yes," he said. "People say that Malkallam has returned to Grimsdell Wood."

"Malkallam?" Will repeated.

"A Black Artist. A sorcerer. One of the worst kind, apparently. He had a feud with Syron's ancestor, going back a hundred years ..."

"A hundred years?" Will repeated, edging his voice with disbelief. "How long does a sorcerer live, anyway?"

Gelderris raised an admonishing finger. "Don't be too quick

to disbelieve," he said. "Nobody knows how long sorcerers can live. I'd say it's pretty much up to the sorcerer himself. But these goings-on in Grimsdell don't have any other explanation. Nor does Lord Syron's strange sickness. Stories go that it was exactly the same sickness struck down his ancestor when he fought with Malkallam."

"So if this Malkallam is in Grimsdell Wood, why doesn't someone from Macindaw take a few soldiers in and give him a see-ing to?" Will asked. "Somebody must have taken charge if Syron's incapable?"

"You don't just march into Grimsdell Wood, Will Barton. It's a tangle of trees and undergrowth in there, with paths that twist and turn on themselves and branches above you so thick you only see the sun at noon. There's the mere as well. Step in that and you'll sink to the bottom and never be seen again."

Will considered that fact for a few moments. The tavern keeper was turning out to be a mine of information.

"So there's nobody in charge at Macindaw?" he said, and added, "That's a blow. I was hoping to winter there—at least a few weeks."

Gelderris pursed his lips. "Oh, you'll most likely find a position there. Syron's son has taken over the running of things. Strange cove he is, too," he added darkly. Will looked up quickly.

"Strange, you say?" he prompted, and Gelderris nodded emphatically.

"There are those who say he might even be behind his father's illness. He's very withdrawn, very mysterious. Wears a black robe like a monk, although he's no man of the church. A scholar, he calls himself. But what does he study, I want to know."

"You think he might be this . . ." Will hesitated, seeming to search for the name, although he knew it well enough. "Malkallam?" he concluded. Gelderris looked a little uncomfortable now that he had been asked point-blank to make a statement one way or the other. He shifted in his seat.

"I'm not saying that it's so," he said finally. "But I'm saying I wouldn't be too surprised if it were. Word has it that Orman spends all his time in his tower room, studying books and old scrolls that he's got his hands on. He may be lord of Macindaw, but he's no leader of men—no warrior. Thankfully, Sir Keren is there to look after that side of things."

Will raised an eyebrow at the new name. Gelderris needed no further prompting.

"Syron's nephew—Orman's cousin. He's a fine warrior—some years younger than Orman but a natural leader and popular with the men-at-arms. I often thought that perhaps Lord Syron would have preferred it if Keren were his son, rather than Orman."

"This close to the Picta border, you'd have need of a good warrior in the castle," Will mused, and the tavern keeper nodded assent.

"That's a fact. There's more than one of us is glad Keren is there. If the Scotti ever got wind that a weak leader like Orman was in charge, we'd all be wearing kilts and eating haggis before the month was out."

Will rose and stretched. "Ah well, it's all politics and that's beyond a simple man like myself. As long as I can get a bed and lodging at Orman's castle and make a little money to see me on my way, I'll be content. But tonight, of course, I'll spend in your castle."

Cullum seemed content with the news. He gestured to the coffeepot warming by the fire.

"Fine by me. Want some more coffee while it's fresh?"

Good intentions flew out the window. Will reflected that gathering intelligence was thirsty work. He picked up his mug.

"Why not?" he said.

16

WILL LEFT LATE THE FOLLOWING MORNING, HIS PURSE A GOOD deal heavier than it had been when he arrived. The tavern keeper had been right. Once word spread that there was a jongleur in the village, people had flocked in from the surrounding countryside. The tavern had done a roaring trade and Will was kept singing until well past midnight, by which time he had exhausted his repertoire and was having to resort to the pretense that people had asked him to repeat songs he had already performed—another trick Berrigan had taught him.

Gelderris stood by as Will tightened the girths on Tug and his packhorse. "A good night," he said. "Call by again when you're passing south, Will Barton."

He didn't resent Will's leaving. He was realistic enough to know that simple country folk couldn't afford more than one night of overspending in the tavern.

"I'll do that," Will said, swinging easily into the saddle. He reached down and clasped Gelderris's hand. "Thanks, Cullum. I'll see you then."

The tavern keeper sniffed the damp air and looked uncertainly at the clouds gathering in the north.

"You'll do well to keep an eye on the weather. There's snow in those clouds. If it starts to blizzard, take shelter in the trees until it eases. A man can lose his way all too easily in a whiteout."

"I'll bear it in mind," said Will. He glanced at the clouds himself. "Mind you, chances are I'll reach Macindaw before it snows." He touched Tug with his heel and the little horse moved away, the pack animal following stolidly behind. The dog went ahead, head down and belly low, glancing back continually to be sure Will was following.

"Maybe so," said Gelderris, more to himself than to Will's retreating form. But he didn't sound convinced.

He was right. Will was barely a third of the way on his journey when the big, fat flakes began to drift down from the sky. He had felt the temperature dropping, then there was the inexplicable moment when it rose a few degrees, signaling the onset of the snow. Then it was falling, without any other warning. He pulled his hood up and huddled inside the warmth of his cloak. It intrigued him how snow falling seemed to deaden all sound, although perhaps this was an illusion, he thought. It seemed logical to expect such large objects to make a noise when they fell to earth—after all, you could hear rain when it fell. Perhaps it was this lack of any falling sound that created the illusion of overall silence. Of course, as the snow on the ground grew deeper, it muffled the sound of his horses' hoofbeats. There was only the slight squeaking sound of the dry, powdery crystals being compressed with each stride.

Noticing that the snow was rapidly accumulating, he whistled softly to the dog and pointed to the packhorse. The dog, ears pricked at the sound, waited until the horse was level with her, then sprang up into the nest created for her in the center of the packsaddle. It

was a move the packhorse was familiar with now and she took it
with no sign of alarm or resentment.

He rode on. The snow was heavy but it was nowhere near
whiteout conditions and he was confident that he could find his way
easily enough. The surface of the road might be covered, but the
way was still clearly visible, cut between the trees as it was.

From time to time, there was a slithering rush as built-up snow
on a branch finally became too heavy and slid off onto the ground
below. Once, there was a splitting crack as a tree gave way, weakened by the intense cold and the weight of the snow until it sagged
drunkenly against its neighbors. A black-and-white head rose above
the packsaddle at the noise, ears pricked, nose quivering.

"Easy," Will said, grinning. His voice seemed strangely loud in
his ears. She gave a small snuffle, sank her head back onto her paws,
eyes closing. Then they opened again as she shook her head in that
ear-rattling way dogs have, clearing the fallen snow from her fur.
Content, she settled again.

Will's face was chilled but the rest of him was relatively warm.
There was no wind to cut through his protective clothing and the
subzero temperature meant that the snow stayed dry as it gathered
on his shoulders and cowl—not melting and soaking the material of
his cloak. From time to time he would dust it off, smiling as he reminded himself of the dog shaking her coat clear.

Two hours later, he crossed a ridge and there, before him, stood
Castle Macindaw. It was a thickset, ugly building. The dark stone
of its walls seemed black against the pure white snowscape that surrounded it. As was the custom, it was built on a small hill and the
forest trees had been cut back on all four sides, preventing attackers
from approaching unseen. It might be ugly, he thought, but it looked

effective enough in design. The walls were solid, made of stone and at least five meters high. Towers at each of the four corners added another few meters to the overall height, and there was the usual dominant keep tower in the center, soaring above the others. The southern side held the main gate, with a drawbridge over a dry moat. The moat, he noticed, didn't continue too far around the side walls. He assumed it was only there to make access to the main entrance more difficult.

Halt and Crowley had told him that the normal garrison consisted of thirty men-at-arms and half a dozen mounted knights. That would be more than enough to hold the walls against any Scotti raiding party, he thought.

He pushed back his hood and produced the narrow-brimmed hat that Berrigan had given him. Adorned with a green-dyed swan's feather, it marked him as a jongleur and should guarantee easy entry to the castle yard. He pulled the hat down tight and rode toward the gate.

17

TUG'S HOOVES RANG ON THE HEAVY PLANKING OF THE DRAW-bridge as Will rode under the portcullis. The hollow sound changed to a sharp clatter as the horses stepped onto the cobbled courtyard. The area was filled with people moving from one place to another, going about their normal day-to-day tasks. Only a few of them looked up at him, looking away almost immediately.

Something was missing, he thought. Then he realized: there was none of the usual buzz of conversation, no sudden bursts of laughter or raised voices as people greeted companions, sharing a joke or a story. The people of Norgate were quiet, moving with their eyes cast down, seemingly disinterested in what was going on around them. It was an unfamiliar experience for him. As a Ranger, he was accustomed to drawing attention—albeit guarded—whenever he arrived in a new place. And in the past weeks as a jongleur, he had experienced the same surge of interest—although for a different reason.

In a remote, isolated place like Macindaw, he had fully expected to be greeted eagerly, if not warmly. He looked about curiously but could find nobody willing to meet or hold his gaze.

It was fear, he realized. People in Norgate were living close to a dangerous border. Their lord had been struck down by a mysterious ailment and there was a distinct belief among them that it was the work of a sorcerer. Small wonder that they would not show interest in or greet a stranger arriving in their midst. He hesitated, uncertain whether or not he should dismount. Then the question was answered for him as a rotund man, with a seneschal's chain and keys and a look of perpetual worry, emerged from the keep. The seneschal—basically the person who managed the day-to-day domestic affairs of the castle for its lord—saw him and moved toward him.

"Jongleur, are you?" he asked. It was an abrupt enough greeting, Will thought. But at least it was a greeting. He smiled.

"That's right, Seneschal. Will Barton, from places south, bringing my small measure of pleasure to the castles of the north." It was the sort of florid speech that he had been taught to deliver. The seneschal nodded distractedly. Will guessed that he had a lot to distract him.

"We can use some. There's been precious little to smile about here, I can tell you."

"Really?" Will asked. The seneschal glanced up at him appraisingly.

"You've heard nothing of events here?" he asked. Will realized it would be foolish to try to pretend complete ignorance of events. An entertainer traveling through the country would have heard the local gossip—as indeed he had. He shrugged.

"Rumors, of course. The countryside is always alive with them wherever you go. But I'm used to discounting rumors."

The rotund man sighed heavily. "In this case, you can probably believe most of them," he said. "And add to them as well. You could hardly exaggerate the situation here."

"Then the lord of the castle is truly . . ." Will hesitated as the other man looked up warningly.

"If you've heard the rumors, you know the situation," he said quickly. "It's a subject that's best not discussed too much."

"Of course," Will replied. He shifted in his saddle. He was tired and he felt that, troubled or not, it was time the seneschal showed him a little of the normal courtesy. The other man saw the movement and gestured for Will to dismount.

"I'm sorry. You'll understand that I'm a little distracted. You can put your horses in the stable. I take it the dog is with you?"

The border shepherd had been lying on the cobbles watching the conversation. Will nodded, smiling, as he swung down from the saddle, stretching his legs and back muscles.

"She assists me in my act," he said.

The seneschal nodded. "Keep her with you then. You're lucky, we're not too crowded at the moment, not that that's a surprise. So you can have a room to yourself."

That was an agreeable development. Will had been expecting to be assigned one of the curtained-off sleeping stalls that lined the annex to most castle great halls. Particularly in winter, when you would normally expect a castle to be crowded.

"Not too many visitors, then?" he asked, and the seneschal shook his head.

"As I said. Not that it's a surprise. We do expect a Lady Gwendolyn of Amarle to be passing through in a week or two— she's traveling to meet her fiancé in the next fief but one and sent word requesting lodging until the snow clears from the passes. But apart from her, there are just the normal castle folk. And there are fewer of them than normal," he added darkly.

Will chose not to pursue the matter. He set to work loosening the girth straps on the two horses. The seneschal glanced around him.

"Forgive me if I leave you to it," he said. "That firewood will never get stacked if I don't see to it myself. Stables are over that way." He gestured to the right of the courtyard. "Once you've got your horses settled, ask in the castle for Mistress Barry—she's the housekeeper. Tell her I said you were to have one of the tower rooms on level three. My name's Agramond, by the way."

Will nodded his thanks. "Mistress Barry," he repeated. The seneschal was already turning away, yelling at two of the castle workers who were slowly stacking cut firewood in one corner.

"Come on, Tug," said Will. "Let's find you a bed."

The Ranger horse's ears pricked at the sound of his name. The packhorse, placid and unimaginative, followed Tug docilely as Will led the way to the stables.

Once the horses were tended to, Will found the housekeeper. Like most women of her calling, she was a stoutly built, capable woman. She was polite enough, he thought, but she had the same air of distraction that he'd noticed in Agramond. She showed him to his room—fairly standard accommodation for a castle of this size. The floors and walls were stone, the ceiling timber. There was a narrow window, fitted with a frame covered in translucent hide that allowed a half-light to filter through. A wooden shutter was available for severe weather. A small fireplace warmed the room and there was a bed in a curtained-off alcove. Several wooden seats and a small floor rug completed the home comforts. A washstand was on a small wooden table against the curved wall. Will hadn't spent a lot of time in tower rooms, and he realized now, looking around, that it could be no easy task finding furniture to fit a room where the greater part of the wall was semicircular.

Mistress Barry glanced at the mandola case as he set it down.

"Play the lute, do you?" she asked.

"It's a mandola, actually," he replied. "A lute has ten str—"

"Whatever. I imagine you'll be playing tonight?"

"Why not?" he said expansively. "It's a fine night for music and laughter, after all."

"Precious little laughter you'll find here," she said dourly. "Although I daresay we could use some music."

And on that cheery note, she moved to the door. "If you need anything, ask one of the serving girls. And keep your hands to yourself. I know what jongleurs are like," she added darkly.

You must have a long memory then, Will thought to himself as she left the room. He imagined many years must have passed since a jongleur had chosen to pinch that ample backside. He grimaced at the dog, lying on the floor near the fireplace and watching him intently.

"Friendly place, eh, girl?" he said. She thumped her tail at the sound of his voice.

The evening meal in the dining hall of the castle was a somber affair, presided over by Lord Syron's son, Orman.

He was a man of medium height, perhaps thirty years of age, Will thought—although his receding hairline made it difficult to judge. He was dressed in a dark gray scholar's robe and his mood seemed to match the color of his clothes. He was sallow-faced, and looked as though he spent the greater part of his time indoors.

Altogether not the sort of man to inspire confidence in a community living in the shadow of fear, as Macindaw was.

He made no acknowledgment of Will's presence as he took his place at the head table in the dining hall. As was the usual custom, the tables were arranged in the form of a T, with Lord Orman and his companions, including Agramond, at the crosspiece. Will noted that there were several empty places at the head table.

The rest of the diners were seated at the table that made up the stem of the T, in descending order of importance. Will was placed a little more than halfway up the stem. As a Ranger, he would normally be accorded a seat at the head table—he'd had to resist the automatic urge to move toward it. Mistress Barry, supervising the serving of the meal, indicated his place at the table and he found himself seated with several of the lower-ranking Craftmasters and their wives. No one spoke to him. But then, he realized, they didn't speak to one another either, other than muttered requests for condiments and dishes to be passed.

As usual, Will silently cursed the flamboyant jongleur's outfit he wore, with its wide, flowing sleeves. More than once he managed to trail them in the gravy of passing dishes.

The standard of food served matched the overall atmosphere— a plain mutton stew, with a rather chewy venison roast and platters of stringy boiled vegetables that seemed to have come from long storage in the cellars.

The meal, without conversation or diversion of any kind, was soon finished. Then Agramond left his seat and spoke quietly into Orman's ear. The temporary lord of the castle listened, grimaced slightly, then looked down the table until he picked out Will.

"I believe we are privileged to have an entertainer with us," he said.

If he felt privileged, the tone of his voice certainly didn't betray it. There was a weary acceptance of the inevitable and an unmistakable air of disinterest in his words. Will, however, chose to ignore the insulting delivery of the introduction. He stood and moved slightly away from the table to deliver an ornate bow, deep and accompanied with much flourish. Then he smiled widely at Orman.

"If it pleases my lord," he said, "I am a humble jongleur with songs of love, laughter and adventure to share with you."

Orman sighed deeply. "I very much doubt that it will please me in any way," he said. His voice was nasal and high-pitched. Altogether, he was a most unimpressive specimen, Will thought, with not one saving grace evident.

"I suppose you have the usual repertoire of country jigs, folk songs and doggerel to put before us?" he continued. Will thought the best answer was to bow once more.

"My lord," he said, grinding his teeth as he kept his eyes down, and wanting to step up to the head table and throttle the sallow-faced man.

"No faint chance that you might know something of the classics? Some of the greater music?" Orman asked, his tone making it obvious that he knew the answer would be in the negative. Will smiled again, wishing that he had the skill to suddenly burst into the first movement of Saprival's *Summer Odes and Interpretations.*

"I regret, my lord, that I am not classically trained," he said, around the fixed smile. Orman waved a dismissive hand.

"As do I," he said heavily. "Well, then, I suppose we must endure the inevitable. Perhaps my people will find some enjoyment in your performance."

Not likely after that introduction, thought Will, as he passed the strap of the mandola over his head. He hesitated, looking around the room, taking in the stolid expressions of all present. I think I am about to learn what it is to die on stage, he thought to himself, as he struck up the opening bars of *Katy Come and Find Me*, a lively reel from Hibernia. It was a safe song for him, one of the first he had ever learned, and the opening instrumental passage was simple but stirring.

And of course, still seething with anger at Orman's attitude, he managed to botch it totally, playing in such a ham-fisted manner that he had to abandon the melody line and strum the chords instead. His ears burned with embarrassment as he plowed doggedly through the song, mistake building on mistake, missed note following missed note. He finished with a thwarted note on the bass string that summed up the ineptitude of the total performance.

Stony silence greeted him for what seemed like minutes. Then, from the back of the hall came the sound of ringing applause.

18

WILL TURNED TO LOOK. A GROUP OF FIVE MEN, DRESSED IN hunting clothes, had entered the hall as he sang. Now they applauded, encouraged by the one who was obviously their leader.

Stocky and muscular, he had a square, open face and a wide grin. He moved down the hall now toward Will, continuing to clap as he moved closer. Then he held out his hand in greeting.

"Well done, jongleur, particularly in view of the frosty reception you've been given!"

Will took the hand that was offered. The handshake was firm, and the hand felt hard and callused. Will knew that feel. It was the hand of a warrior.

"What's your name, jongleur?" the man said. He was taller than Will and looked to be in his thirties. He was clean-shaven, with dark, curly hair and lively brown eyes. His four companions stood slightly behind him. Warriors as well, Will noted.

"Will Barton, my lord." The quality of the man's clothing left him in no doubt that this was the correct address. The title was greeted with laughter, however.

"No need for ceremony here, Will Barton. Keren's the name.

Sir Keren perhaps on formal occasions, but Keren's good enough any other time." He turned to the top table, raising his voice as he addressed Orman.

"Apologies for our late arrival, cousin. I trust there are some scraps of food still left for us?"

Keren, thought Will, remembering the name. He was Syron's nephew and, by all reports, he was the one holding the castle together in the Lord's absence. He was said to be a capable warrior and a good leader. And, if first impressions were anything to go by, he was a totally different kettle of fish to his cousin.

Orman was speaking now, the distaste in his voice obvious. "The hall is used to your ill-mannered late arrivals by now, cousin," he said. Keren looked back at Will and gave him a conspiratorial grin, accompanied by a histrionic raising of the eyebrows.

"If you'll take your place, I'll have the servants bring food," Orman continued.

Obviously, the empty places at the head table were intended for Keren and his companions. But Keren waved the suggestion aside.

"Let's have places set here," he said, indicating the table close by Will. "We'll eat while we enjoy some music from Will Barton. It's about time a little fun blew through these dowdy old walls," he added, with a glint in his eye. "Let's hear something lively, Will! Do you know *Old Joe Smoke* by any chance?"

"Indeed I do," Will replied. He was glad he had spent the previous weeks practicing the correct words to the song. He was confident now that he wouldn't make the mistake of mentioning "Graybeard Halt." Halt, after all, was a name famous throughout the kingdom and it would do no good to suggest that he had any connection with the legendary Ranger.

It was amazing what a difference a small group of interested listeners could make. As he began the rippling melody, his fingers were sure and confident. Keren and his friends stamped and clapped along, joining in the chorus—and, gradually, so did the others in the room.

Not Orman, of course. As the applause for *Old Joe Smoke* died away, Will heard the noise of a chair scraping back at the high table. He glanced around to see the castle's lord leaving by a side door, his face set in a scowl.

"Well, that lightened the mood!" Keren said cheerfully. Will wasn't sure if he was referring to the song or his cousin's departure. "Let's have another, what do you all say?"

He looked around the table at his companions. For a moment there was little response from any of them. Keren leaned forward. His smile widened and he spoke a little louder.

"I said, let's have another. What do you all say?"

There was a sudden surge of enthusiasm as they chorused their agreement. Will regarded them with some surprise. Keren seemed to be extremely popular among his followers. Whatever he wanted, they seemed happy to go along with. But Will certainly wasn't complaining. After Orman's dismissive comments, it would make a nice change to have an enthusiastic audience.

He grinned around at them and flexed his fingers experimentally. The night was going to be better than he had expected, he thought. Much better.

The evening continued for another hour and a half. Then people began drifting off to their beds. Will, satisfied with his night's work, packed the mandola away and was ready to follow them when Keren stopped him. The cheerful grin had disappeared and his face was serious as he gripped Will's forearm.

"I'm glad to see you here, Will Barton," he said in a lowered tone. "People here need some diversion from their troubles. And they get precious little from my sour-faced cousin. Let me know if there's anything you need while you're with us."

"Thanks, Sir Keren," Will began, but the hand squeezed his arm a little harder and he amended the statement, "Keren, then. I'll do whatever I can to raise the people's spirits." Keren's ready grin lit up again.

"I'm sure you will. Remember, if you need anything, just ask."

And with that, he led his companions away.

Suddenly tired with the letdown that all performers feel after a successful night, Will trudged slowly up the stairs to his room. The dog greeted him with a questioning look and the usual thumping of her tail.

"Not a bad night," he told her. "Not bad at all. You can work with me tomorrow."

She dropped her nose onto her paws and fixed her gaze on his. Those steady eyes held an unmistakable message for him.

"You don't, do you?" he said hopefully. "Surely you could wait till morning?"

The eyes were unwavering and he sighed softly. He buckled on his saxe knife and pulled the black-and-white cloak around his shoulders.

"All right," he told the dog. "Let's go."

She padded obediently behind him as he made his way down the stairs and into the castle courtyard. It was a cold, clear night, with a definite hint of frost in the air. Above him, the stars blazed down, while a quarter moon hung low in the east.

Revived by the cold air, he breathed deeply as he looked around the courtyard. There was enough light from the stars and moon to throw definite shadows across the yard and it occurred to him that this might be as good a time as any to look around the vicinity.

The thin powdering of fresh snow on the cobbles squeaked under his boots as he made his way to the postern gate beside the massive portcullis. One of the sentries stopped him as he made his way into the post beside the gate.

"Where are you off to then, jongleur?" he asked. His manner was neither friendly nor unfriendly.

Will shrugged. "Can't sleep," he said. Then, gesturing to the dog, "And she's always ready for a walk."

The sentry raised an eyebrow at him. "This is not a good place to go walking at night," he said. "But if you must go, you'd be best to stay away from Grimsdell Wood."

"Grimsdell Wood?" Will said, assuming a slightly amused, skeptical tone. "Isn't that where the ghoulies and ghosties gather?" He smiled cheerfully at the sentry to let him know that such superstitions meant little to him. The sentry shook his head.

"Make fun of it if you like. But a wise man would give it a wide berth."

"Well then, perhaps I will," said Will, sounding totally insincere. "Where is it exactly, so that I can make sure I stay away from it?"

There was a long pause while the soldier looked at him, recognizing his disbelief and bridling slightly at the ridicule underlying the minstrel's words. Jongleurs, he thought, they're always so clever, always so quick to joke about things. Finally, he pointed to his left.

"It's that way," he said, holding in his anger. "About a kilometer. And you'll know it when you see it, believe me. I'll let the sentries on the wall know you've gone out," he added, "in case you make it back."

And, feeling that he had had the last word, he opened the small postern gate beside the portcullis, allowing Will and the dog to slip through. The gate banged shut behind them and Will heard the bolts sliding home almost immediately. In country like this, one didn't leave gates open any longer than necessary once the sun was down.

For the same reason, the massive drawbridge was up. It wouldn't be lowered again till after sunrise. But there was a narrow two-plank access bridge across the moat that protected this side of the castle. Will stepped across it easily, the dog a little less so. He'd noticed before that she didn't like the feeling of uncertain footing underneath her.

He looked back at the castle, a crouching black mass above him. He could see one or two dark shapes moving on the battlements and realized these would be the night guards.

Resisting the temptation to wave, he struck out in the direction the sentry had indicated. The dog followed him then. As he snapped his fingers and said the word "Free," she quested ahead, running in a wide arc some twenty meters ahead of him, stopping and sniffing at new scents, cocking an ear at new sounds, but continually checking back to make sure Will was following.

There was a wild beauty to the countryside under its cover of snow. The road itself held only the thin dusting that had fallen that night. But in the fields and trees beside the road, the snow still lay thick and heavy from previous falls. Will had always loved the sight of a snowscape at night and he walked on contentedly, thinking over the events of the evening and the total disparity in the characters of Lord Orman and his cousin.

Gradually, the open countryside and the cleared fields began to give way as trees and bushes encroached closer to the road. It was darker here, without the fields and their cover of snow to reflect the ambient light, and Will felt a sense of the countryside pressing in on him. Crowding him. Watching him. He loosened the saxe knife in its sheath and touched the hilt of the throwing knife behind his neck. He told himself that this was nothing to do with superstition. It was just good sense in a potentially dangerous piece of country. He noticed that the dog's questing had fallen into a narrower arc than before. She obviously preferred the clear ground as well. But he reasoned that she would sense any ambush ahead of them and give him warning, so he continued.

And found himself at the edge of Grimsdell Wood.

19

GRIMSDELL WOOD LOOMED—THERE WAS NO OTHER WORD FOR it. The trees here were taller, darker and more closely packed. The shadows under them were dense and impenetrable. The wood was brooding and dark and seemed determined to conceal its secrets from strangers.

The sentry had been right, he thought. He did know it when he saw it.

He walked slowly along the edge of the trees, clicking his fingers once to bring the dog back beside him. Her ears were pricked, he realized, and her eyes swept from him to the wood and back again, as she sensed where his attention was focused.

Then her hackles went up and she growled softly, her gaze riveted to one side. Will looked in that direction but for the moment saw nothing through the tangle of trees and undergrowth. Then he dropped into a crouch and for a moment saw a faint red glow moving among the shadows. Just for a moment. Then it was gone.

He felt the hairs rising on the back of his neck as he stood erect once more. He shook his head and laughed softly.

"It's a light," he told himself. "Nothing more."

She growled again, and this time Will saw the movement from the corner of his eye. A blue glow this time—that seemed to flare briefly in the tops of the trees and then disappear. He wasn't even sure than he had seen anything—but the dog's behavior confirmed that he had.

Then the red glow was back once more—and gone again before he could focus on it clearly. This time it was in a part of the wood several hundred meters from where it had first appeared. Will felt his heart beating faster, and his hands dropped to the saxe knife once more.

"Come on, girl," he said. "There must be a path into this wood somewhere."

He found one some thirty meters farther along. It was narrow and twisting, with barely enough room for one man. Perhaps it was a game trail. Or perhaps it had been made by man. Either way, he went forward into the wood, the dog moving a pace or two ahead of him, head down, nose to the ground.

After twenty paces, Will looked behind him and could no longer see the way out of the wood. The path twisted so much and the undergrowth and creepers and trees twined together so closely that his world had become confined to a space of a few meters. He continued on, his hand still on the saxe knife hilt. Years of Ranger training meant that he moved with virtually no sound and now he began instinctively to use the shadow patterns as cover for his movement.

There was no further sign of lights among the trees. Perhaps, he thought, the light bearers had been scared off when he entered the wood. The thought made him a little more relaxed. Maybe he wasn't the only one in this wood feeling nervous. He smiled at the thought and moved on.

Then the whispering started.

It was right at the limit of hearing, so that at first he wasn't to-tally sure he could actually hear anything. Then, he thought that perhaps it was the wind through the leaves—except there was no wind. It was an almost imperceptible susurration that seemed to come from everywhere and nowhere. He looked at the dog. She had stopped, one forepaw raised, head cocked to one side, listening. So the sound was there. But it was impossible to determine where it came from, and that made it impossible to make out whether it was voices or just a sound. It ebbed and flowed at the very edge of his senses, sometimes drowned by the accelerated sound of his own heartbeat, sometimes becoming almost clear, almost comprehensi-ble. And then, in the middle of the indeterminate muttering, he began to make out individual words.

Unpleasantly evocative words. Once, he thought he clearly heard a voice say: *pain*. And then the muttering died until he heard, or thought he heard, the word *death*. And *suffering*, *darkness* and *ter-ror*. Then more meaningless, wordless whispering.

He looked at the dog again. She remained alert but the actual words, of course, held no meaning for her. She was reacting only to the sound. His mind went back to the terror he had felt years be-fore, when he and Halt and Gilan were hunting the evil Kalkara beasts across the Solitary Plain. Then, as now, the terror of un-known sounds had seized and threatened to overwhelm him. But then, he'd had the reassuring presence of Halt to quell his fears. Now he had only himself.

He took a deep breath. The saxe knife made a soft hiss as it slid from its oiled scabbard and he said, clearly and firmly, to the shad-ows around him:

"Steel."

The whispering stopped.

The dog looked at him. Her tail wagged once. Her hackles lowered and he felt better. *Face your fears*, Halt had always taught him, *and more often than not they will fade like mist in the sunshine.* Whispering and words were one thing, he thought. The razor-sharp, heavy saxe knife was another altogether. More practical. More real. More compelling.

And altogether more dangerous.

"Lead on, dog. Let's find these whisperers." He gestured for the animal to continue. He followed a few steps behind her, confident in her ability to sense danger.

It was as well he let her lead. Otherwise he might have walked straight into the black waters of the mere that suddenly appeared as they rounded a bend.

The path skirted its edge to the right. Set among the trees, it was an expanse of black water thirty meters across. At its edge, the trees trailed creepers into the water and leaned over to meet each other—some so tall that they nearly touched hands with their opposite neighbors—so that there was clear sky only above the center of the lake.

Vapor rose from the water's surface, twisting in wreaths of fine mist that dissipated as they rose to the trees. And bubbles broke the surface where rotting vegetation lay below. Or where some large creature breathed, he thought. On the far side of the water, opposite where he stood, the mist seemed to be thicker, forming what was almost a curtain. He stopped to study the phenomenon, wondering why the mist should be thicker in that one spot. The dog sank to her belly, watching him intently, ready to move off if he started walking again.

Then, in a heart-stopping moment of absolute terror, a giant figure loomed out of the mist, towering high above the mere, seeming to rise from the black water itself.

It happened as quickly as that. One moment there was nothing. Then, in the blink of an eye, the figure was there, fully formed. Huge and menacing, black against the mist, a shadow of a giant warrior in ancient, spiked armor, with a massive winged helmet on its head. It must have been twelve meters high, he thought as he stood, rooted to the spot in horror. The helmet was a full-face design, but where the eyeholes pierced it, there was empty space.

The figure seemed to shiver slightly and for one ghastly moment he thought it was moving toward him. Then he realized it was simply the movement of the mist curtain. Will's heart hammered inside his ribs, and his mouth was dry with fear. This was no mortal figure, he knew. This was something from the other side, from the dark world of sorcery and spells. Instinctively, he knew that none of his weapons could harm it.

The figure towered, unmoving apart from the slight quivering of the mist. The empty eyeholes seemed to seek him out. Then he heard the voice.

It was deep and seemed to echo around the black lake, as if he were hearing it in some vast cavern rather than the open woods.

"Beware, mortal!" it boomed. "Do not awaken the shade of the Night Warrior. Leave this place now while you are still able!"

The dog sprang to her feet at the sound of the massive voice. A growl rumbled in her throat and Will quieted her in a voice that was nowhere near steady.

"Still, girl!" he croaked, and the growling stopped. But he could see that the ruff around her neck had raised in a primeval reaction of either anger or fear. He could feel the hairs on his own neck standing on end in the same way. Across the lake, the mist seemed to thicken and the terrifying figure seemed to grow more and more substantial, as if it were drawing power from the mist. This time, when it spoke, the voice was even louder than before.

"Go now while I grant you the chance! Leave!"

The final word echoed around the mere and Will found himself involuntarily moving back the way he had come, stepping away from the black lake and the hellish warrior. He stumbled on a tree root, looked down to recover himself and then, as he looked up, the Night Warrior was gone.

Just like that. In an instant, like a candle extinguished. He glanced fearfully around the mere, wondering if the warrior might reappear somewhere closer. Then the voice came again. It was low this time, nowhere near the volume of the original, and this time there were no words. Just a deep, menacing chuckle. Will's last reserves of courage left him.

"Come on, girl!" he called and, turning, he ran blindly back out of Grimsdell Wood, the dog slipping past him to lead the way to where they could see the clear night sky and the brilliant stars overhead. Only then did Will stop running. His breath came in ragged clouds of steam in the cold while his heart thumped at double time. He waited several minutes, until his breathing settled to a more natural rhythm.

When they came in sight, the black bulk of Castle Macindaw seemed welcoming and comforting to him. The torch burning by the postern gate was a beacon of safety and he hurried toward it, anxious to be inside the walls.

20

WILL SLEPT BADLY FOR THE REST OF THE NIGHT, AS WAS TO BE expected. His sleep was patchy and uneven, populated by dreams of the towering Night Warrior. It was only toward dawn that he managed to fall into a deep sleep and inevitably, shortly after he had, he was woken by the early morning sounds of the castle rising.

He lay for a moment on the bed, wondering if he really had seen and heard the horrific figure the night before. For a minute or two, his brain muddled by sleep, he thought it might have been a nightmare. He rose, stretching stiff limbs and muscles, realizing that his entire body had been tensed as he slept. The dog, chin on paws, belly down on the warm flagstones by the embers of the fire, cocked her ears at him and thumped her tail twice in greeting.

"It's all right for you," he said morosely. "You have no idea how terrifying that was last night." He opened the shutters and looked out at the new day. It was bright and sunny, the morning light glistening off the snow-covered countryside surrounding Macindaw. Training and discipline demanded that he should take time to review the events of the night before while they were fresh in his mind, trying to find some logical explanation for them. After ten minutes' analysis, he came to the reluctant conclusion that he *had* seen the figure. He *had* heard its voice. And he had been terrified as never before.

The light of day brought no logical explanation, no physical solution. There was something terrible in Grimsdell Wood. He let out a long sigh. He thought again of Halt's briefing, and his opinion that, in ninety-nine cases out of a hundred, there was an explanation for such phenomena.

"I suppose I'm going to have to go back and find out what it is," Will said quietly.

Not surprisingly, he had little appetite when he went for breakfast in the dining hall. But he managed to cram down a couple of warm rolls, smearing them with a preserve made from raspberries, and by the time he was halfway through his second cup of coffee his jangled nerves were almost back in place. Not looking for company, he sat alone at one of the long tables in the hall, staying away from the small groups that clustered together, chatting quietly over their breakfast. It was there that the page found him.

"Jongleur?" he said coolly. He was old for a page. He must have been in his early forties, which meant he had found no favor at all in the eyes of his superiors. The majority of young boys employed as pages in a castle moved on to positions as squires or assistants to the Craftmasters. Those who didn't were usually lazy, truculent or stupid. Or all three. His next statement decided Will that the fourth option was the correct one. As he glanced up from his coffee cup, the page continued.

"See Lord Orman at ten of the clock."

He turned and walked away. For a moment, Will was tempted to call the page back and give him a dressing down for his lack of manners. As a Ranger, he was used to being treated with respect.

Then he realized that he wasn't a Ranger at the moment. He was a jongleur. Ruefully, he decided that Orman's undisguised contempt for country minstrels must have rubbed off on some of his staff.

There was a water clock in the dining hall and he saw that he had over an hour before his interview with Orman. He wondered briefly why the lord of the castle wanted to see him. His immediate thought was that it had something to do with the events in Grimsdell Wood, but then he realized that this was probably his imagination working overtime, since Grimsdell was foremost in his mind.

More likely, he thought, Orman wanted to see him about the earlier scene with his cousin Keren. The more he considered it, the more he felt that was the case. Orman had been embarrassed in front of the entire assembly. Chances were he would be ready to take out his anger on Will, and he faced the prospect philosophically. There was nothing he could do about it, so there was no point worrying about it. But he realized that he would have to tread a careful path in the future. There was no point in alienating the castle lord, no matter how unpleasant he might be.

He passed the time in the castle's small library, situated in one of the corner towers, hunting through the dusty shelves of books and scrolls to see if there were any references in local histories to the Night Warrior, and looking at random for volumes on sorcery and spells. On both counts, he came up empty-handed. There was only one small volume on sorcery, although he noticed several empty spaces in the shelves beside it. And the few sketchy accounts of local history that he found held no mention of any Night Warrior.

Frustrated and distracted by the memory of his reaction in the wood the night before, he made his way to Lord Orman's suite of rooms, on the fourth floor of the keep tower.

Orman's secretary, a small man with a bald head except for tufts of white hair above either ear, looked up as he entered the anteroom. He reminded Will of a bald squirrel, his head moving quickly from side to side, as if to see Will better.

"The Lord Orman wanted to see me," he said briefly. He saw no reason to introduce himself to the secretary.

"Aaah yes, yes, the jongleur, aren't you? Come this way then. Lord Orman is free at the moment."

He rose from behind a table that was laden with paperwork, half-unrolled scrolls and thick ledgers, and knocked on the massive door that led to Orman's chamber. From the other side, Will heard the thin, nasal voice reply.

"Come."

Gesturing for Will to follow, the secretary opened the door and entered. Orman was by the window, looking out at the view of the castle yard below. It was a large room, lit even in daylight by candles and oil lanterns placed at strategic points. A fire in one corner heated the room, which was lined with shelves of books and heavy wooden cabinets. One of these was open and Will saw a display of scrolls inside. Orman had a reputation as a scholar, he thought. His room certainly seemed to reflect it.

"The jongleur, my lord," said the secretary, indicating Will. Orman turned away from the window and studied Will for several seconds without speaking.

"That will be all, Xander," he said, and the secretary bowed and quietly left, closing the door behind him. Orman, still studying Will through unblinking eyes, sat at a table beside the window. There were two other chairs at the table but he made no sign for Will to take one, so he remained standing. He could feel the color mounting in his neck and face at the castle lord's arrogant treatment. Forcing himself to look casual, Will looked away from Orman, allowing his gaze to wander around the room, taking in the stacks of open books and papers on the huge desk against an inner wall.

"My cousin Keren is a disruptive influence," Orman said finally. "You would do well to remember that in the future."

Will said nothing, but bowed in acquiescence. So his prediction had been right. Orman seemed to expect no reply and went on.

"It's easy to be 'popular' when you have no responsibilities, of course. And there are those in this castle who would like to see Keren in charge . . ." He hesitated and Will had the strange feeling that the other man almost expected him to comment. Still, he held his peace.

"But he is not," Orman continued. "I am in authority here. No one else. Is that understood?"

The last few words were almost spat out, with an intensity that surprised Will. A little taken aback, he met the hot, angry gaze of the other man and bowed.

"Of course, my lord," he replied. Orman nodded once or twice, then rose from his chair and began to pace the room.

"Then mind your manners in the future, jongleur. I *will* be treated with the respect that my position demands. I may be only the temporary lord of this castle but I will not be undermined—by you or Keren. Is that understood?"

"Yes, Lord Orman," Will said evenly. He was puzzled. He had the strange feeling that, in spite of his anger, Orman seemed to be almost pleading for respect and recognition.

Orman paused in his pacing and took a deep breath.

"Very well. That said, I realize it is not your fault that you fail to live up to the standards that I consider should be the norm for a jongleur. Country ditties and folk songs are all very well, but they are no substitute for the classics. The kind of simplistic doggerel you sing merely stultifies the minds of the common people. I believe it is a performer's role to lift people. To elevate their perceptions. To expose them to a greatness beyond their own limited horizons."

He stopped, looked at Will and shook his head slightly. Will was in no doubt that Orman found his potential for elevation sadly lacking. He bowed again.

"I regret that I am a simple entertainer, my lord," he said. Orman nodded sourly.

"With the emphasis on simple, I'm afraid," he said.

Head lowered, Will felt his cheeks beginning to flush. Get over it, he told himself. If you plan to be a jongleur, you have to develop a thick skin for criticism. He breathed deeply a few times, regaining control of himself. Orman watched him curiously. The barb had been intentional, Will realized. The castle lord wanted to see how he might respond.

"And yet," Orman said, in almost grudging recognition, "the instrument you play is an uncommonly good one. It's not a Gilperon, by any chance, is it?"

"It's a mandola," Will began his usual response. "It has eight strings, tuned in . . ." He got no further.

"I *know* it's a mandola, for pity's sake!" Orman interrupted him. "I was asking if it were made by Axel Gilperon, probably the kingdom's foremost luthier. I would have thought that any professional musician would have heard of him. Even you."

It was a bad slip, Will realized. He tried to cover as best he could.

"My apologies, my lord. I misheard you. My instrument was made for me by a local craftsman in the south, but he is well known for copying the style of the master. Naturally, a poor country musician like myself could never afford a real Gilperon."

He laughed in a self-deprecating way, but Orman continued to stare at him, suspicion all too evident in his gaze. There was an awkward silence, finally broken by a tapping at the door.

"What?" Orman demanded angrily, and the door opened just far enough for his secretary to peer nervously into the room.

"Your pardon, Lord Orman," he said, "but the Lady Gwendolyn of Amarle has arrived and insists on seeing you."

Orman scowled. "Can't you see I'm busy?"

Xander opened the door a fraction wider, making covert gestures toward the anteroom behind him. "She's *here*, my lord," he said, keeping his voice as low as possible. Orman made an ill-tempered gesture, realizing that the visiting noblewoman was already in his anteroom.

"Very well, show her in," he said. He glanced at Will, who had moved toward the door. "You wait. I'm not finished with you yet."

Xander nodded gratefully and withdrew. A few seconds later, he opened the door wide and entered, standing to one side as he ushered in the new arrival.

"Lord Orman, may I present Lady Gwendolyn of Amarle." He bowed low as the lady entered the room. Blond, tall and beautiful, she was dressed in an exquisite sea-green silk gown and carried herself with the unconscious dignity and grace of a born noble. Will suppressed an exclamation of surprise.

Lady Gwendolyn of Amarle was Alyss.

21

ALYSS SWEPT TOWARD THE GRAY-GOWNED CASTLE LORD, ignoring Will. "Lord Orman," she said, "it is so good of you to shelter me for these next few weeks!" She held out her hand, palm downward, to Orman, leaving him in no doubt as to whom she considered to be more senior in rank.

Orman grudgingly bent over the hand and brushed his lips to it. "Weeks, my lady?" he said. "I thought it was a matter of a few days? A week at most?"

"But surely not!" Alyss recoiled a little at his *gaucherie*. "The roads to my fiancé's castle are thick with snow and I have heard that there are wolves and bears in this countryside! I cannot possibly progress further until the roads clear—anxious as I am to be with my beloved Lord Farrell. Surely, Lord Orman, you would not begrudge me the hospitality promised by your poor dear father."

Orman was trapped. It was interesting, Will thought, how the noble pecking order worked. Sour and ill-mannered as he might be, and a potential murderer to boot, Orman was overwhelmed by Alyss's presumption of superior rank.

"Of course not, Lady Gwendolyn!" he said. "It was a mere inquiry, nothing more."

But Gwendolyn had already dismissed him and was staring at Will as if he were some kind of inferior insect.

"And whom do we have here?" she asked, arching one eyebrow.

"A jongleur, my lady, arrived only a day ago himself."

"Does this jongleur have a name?" she replied, her gaze fixing on Will. He hesitated. It was Orman's place to introduce him. Someone of common rank could not initiate a conversation with a noblewoman such as Gwendolyn. As he watched the byplay between the two, Will was immensely impressed by her ability to play the role she had taken.

"Will Barton, my lady," said Orman. By having him introduce Will to her, she had reinforced her superior rank once again. Will bowed deeply.

"At your service, my lady," he said. Alyss studied him thoughtfully, one elbow cupped in her hand while her long, elegant fingers stroked her cheek.

"Are you a skilled performer, Will Barton?"

Will glanced sidelong at Orman. "I am a simple entertainer, my lady," he said.

Orman shook his head disparagingly. "Folk songs and country ditties are his limit, I'm afraid, my lady. Hardly what you would call one of the higher rank."

"Folk songs?" Alyss said, and broke into a shrill little laugh. "What fun! Very well, jongleur, you may attend me in my suite in an hour's time. Perhaps your ditties can help me forget the misery of separation from my beloved." She glanced at Orman. "I trust you have no objection, Orman?"

Orman shrugged. "None at all, my lady," he said. "Please avail yourself of all our facilities."

Will's eyebrow shot up. So he was a "facility," was he? Fortunately, he had his expression under control again before Orman noticed. The castle lord's attention was fully occupied by Alyss, as she forged on with her superb impression of an overbearing noblewoman.

"Then perhaps you could have your kitchen deliver a light meal to my rooms as well, Orman?" she said. "I'm tired and hungry after my travels through this dismal countryside of yours. You may present your household to me tomorrow, but for the remainder of the day I prefer to rest."

Orman bowed. "Of course, my lady." Really, thought Will, there was little else he could say. He realized that Alyss was looking at him once more.

"But before I retire, there are one or two things we might discuss, Orman . . ." she said meaningfully, and Orman took up her cue.

He made a covert shooing gesture to Will. "Very well, Barton, you may go. We'll continue our discussion another time."

Will bowed deeply. "Lady Gwendolyn, my lord," he said, and backed toward the door. They ignored him, which was only fitting, as Orman ushered Alyss to a chair.

"Remember, jongleur," she called imperiously as Will reached the door, "my rooms in an hour. I may not be ready for you then, so you may have to wait, but be there anyway."

Will bowed again. "Of course, my lady," he said.

As he exited, he heard her saying breathlessly to Orman: "Now, Orman, you must tell me what ails your poor dear father! Is there anything I can do to help?"

Xander eased the heavy door closed behind Will before he could hear Orman's reply.

As befitted her assumed rank, Alyss was traveling with a sizeable retinue. A chamberlain, two maids and half a dozen men-at-arms made up the group. The soldiers were accommodated in the castle dormitory while Alyss and the others occupied a large suite in the keep tower. Will presented himself in her anteroom at the appointed time. He wasn't sure what to expect, not knowing how many of Alyss's party were aware of her true identity. The chamberlain greeted him coolly and motioned him to a seat.

"The Lady Gwendolyn said you are to wait," he said loftily. He glanced at the instrument case as Will set it down. "Brought your lute, have you?"

Will took a breath, preparatory to speaking, then decided to give up. If the entire population of the world wanted to assume he played a lute, who was he to disabuse them? The chamberlain had lost interest in him and disappeared into an inner room, leaving him alone.

Several castle servants came and went while Alyss kept him waiting at least half an hour. He realized that the delay was totally in keeping with the character she was playing—lords and ladies rarely gave any thought to lesser beings whom they might keep waiting—but he felt she was overdoing it just a little. Finally the chamberlain reemerged and beckoned him in.

"The Lady Gwendolyn is ready for you now," he said. Will muttered under his breath. A keen listener might have made out the words "Not before damn time," but the chamberlain seemed to hear nothing.

He followed the other man into the large sitting room. Alyss was standing by the window, her face a mask until the chamberlain closed the heavy door behind them. Then her mouth widened into a warm smile and she came forward to take his hands in hers, brushing soft lips against his cheek.

"Will," she said softly, "how wonderful to see you again!"

His annoyance evaporated instantly and he returned the pressure of her hands.

"I couldn't agree more," he said. "But what on earth brings you here?"

Alyss looked surprised. "I'm your contact," she said. "Didn't Halt tell you?"

He stepped back, confused. "He said it would be someone I'd recognize. I had no idea it would be you. I had no idea that you . . ." He hesitated, not sure how to proceed. Alyss laughed softly. It was her natural laugh, not the shrill neigh of self-amusement she assumed as Lady Gwendolyn.

"You had no idea I got involved in this sort of cloak-and-dagger business?" she said. When he nodded, she smiled and continued. "Well, you've seen my dagger. Did you think Couriers simply carry messages around the kingdom?"

He smiled in return. "Well . . . yes, as a matter of fact. But then, this is my first assignment like this."

She released his hands and became businesslike all of a sudden. "We're wasting time. I'll explain more later. But first, we need to hear you play."

That startled him. "Hear me play?" he said, and she nodded quickly, gesturing to the instrument case.

"Your mandola. It is a mandola, isn't it?" she added, and he nodded. Somehow, he wasn't surprised that Alyss could name it correctly. He unstrapped the fastenings, still puzzled. He realized that the chamberlain had moved a little closer and was watching carefully as Will adjusted the tuning. He strummed a chord.

"Just the instrument. Don't bother to sing," Alyss said.

Frowning, Will began the introduction to *Wallerton Mountain*. The chamberlain drew closer, his head to one side, listening intently. Alyss's eyes were fixed on the man. After sixteen bars or so of the old folk tune, he looked up at her and nodded briefly and she gestured for Will to stop. Still puzzled, he played the last few notes and frowned a question. In a low voice, she gestured to the chamberlain.

"Give the mandola to Max," she said. "He'll play while we talk."

Understanding dawned as Will passed the instrument to the older man. Max took it and, without any of the usual re-tuning or fiddly adjustments that most musicians undertook when they borrowed another's instrument, he began playing immediately. Will realized that the man was copying his own style exactly. There was the occasional thwarted note in the lower range, and the slight hesitation as he moved up the neck for treble arpeggios—faults that Will was constantly at pains to correct.

Alyss drew him to one side, closer to the window but not so close that they could be seen from outside.

"Now we can talk," she said, "while any eavesdroppers will hear the jongleur serenading that stuck-up twit, Lady Gwendolyn."

"Who dreamed up Lady Gwendolyn, by the way?" he asked her. Alyss shook her head.

"Oh, she's real enough. A bit of an intellectual lightweight, but terribly loyal. When we found that she had arranged to travel here this month, she agreed to allow me to take her place. It was an ideal situation, really. She'd been invited to winter here by Lord Syron before all this business began. Orman could hardly go against his father's offer of hospitality. I spent days practicing her half-witted giggle, you know," she added.

Will smiled. "Is all this really necessary?" he said, indicating Max, now stumbling slightly over the introduction to *Heart of the Wildwood*. Alyss shrugged.

"Maybe not. But we can't be sure who might be listening or watching and it's better to assume that someone is. That's why I felt I should keep you waiting—sorry about that."

He shrugged the apology away. What she said made sense. He recalled the castle servants who had seen him in the anteroom. Any of them could be reporting to Orman right now. He glanced at Max.

"He's very good," he said, then amended the statement, "I mean, he's very good at being bad." He grinned. "Do I really sound as bad as that?"

Alyss touched his hand. "Oh, come on. You're not so bad. But we couldn't have him playing like a virtuoso and expect people to believe it was you. Now tell me, what have you found out so far?"

Will shook his head. "Not a lot that we don't already know. The entire countryside is terrified all right. Nobody will talk. I haven't seen Syron, but Orman seems like a nasty piece of work altogether."

Alyss nodded. "I agree. Did you notice the books on his desk?" she said. Will shook his head and she continued. "*Spells and Incantations* was one. *Wizardry and the Black Art* was another. There were more but they were the only two titles I could make out."

Will nodded, understanding. "That explains the gaps on the shelves in the library," he said.

Alyss sat on a two-seat settle, tucking her feet up under her. Will found it a particularly appealing motion. "What about the cousin? Keren?" she asked. "Have you met him?"

"Just once. He seems like a good man to have around. Straightforward. No-nonsense. And there's no love lost between him and Orman. Orman virtually warned me to stay away from him just before you arrived," he added. Alyss's face took on a thoughtful expression.

"So it might be awkward for you to make further contact with him?" she said. Will nodded and she continued. "Perhaps I could do it. I suppose it would be in character for Lady Gwendolyn to flirt with him—particularly since he's beneath her in rank. That way she could be sure nothing would come of it."

Will was a little surprised to find that he didn't like that idea too well. Keren was good-looking, friendly, and, he assumed, would be attractive to women with his open, easygoing manner. He realized that Alyss was smiling at him, as if she could read his thoughts.

"It'd only be Lady Gwendolyn doing the flirting, Will," she said. "And she is betrothed to be married, so it would amount to nothing, as I said."

She might be betrothed but you're not, Will thought to himself. Then he shook away the sour thought. Alyss was only doing her job, he realized.

Alyss continued. "I've left a man outside the village you came through, in case we need to contact Halt and Crowley. He's camped in the woods there with half a dozen message pigeons if we have anything to report."

Will cleared his throat nervously. "Actually, there is something I think we should let them know," he said. Alyss paused and looked at him curiously. He hesitated, knowing that what he was going to say would sound ridiculous, then went ahead anyway.

"Last night, I saw the Night Warrior in Grimsdell Wood."

22

ALYSS LISTENED INTENTLY AS WILL RECOUNTED THE EVENTS OF the previous night. Max was obviously paying attention as well, he thought. When he reached the moment where the giant figure had emerged from the mist, he noticed that the musician missed several beats. He smiled ruefully. He didn't blame the other man. He had a distinct memory that his heart had done much the same thing— and had kept on doing it, when he had been in the dark, menacing wood.

As he related his tale, Alyss had jotted occasional notes in a small leather-bound journal. She studied them now, frowning slightly, her chin on her hand. Finally, she looked up at him.

"It must have been terrifying," she said.

"It was." Will had no hesitation about admitting his fear to her. They had known each other too long for him to try to pretend otherwise. In addition, his training and his honest nature compelled him to give a true and accurate account of events—including his reactions to them. She drummed her fingers on the table for a few seconds, studying her notes once more. Then she touched her quill to one of the jotted points.

"Your dog . . ." she began. "What's her name, by the way?"

Will hesitated. He was getting tired of that question. He racked his brains for a name but inspiration deserted him. "I was thinking of calling her Blackie . . ." he said.

"Blackie?" Alyss's tone left no doubt that she didn't think too much of his choice.

"But I have a few other ideas as well," Will added hastily. She waved the matter aside. It wasn't important.

"Whatever. You said she growled when you first saw the lights moving?"

He thought back to the scene in the wood, trying to reconstruct exactly what had happened. "Yes," he said finally. "She had her head cocked—the way dogs do when they hear a strange sound."

"Then . . ." She paused and went back to the notes. "You saw the Night Warrior and *then* you heard him speak, correct?"

He nodded.

"How long was it between the time you saw the figure and heard him speak? Was there a pause?"

He thought carefully. He knew how important small details could be and he wanted to be absolutely sure he had them correct. "There was a definite pause," he said. "Perhaps twenty seconds. No less then that. It's hard to be accurate; I was a little distracted by what was going on," he added, and she nodded her sympathy.

"I don't blame you. I would have been running, screaming the place down, long before you reached that point," she said. Then she touched on the detail that had been bothering her.

"You said when the figure spoke, the dog jumped up and growled?"

"That's right." And suddenly a light dawned in his mind, a fraction of a second before Alyss stated it.

"So she wasn't bothered by the apparition?"

Will shook his head. "No. She came to her feet and growled when we heard the voice. So when the figure appeared, she must have been lying down . . . relaxed."

Alyss nodded at him. "So she reacted to the sounds, and the lights—which you'd expect a dog to do if they were real—but when it came to the twelve-meter-high figure of the Warrior . . . ?"

She let the sentence hang and Will completed the thought.

"She didn't see it. Or, if she did, it didn't bother her or threaten her."

Alyss sat back in her chair. "You know, Will, I'm no expert on the paranormal, but I have always heard that animals sense the presence of manifestations long before humans do. Yet the dog simply lay there, doing nothing, while you were seeing a giant warrior in the mist."

"That's the point. I did see it. It was there." Will frowned as he tried to piece together the puzzle.

"I know you saw it. I know you're not the hysterical type. But I'm saying it wasn't a spirit. It was some kind of trick. And the dog ignored it because the dog sensed that it wasn't real. The sounds, the voices, the lights—they were all real, physical events. But the figure was some kind of trick—an illusion of some kind."

There was a long silence while they looked at each other. Will knew they were both thinking the same thought.

"I'm going to have to go back in there and find out, aren't I?" he said, at length.

"*We're* going to have to go in there and find out," Alyss corrected him. He was grateful for the idea of company—and at the thought that her analytical mind would be applied to the task. But even so . . .

"This time, I'm going in daylight," he said, and Alyss grinned at him.

"After what you've told me, wild horses couldn't drag me into that wood after dark," she said.

Will played in the dining hall again that night. Alyss, as she had told Orman, stayed in her suite, presumably recovering from her journey, and made no public appearance. There was a good deal of interest in her, particularly among the ladies of the castle. A noblewoman from the south would probably wear the latest in fashion and the local ladies couldn't wait to see it. They were mildly disappointed by her absence and, as a result, it was a low-key night. Orman left the dining hall shortly after the meal was cleared and before Will played. There was no sign of Keren and his entourage, and Will wondered whether the likeable young warrior had been warned off by his cousin as well.

Will's performance was adequate, he thought. He was becoming sufficiently at home as a performer to now be able to gauge the level of his own work. The audience enjoyed themselves without becoming overly enthusiastic, which suited his plans admirably. He and Alyss had arranged to meet early the following morning and he didn't want a late night in the smoky atmosphere of the hall.

Accordingly, an hour after sunrise, he rode out under the portcullis. The massive gate was raised at dawn each day, as soon as it was evident that there was no sign of enemies in the immediate vicinity. The guard looked up at him as he passed.

"Hunting, jongleur?" he asked, nodding at the small hunting bow Will had slung over his shoulders, and the quiver of arrows hanging from his saddle.

"Nothing like a brace of snowshoe hare or the odd grouse to

liven up a meal," Will told him, and the man raised an eyebrow as he indicated the bow.

"You'll need to get mighty close with that bow," he said. "Mind you, there's precious little in the way of game at the moment."

Will grinned easily. "Ah, well, they say hunting is just a way to ruin a pleasant ride," he said, and the sentry smiled at the old joke.

"Good luck, in any event. And be careful. There's talk that a bear's been sighted hereabouts."

"I never eat bear," said Will, completely straight-faced. For a moment, the guard didn't realize he was joking. Then he chuckled as he caught on.

Will took the northwest road away from the castle, reflecting on how his reactions to people had changed since he had assumed an entertainer's role. As a Ranger, he was accustomed to remaining silent around people, and never making an unnecessary remark—certainly never a joke. It was part of the Ranger mystique, he had been taught. There was a practical side to it as well: people who weren't talking found it easier to listen to what others were saying, and information was a Ranger's stock-in-trade. As a jongleur, however, it was totally in character for him to make jokes at the slightest opportunity. Even bad ones. Especially bad ones, he amended.

He went northwest for several kilometers. The dog loped silently along, in the lead as usual, glancing back from time to time to make sure he and Tug were following. The little horse watched their new companion with good-natured tolerance.

They had planned the rendezvous in Alyss's chambers the night before, poring over a chart of the area that she had produced. "I'll leave at first light and go east," she had said. "You go northwest an hour later. Then loop around by this track here and meet me at the edge of Grimsdell Wood."

He found the narrow track she had indicated and turned Tug onto it. It was an overcast day, with a wind keening through the bare treetops, but there were still glimpses to be had of the watery sun. He caught sight of it now and decided he was a little behind schedule. A slight pressure with his knees and Tug broke from a trot into a slow canter. The dog, hearing the change in gait, sped up her own pace accordingly. Will looked at her with interest. She showed a great deal of economy of motion, never going faster than necessary. He guessed that, like a Ranger horse, she could maintain that steady pace all day if asked.

It was the dog who first registered Alyss's presence as they approached the outskirts of Grimsdell Wood. The bushy, white-tipped tail began sweeping back and forth in greeting and she ran up to the girl, half-hidden in the shadows beneath a grove of trees. Tug stirred, as if to say *I saw her too*, and Will patted the little horse's neck.

"I know," he said.

The previous day, Alyss had dressed as a noblewoman, in a fine, fashionable gown. There was no sign of that elegant creature now. Today, she wore a short tunic, gray tights and knee-high riding boots. A waist-length cloak swung from her shoulders and her gleaming blond hair was held in place by a feathered hunting cap. The gray tights showed off her long and very shapely legs to great advantage and Will found he preferred this Alyss to the perfectly coiffed, elegant Lady Gwendolyn. Her long dagger, in a beautifully worked leather scabbard, hung from a wide leather belt that gathered the tunic around her waist. She grinned up at him as he approached.

"You're late," she said, holding up her hand to him. He took hold of her by the wrist and heaved as she sprang up behind him.

She settled herself on Tug's withers and put her arms around his waist.

"Where's your horse?" Will asked—not that he minded having her ride with him and not that he minded her arms around his waist either.

"It's riding on with my escort," she said. "And with an excellent dummy of Lady Gwendolyn tied in the saddle, covered with her riding cloak."

Will half-turned to look at her. "Was that totally necessary?" he asked. Alyss shrugged.

"Perhaps not. But shortly after they rode off, a couple of men-at-arms from the castle rode past after them. It might have been coincidence, but who knows? Is this Grimsdell?" She pointed to the grim, dark line of trees in the near distance. Will nodded.

"That's it all right," he said, feeling a tightening in his stomach.

They rode back south along the fringe of the wood until they located the split oak tree that marked the spot where Will had entered Grimsdell two nights previously. By daylight, he felt no need to dismount. They rode into the trees, occasionally bending forward to avoid branches and creepers that grew across the narrow trail, the dog moving silently ahead of them.

Will's training reasserted itself. In spite of his growing nervousness at entering this unfriendly place again, he was able to retrace the path he had taken.

"Where did you see the lights?" Alyss asked, and he hesitated, thinking for a second, before pointing.

"They were moving in that direction," he said. "Hard to tell how far away they were."

Alyss looked critically at the tangle of trees and creepers around them. "Couldn't have been too far or you'd never have seen them through all this. Come on," she added, and slid down from the saddle. Will dismounted and she pointed in the direction he had indicated.

"Let's take a look in that direction," she said. Will signaled for Tug to stay on the track. He clicked his fingers and pointed, gesturing for the dog to move ahead of them, and she slid easily though the undergrowth and beneath the lower branches. The going was harder for Will and Alyss, however, and before long he found it necessary to unsheath his saxe knife and hack a way through the tangle. Alyss smiled quizzically at the way the heavy blade sliced through tough creepers, thick vines and even small saplings.

"That's a handy weapon to have," she said, and Will nodded, grunting as he chopped through a thick branch and tossed it aside.

"It's a weapon and a tool," he said. Then, unexpectedly, the way ahead was clear.

"Well, what do you know?" Alyss said, nodding her head in satisfaction.

The dog waited for them, sitting on a narrow, but unmistakably man-made, track through the woods, running parallel to the main trail they had been following.

23

ALYSS GLANCED FROM SIDE TO SIDE ALONG THE NARROW LANE that had been cut through the trees. "Which way were the lights moving, do you remember?" she asked. Will was already nodding in anticipation of the question.

"I can't be totally sure," he said, "but I'd say they were moving along this track."

Alyss pointed to the ground. "I'm no tracker," she said, "but they say Rangers are. Any sign of traffic along this path?"

Will dropped to one knee and studied the ground. He frowned after a moment or two. "Could be," he said. "Difficult to say, really. There are faint marks here. But you'd expect that on a track like this, wouldn't you?"

"But not the sort of thing you'd expect if someone were running back and forth carrying a lantern?" she asked, a slight tone of disappointment in her voice. Will shook his head. Then, remembering one of Halt's earliest lessons, he looked up into the forest canopy above them. *Always remember to look up,* his mentor had told him. *It's the one direction most people never think to check.*

Now his eyes narrowed as he saw something in the trees, something out of place. Alyss, seeing the change of expression on his face, looked up as well.

"What is it?" she asked, as Will moved toward one of the larger trees, his eyes seeking and finding the hand- and footholds he would need.

"Vines," he said, at length. "I've seen them growing down from the higher parts of trees. But I've rarely seen them growing at right angles to them."

He was a natural climber and he swarmed up the tree in seconds, seeming to Alyss to glide up the apparently smooth trunk. Four meters from the ground he stopped, and she saw he was studying a green creeper that grew along one of the larger branches, then led off toward the neighboring tree, sagging in a loop between the two of them.

"It's rope," he called down to her. "Dyed green to look like a vine, but rope sure enough." He traced the line of the rope as it led from one tree to the next, running along above the track they had discovered. He nodded to himself, satisfied, then slid lightly down to the ground beside her again.

"No need for someone to run up and down with the light," he said. "They could sling it on that rope on a pulley and haul it back and forth with a light line."

Alyss ruffled the dog's head affectionately. "And this young lady sensed the people doing it—maybe scented them or heard them. That's why she growled," she said. "My bet is if we looked we'd find other trails like this and other horizontally growing vines."

"It doesn't explain the Night Warrior," Will pointed out, and Alyss smiled at him.

"Perhaps not. But if he were real, why bother with trick lights?" she said. "Odds are he was another trick—even less substantial than the lights, judging by the dog's reaction. Now show me exactly where you were when you saw it."

She led the way back to where Tug waited on the main trail. The little horse looked at them quizzically, as if wondering what he'd missed. Will reached up to the bedroll behind the saddle and untied it. Alyss watched curiously as he withdrew the component parts of the recurve bow. He fitted them together and strung the bow in a series of deft movements. Then he tested the draw and met her gaze with a look of fierce satisfaction.

"That's more like it," he said, laying an arrow on the string. "If we're going looking for this damn Night Warrior, I'd rather do it with a bow in my hands."

He led the way forward until they reached the edge of the mere. Even by daylight, it was a sinister place, with curtains of mist rising from the far side. The water itself was like black marble, smooth and impenetrable to the eye. Bubbles rose to the surface further out, hinting at the presence of creatures lurking below in the depths.

"Here," Will said. "As near as I can remember. And the figure was out there . . . toward the far side of the mere."

Alyss looked shrewdly in the direction he indicated, then looked along the edge of the mere, where the path ahead of them followed the bank. At one point, it cut inside a small promontory, covered in trees and shrubs.

"Let's take a look over there," she said.

Will followed her, his curiosity mounting. "What have you got in mind?" he asked. It was clear to him that Alyss had formed a theory of some kind. But she held up a hand to forestall his questions.

"It's just an idea," she said vaguely. Her eyes were searching the ground ahead of them and to either side of the path. "You're better at this than I am," she said. "Check the ground in any clear spot."

Will complied, his trained tracker's eye running over the ground. There was faint evidence that someone had been there before them—perhaps as recently as two nights ago, he thought.

"Am I looking for anything in particular?" he asked, his eyes quartering the ground.

"Scorch marks," said Alyss, and as he heard the words, he saw the large bare patch of ground, where the snow had melted and the grass beneath was dry and singed.

"Here," he said. Alyss joined him, dropping to one knee and running her fingers over the dry, brittle grass. She let go a small grunt of satisfaction.

"All right," Will told her. "I've found your scorched grass. Now what does it mean?"

"You've seen a magic lantern show?" she said. As children in the Ward at Castle Redmont, they had often seen a traveling entertainer's magic lantern show, where the shadows of cutout figures—stars, half moons, witches and their cats—were projected onto the wall of a room by a candle's light.

"I'm guessing," she said, "that your Night Warrior is the same thing in principle."

"But he was huge!" Will protested. "And he must have been thirty or forty meters from here. You'd need an awfully powerful light to manage that."

Alyss nodded. "Exactly. And a powerful light would mean an awful lot of heat—hence the scorched ground here."

"But the distance . . ." Will began. After all, the shows they'd seen as children had been staged inside rooms, with the shadows barely a few meters from the light source.

"There are ways of focusing light so it becomes a beam, Will. It is possible, believe me. It's very expensive and there are only a few craftsmen who can fashion the equipment for it. But it can be done. A powerful light, a focusing device and a cutout figure, and hey presto, your giant warrior appears thirty meters away."

Will was still perplexed. "On what?" he asked. "There's no wall there to project on."

"On the mist," Alyss said. "It's like a curtain it's so thick, and look how it rises from the mere in a line. That would give the flickering, pulsating effect you noticed too—as the mist eddied and moved."

It made sense, he saw. He was willing to take Alyss's word that it was technically possible. And if that were so, he was ready to pay someone back for the terror he'd experienced in the wood two nights ago.

"Someone is going to a lot of trouble to keep visitors away," Alyss said thoughtfully. "I wonder why?"

The anger was rising in Will now, along with a sense of relief—relief that there might be a logical explanation for all of this, and a living, breathing person to account for it all. At that moment, he wanted nothing more than to bring that person to account.

"Let's find him and ask him," he said, grim-faced. But Alyss was glancing at the sun and shaking her head.

"We're out of time," she said. "My escort will be back in a few minutes to pick me up. And since they are being followed, they can hardly ride around in aimless circles while I frolic in the woods."

"Fine," said Will. "You go on back. I'll keep looking for this . . . whoever it is."

Alyss laid a hand on his arm, and kept it there until he met her gaze. She shook her head slightly, seeing the anger, seeing the determination in his eyes.

"Not now, Will," she said. "Leave it for now and we'll come back later—together."

He said nothing and she continued. "Let's do a little more research, find out a little bit more about all this. The more we know when we go looking, the better. You know that."

Reluctantly, he nodded. His training had taught him that when you were entering enemy territory, it was best to find out all you could beforehand. Alyss saw the angry light go out of his eyes and took her hand from his arm. She smiled at him.

"Now give me a ride back to the forest edge."

"You're right," he said as he swung up astride Tug, then leaned down to help her mount behind him. "It's just that I wanted someone to pay for the way I felt the other night."

Alyss, her arms around his waist, squeezed him gently. "I don't blame you," she said. "And you'll get your chance, believe me." She was silent for a few moments as they rode back through the forest, bending low over Tug's neck from time to time to avoid the low-hanging creepers and branches that obstructed the trail. Then she spoke again.

"You know, it might be a good idea if we sent in a report to Halt and Crowley, to let them know what we've found so far. They might have some ideas about all this. We'll send it by message pigeon."

Message pigeons, Will knew, were trained by the Diplomatic Service to return to their last place of rest. Once a pigeon had flown back to its home base, it would be ready to return to the spot from which it had been released. Nobody knew how the birds managed to fix the positions in their minds, but they were invaluable for communication in the field. Alyss continued.

"I'm being watched, so I have to get back to the castle. But could you ride back, make contact with the pigeon handler, and send off a report?"

Will nodded agreement. There was certainly plenty to tell his superiors—even if, so far, there were no conclusions to be drawn.

"How will I know your man?" he asked.

"He'll know you. When he sees you, he'll make contact."

They were back at the edge of the forest now and the going was clearer. Will touched Tug with his heels and the little horse broke into a canter. As they reached the small copse of trees where he'd met Alyss, she slid quickly from the saddle, glancing anxiously along the road to the point where her escort should appear. So far, there was no sign of them and that meant there was no sign of the men following them either.

"You'd better make yourself inconspicuous," she said, and Will nodded, urging Tug into the shadows under the trees. The dog followed, lying prone in the long grass.

From his position, Will could see the bend in the road a couple of hundred meters away. Now he saw the first rider in Alyss's escort rounding the bend.

"They're here," he said softly, and Alyss ran quickly to a thick clump of bushes at the edge of the trees, unfastening her short cloak and pulling the tunic over her head as she did so. She was wearing only a brief shift underneath the tunic and Will turned away hurriedly as he caught a glimpse of bare shoulders and arms. He heard rapid rustling from the bushes, then Alyss called to him.

"You can open your eyes now." She sounded vaguely amused at his embarrassment.

She had donned a long white riding habit over her tights and riding boots. The cloak, tunic and knife belt were bundled together at her feet. Will glanced along the road. The four-man escort,

grouped around the mannequin tied to Alyss's horse, was almost up
to them. From the shelter of the bushes, Alyss signaled to them. She
turned and waved at Will, a conspiratorial grin on her face.

"See you back at the castle," she said. Then, in what was obviously a carefully rehearsed piece of confusion, the escort was alongside her. The horses milled back and forth, confusing the scene, and
one of the men released a slip knot, allowing the mannequin to slide
sideways off the horse. Before it hit the ground, Alyss had swung up
into the saddle. Another member of the escort bent quickly to re-
trieve the mannequin and within a matter of seconds the group was
riding on, the mannequin already half folded and out of sight.

As they moved away, Will waited, unmoving, in the trees. They
were still in sight when Tug's ears twitched and the dog let out a
low rumble.

"Still," Will told them both. Sure enough, two men-at-arms
were rounding the bend, looking cautiously along the trail to make
sure they hadn't closed up too far on the party they were following.
Will sat, unmoving, as they rode past. He gave them several minutes' grace, then he rode out, heading south to find Alyss's pigeon
handler.

24

WILL PERFORMED IN THE MEN-AT-ARMS' BARRACKS THAT EVE-ning. It was normal practice for a jongleur to spread himself around. After all, if he were to perform in the main hall every night, the audience there would soon grow bored with his repertoire. And the soldiers in a remote castle such as Macindaw could often prove to be more than generous. They had little to spend their money on in a small, remote shire like that one. As a result, he could expect to make his purse considerably heavier if they enjoyed his work.

Furthermore, while a visiting entertainer might expect a small cash bonus from the castle lord at the end of his tenure, his chief payment came in the form of shelter, food and accommodation. A performer looking for hard cash would usually find it among the soldiers, or at the local tavern, if there were one.

In addition to all these excellent reasons, Will had another motive for taking himself to the barracks room that night. He wanted to get the men talking, to hear the local gossip and rumors about the forbidding Grimsdell Wood and the black mere. And nothing loosened men's tongues like an evening of music and wine, he thought wryly.

By now, he had become an accepted part of Macindaw life and people would be more likely to open up to him. In addition, the men-at-arms would feel more secure than the country folk who went home each night from the Cracked Flagon to their isolated, unprotected homes and farms. The men here were well armed and relatively secure behind the solid walls of a castle. That, if nothing else, would help to make their tongues a little looser.

He was greeted cheerfully when he arrived—all the more so when he produced a large flagon of apple brandy to help the night along. His standard repertoire of country folk songs, jigs and reels was exactly what this audience wanted. And he added a few of the bawdier numbers he had been taught by Berrigan as well: *Old Scully's Daughter* and a rather coarse parody of *The Knights of Dark Renown* titled *The Knights Whose Pants Fell Down*, among others. The evening was a success and the coins showered into his mandola case as the hours passed.

At length, he and half a dozen of the group were left lolling around the dying fire, brandy tankards in their hands. He had set the mandola aside. The singing was over for the night and the men were content with that. He had given them good value and now he once again experienced that strange phenomenon where, having performed for an audience for an hour or so, he was accepted into their midst as if they had known him all their lives.

The talk was the usual chatter of bored soldiers. It concerned the shortage of available females in the area, and the boredom of life in a remote castle, hemmed in by the winter snows. It was a boredom tinged with fear, however. There was no telling when the Scotti tribes might launch an attack across the border and, of course, there was the troubling mystery surrounding the lord's illness. As the men talked more freely, Will probed subtly and discovered that they had little respect for his son, Orman.

"He's no warrior," one of them said in a disgusted tone. "I doubt he could hold a sword, let alone swing it."

There was a rumble of agreement from the others. "Keren's the one for us," said another. "He's a real man—not like Orman, a jumped-up bookworm with his nose forever stuck in a scroll."

"That's when he's not looking down it at such as us," a third put in, and again there was an angry growl of assent. "But as long as he's Syron's heir, we're stuck with him," the man added.

"What sort of man is Syron?" Will ventured to ask. Their eyes turned to him and they waited for the most senior among them, the sergeant major, to answer.

"A good man. A good laird and a brave fighter. A just leader, too. But he's to his bed now and little chance he'll recover, if you ask me."

"And we need him now more than ever, with Malkallam on the loose again," said one of the soldiers. Will looked at him and recognized the sentry he had spoken to when he had left the castle several nights previously.

"Malkallam?" he said. "He's this wizard you talk about, isn't he?"

There was a moment of silence and several of the men glanced over their shoulders into the shadows beyond the flickering light of the fire. Then the sentry answered him.

"Ay. He's laid a curse on our Laird Syron. He lurks in that forest of his, surrounded by his creatures . . ." He hesitated, not sure if he had said too much.

"I went by there the other night," Will admitted. "You made me curious with your warnings. I tell you, what I saw and heard there was enough to keep me out of Grimsdell Wood in the future."

"Thought you would," said the sentry. "You young 'uns always know better than those who seek to advise you. You're lucky you got away. Others haven't," he added darkly.

"But where did this Malkallam come from?" Will asked. This time another man joined the conversation—a grizzled soldier whose gray beard and hair bespoke his long service in the castle.

"He was among us for years," he said. "We all thought he was harmless—just a simple herbalist and healer. But he was biding his time, letting us become unwary. Then strange things began to happen. There was a child who died, when all knew that it was within Malkallam's power to heal him. Malkallam let him die, they say. And others say he used the spirit for his evil purposes. There were those who wanted to make him pay for his sins, but before we could do anything about it, he escaped into the forest."

"And that was the end of it?" Will asked.

The soldier shook his head. "There were stories—dark stories— that he surrounded himself with monsters. Misshapen, ugly beings, they were. Creatures with the evil eye and the mark of the devil on them. Occasionally, they'd be seen at the edge of the forest. We knew he was doing the devil's work and when Lord Syron fell under a spell, we knew who had cast it."

"No coincidence there," said the sentry. The others nodded assent.

"And what does Orman do?" continued the old soldier. "He reads those weird scrolls of his late into the night, when decent folk are in their beds. While what we need is leadership—and someone with the guts to face up to Malkallam, and drive him out of Grimsdell once and for all."

"Need more men if we're to do that," said the sergeant major. "We couldn't face down his monsters with just a dozen of us. Orman should be recruiting. At least Keren's been doing something about that."

The older man shook his head. "Not sure I like what he's doing there," he said. "Some of those men he's recruited, they're barely more than bandits, you ask me."

"When you need fighting men, Aldous Almsley, you take what you can get," said the sergeant major. "I'll grant you they ain't no bunch of choirboys, but I reckon Keren can control them all right."

Will pricked up his ears at the words. This was something new, he thought. Nevertheless, he was careful to keep his expression disinterested. He even managed a yawn before he asked, as casually as he could manage, "Keren's recruiting men?"

The sergeant major nodded. "As Aldous says, you wouldn't want to look too closely at their pasts. But I reckon the time will come when we need hard men and we won't argue too much about them then."

Will looked around the barracks. "They're not quartered here?" he asked.

This time it was Aldous who answered. "He's keeping them separate. They have quarters in the keep tower. He said that was a better arrangement—it'd avoid any chance of friction."

It was apparent that the members of the normal garrison had accepted this reasoning without any question. Will clicked his tankard against his teeth thoughtfully. Maybe it did make sense, he thought. Throwing two separate groups of fighting men together in the rather basic conditions of the barracks room might well be a recipe for trouble. Still, there was something about the arrangement that was a little unsettling.

"Maybe," said the sergeant major, "when you consider the situation between Sir Keren and Lord Orman, Sir Keren thinks it's wise to have a group of men loyal to him—not that he'd have any trouble from us, mind."

"Although," said Aldous, "we are sworn to obey the orders of the rightful lord of the castle. And with Lord Syron out of action, that's Orman, whether we like it or not."

"Sworn or not," chipped in a third soldier, "I doubt he'd find any of us willing to act against Keren."

The others all mumbled assent. But it was a low mumble and one or two glanced over their shoulders once more, aware of the dangerous nature of the sentiments they were expressing. A silence fell over the group and Will thought it best to move on. He didn't want anyone to register the fact that he'd been pumping them for information.

"Ah well," he said, "one thing's for sure. With Sir Keren's men in the tower, there are fewer to share the rest of this brandy. And there's precious little left."

"Hear, hear!" the soldiers agreed. And as the flagon was passed around, Will's mind was racing. The evening had given him much to think about and he began to wish he'd waited another day before sending a report to Halt and Crowley.

Far to the south, the two senior Rangers were studying the report that the weary pigeon had delivered barely half an hour before. There had been storms and strong winds on its path south but the sturdy little bird had flown on through the weather, arriving at

Castle Araluen wet and nearly exhausted. A handler had gently detached the message from its leg and placed the faithful little bird in a warm hutch in one of Castle Araluen's soaring towers. Now, feathers fluffed out and head tucked under its wing, it slept, its task completed.

Not so Halt and Crowley. The Ranger Commandant paced back and forth in his room as Halt read through Will's truncated sentences once more. Finally, the gray-bearded Ranger looked up at his chief with a frown.

"I wish you'd stop that pacing," he said mildly.

Crowley made a gesture of irritation.

"I'm worried, dammit," he said, and Halt raised one eyebrow.

"You don't say," he said with mild irony. "Well, now that we have established that fact and I have conceded that yes, you are worried, perhaps you might stop your interminable pacing."

"If I stop it, it can hardly be interminable, can it?" Crowley challenged him. Halt pointed to a chair on the other side of the table.

"Just humor me and sit down," he said. Crowley shrugged and did as he was asked. He sat for a full five seconds, then was up and pacing again. Halt muttered something under his breath. Crowley surmised, correctly, that it was uncomplimentary, and chose to ignore it.

"The problem is," he said, "Will's report raises more questions than it answers."

Halt nodded agreement. He was about to come to his former apprentice's defense but he realized that Crowley wasn't criticizing Will's report. He was merely stating a fact. There were a lot of unanswered questions in the brief message: strange sights and sounds in the wood, apparently caused by a person or persons unknown; friction at the castle between Orman and his cousin; Orman's apparent inability to command; and the fact that someone, presumably Orman, had arranged for Alyss to be followed when she went on her morning ride. In most castles, it would have been an interesting set of occurrences. In a vulnerable strategic site like Macindaw, close to a hostile border, it was downright dangerous. Still . . .

"It's early days yet," he said finally, and Crowley dropped into the chair again, sprawling sideways, one leg cocked over the arm. He sighed deeply, knowing Halt was right.

"I know," he said. "I just wonder if there might be more than Will and Alyss can handle up there." Halt considered the point.

"I trust Will," he said, and Crowley made a gesture of agreement. In spite of his youth, Will was highly regarded in the Rangers—more highly than he knew. "And Pauline says Alyss is one of her best agents." Lady Pauline was a senior member of the Diplomatic Service. She had originally recruited Alyss and undertaken her early training. Alyss was as much her protégé as Will was Halt's.

"Yes. They're the right choices for the task, I know. And if we send in too many people we run the risk of exposing our hand and doing more harm than good. It's just I have a . . . funny feeling about this. Like someone is behind me and I can sense them but I can't see them. You understand?"

Halt nodded. "I've got the same feeling. But as you say, if we overdo things, we'll give the game away."

There was a long silence between them. They were both in agreement. But they also both had that same uneasy feeling.

"Of course, we could always send maybe one more person to help out if they need it," Halt suggested.

Crowley looked at him quickly, then said, "One more person wouldn't be overdoing it."

"Someone who could provide a bit of muscle—if they need it," Halt continued. "To cover their backs, as it were."

"I think I'd feel a bit better knowing they had even a little bit more backup," Crowley said.

"And of course," Halt added, "if we send the right person, he might provide more than just a little bit."

The eyes of both men met over the table. They were old comrades and friends. They had known each other for decades, served together in more campaigns than either could remember. Each knew exactly what the other was thinking and each was in complete agreement with the other.

"You're thinking Horace?" Crowley asked, and Halt nodded.

"I'm thinking Horace," he said.

25

WILL HAD NO IDEA THAT HIS SUPERIORS HAD DECIDED TO SEND help to him and Alyss. The pigeon that had carried his report was the only one that had learned the route between Norgate Fief and Castle Araluen. So it was the only one that could carry a reply back to him, and it would take three or four days before it would recover sufficient strength to undertake another journey. Then, of course, it would return to its last roosting place—with Alyss's man some distance from the castle. Until Will made contact with him, he would be unaware that help was on its way.

Had he known, he might have felt a little more secure. Horace was only one man but he had proved his worth many times over. As an apprentice, he had been an extraordinarily talented warrior—a natural, as his teachers put it. He had defeated the rebel warlord Morgarath in single combat and later had served with great distinction in the Skandian war against the Temujai riders. In addition, he had earned a fearsome reputation for his skill in single combat—the name of the Oakleaf Knight was still spoken with awe throughout Gallica. His exploits were such that King Duncan had no hesitation in formally knighting him before he had completed half the allotted time for his apprenticeship.

So the news that Horace was on his way might well have counteracted the unease Will felt on this bright winter morning. Still mulling over the conversation in the barracks room, he planned to see Alyss as soon as he could find a reasonable excuse, to talk it over with her. Already, he was half inclined to seek assistance from Sir Keren. After all, the young garrison commander was obviously not close to his cousin and he had an independent armed force at his command, which could prove valuable. But before Will could take such a radical step, he would have to discuss it with Alyss.

He was also keen to set a time when they might further investigate the mysterious Malkallam—for he must be the one behind the lights, the images and the attempts to discourage visitors to Grimsdell Wood. But before any of the above steps could be taken, he needed to contrive a way to have Alyss send for him. As a lowly jongleur, he could hardly barge in on a lady's quarters uninvited.

In the meantime, he had gone to the stables to make sure Tug was well cared for. And, since the dog was beginning to fret in Will's confined and somewhat stuffy castle quarters, he had taken her to the stables to keep Tug company. Both animals seemed content with the arrangement when he left them together. Tug had adopted an amused, superior attitude to the dog, while she, in her turn, seemed to accept the shaggy little Ranger horse as a reasonable substitute for Will himself. The dog wouldn't stray, he knew, but there was plenty in the way of strange new scents and noises and odd corners to keep her occupied in the castle stables.

It was as well he left her there. As he was crossing the courtyard, a vaguely familiar figure left the gatehouse, striding toward the central keep. He was a tall man, with dark hair and beard, and from a distance Will couldn't make out his features. But the way he moved, the way he held himself, was familiar—as was the heavy war spear he carried in his right hand, hefting it easily in spite of its considerable weight. After a few seconds' hesitation, Will made the connection in his mind.

John Buttle. The man he had left with the Skandian crew in faraway Seacliff Fief.

"What the devil is he doing here?" Will muttered to himself. Hastily, he turned away and dropped to one knee, pretending to fasten a strap on his boot. But fortunately, Buttle wasn't looking in his direction. He entered the keep and Will straightened, his mind racing. By now, Buttle should have been safely ensconced on Skorghijl with the Skandian crew, hundreds of kilometers to the northeast and well out of the way. But his turning up here was a real problem. After all, he had heard the conversation between Will and Alyss and knew that . . .

He stopped in mid-thought. Alyss! If Buttle were to see her, he could easily recognize her. Of course, he reasoned, her hairstyle and clothes were more elaborate now, as befitted a titled lady. When Buttle had last seen her, she had been wearing the simple but elegant courier's robe and her long hair had been down. But Alyss was a striking figure and, given enough time, he might remember her. If he did, he would know she was not the empty-headed Lady Gwendolyn, but a Diplomatic Service Courier.

Whether he might recognize Will was a moot point. He wouldn't look to see him in the bright, garish clothes of a jongleur. He knew Will was a Ranger and he would expect to see him in dull-colored, plain Ranger garb. As Halt had taught him, people tend to look for what they expect to see. Besides, the light had been uncertain in the shadows by the door where they had fought. But once he recognized Alyss, it would be only a matter of time before he made the connection to the other stranger in the castle.

Will's first step was clear then. He had to warn Alyss immediately. She would simply have to keep out of sight until they had sorted out this awkward new development. He started toward the keep door, then hesitated. Buttle had gone through there and Will had no idea where he might be now. He might be just inside, in the main hall. Or he might even be coming back out again. Will looked around for an alternative entrance to the keep. The kitchens, he knew, opened out into the rear of the courtyard. He'd go that way.

Before he could move, a heavy hand fell on his shoulder. He turned and found himself looking into the stern face of the sergeant major. Two other members of the garrison stood close by, their hands on their weapons. There was no sign of the previous evening's friendliness. The three men were all business.

"Just a moment, jongleur," the sergeant major said. "Lord Orman wants a word with you."

Will sized up the situation. The sergeant major was old and slow-moving, albeit an experienced warrior. And the other two were merely men-at-arms—their weapon skills weren't likely to be too advanced. He was confident he could deal with at least two of them before they could draw their weapons. But that would still leave one to sound the alarm—and the gatehouse and drawbridge were thirty meters away and manned by another three or four armed men. He'd never get out of the castle if he tried to fight now. The only thing he could do was try to bluff it out. He made this assessment in approximately half a second.

"Very well, sar'major," he replied, smiling. "I'll drop in on him when I've finished my errand."

The hand didn't budge from his shoulder.

"Now," the sergeant major said firmly, and Will shrugged.

"Of course, now is convenient for me as well," he said. "Lead the way." He gestured for the soldier to go ahead of him but the older man stood firm. His eyes were unamused.

"After you, jongleur," he said.

Will gave what he hoped was an unconcerned shrug and led the way across the courtyard. The three soldiers fell into place around him—the sergeant major behind him and the other two flanking him. Their heavy boots rang on the cobbles as they approached the door.

Will breathed a silent prayer that they wouldn't encounter Buttle on his way out. A man being so obviously escorted would be bound to draw attention and if Buttle looked closely, he might well recognize him, jongleur's clothes or no.

Fortunately, there was no sign of his former prisoner as they entered. The sergeant major prodded him with a hard, blunt object—Will realized that he had drawn the heavy mace he wore at his belt—and they headed for the stairs to Orman's rooms.

As was the fashion, the stairs curved around to the right, so that an attacker fighting his way upward would have to expose his entire body to use his sword while a defender above him could strike with only his right arm and side exposed. He could hear the sergeant major beginning to breathe heavily behind him as they went upward and the two flanking men had to fall behind on the narrow stairway. He could easily sprint away from them here, he realized. But the question remained, where could he go? Once again, he decided to bide his time for a better opportunity. Once he tried to escape, he knew, any chance of pretending innocence was gone. He decided to wait until his chances of success were better. Here, in the heart of Orman's castle, with armed men behind him and nowhere to go but upward, those chances didn't look too bright.

They reached Orman's fourth-floor suite of rooms. Will hesitated at the door to the anteroom but the mace prodded him once more.

"Go on in," the sergeant major's grim voice ordered and, with no choice but to obey, Will did as he was told.

Xander was at his table in the anteroom. He looked up as they entered without knocking. If he was surprised to see the minstrel being escorted by three armed men, he gave no sign of it. He held up a hand, motioning them to stop, then slipped out from behind his paper-laden table and opened the door to the inner office. Will heard his quiet voice.

"The men have brought Barton, my lord," he said. There was an indistinct mumble from inside the room and he bowed his head quickly and emerged, motioning for the sergeant major and Will to enter as he opened the door wider.

The mace prodded Will in the back again. That little habit was starting to annoy him and he was tempted to take the weapon from the sergeant major and do a little prodding of his own. Truth be told, he was curious to know what Orman wanted from him, and as long as he didn't summon more guards, Will was confident he could escape any time he chose.

Orman was behind his own work table. Will noticed that the books on magic were still among his papers, one of them lying open at a page marked with a leather bookmark. Orman was wearing his usual dark robe and he seemed to be hunched over in the large wooden armchair. He moved awkwardly as he waved Xander out, almost as if he was in pain. His voice, when he spoke, confirmed the impression. He seemed to form his words with difficulty and his breathing was heavy and labored.

"Well done, sergeant major. Any trouble from him?"

"None, sir. Came right peaceably," the soldier announced. Orman nodded slowly.

"Good. Good," he muttered to himself. There was a pause as he breathed heavily, then he flicked the fingers of one hand at the sergeant major in a gesture of dismissal.

"Very well, sergeant major. You can leave us. Wait outside, please."

The old soldier hesitated. "Are you sure, my lord?" he asked uncertainly. "The prisoner may try to . . ." He stopped in mid-sentence. He wasn't sure what Will might do. In fact, he wasn't even sure that he was a prisoner. He had been ordered to take two men and go fetch him here right away and so he had assumed that there was trouble brewing. Now, as Orman dismissed him, he began to wonder if this was simply a social matter and he remembered with some concern the prodding he had been doing all the way up the stairs.

"It's all right. Go." Orman's voice was a low whisper but the note of annoyance was clear in it. He was definitely in pain, Will thought. He heard the soldier come to attention behind him, then his boots as he marched to the door. He paused there, still unsure of the situation.

"I'll wait outside then, my lord," he said, then added, ". . . with my men."

"Yes. Yes. Do that if you choose," Orman told him. The door closed as the sergeant major went out. Orman rose awkwardly, favoring his left side. Will could see now that his left arm was held close to his side, almost as if he was suffering from broken ribs. He winced as he moved around the table and stood before Will. His breath came heavily, as if moving that short distance was an enormous effort for him. Will started toward him.

"Lord Orman, are you all right?" he said, but Orman held up a hand to stop him.

"No. As you can see, I'm not. But there's little you can do about it."

"Are you wounded?" Will asked. "I can send for your physician." But Orman was shaking his head, and a harsh laugh escaped his lips.

"I doubt that any healers in this castle could help with what I have," he said. "No. I need help of another kind." He paused, and his eyes burned into Will's as he added, "I need the help of a Ranger."

26

There was silence in the room. Will was speechless. It was the last thing he expected to hear from Orman. He recovered, knowing that his reaction was too late, but determined to try to bluff his way through anyway.

"A Ranger, Lord Orman?" he said. "I'm just a simple jongleur." He forced a self-deprecating smile and continued, "And, as you've pointed out several times, a pretty disappointing one."

Orman made a dismissive gesture and sank painfully onto one of the straight-backed chairs in front of his table.

"Don't bandy words with me. I don't have the strength. Look, I need help and I need it quickly. They've finally gotten to me, just as they got to my father. As you can see, I'm sick, and before too much longer I'll sink into a coma and then there's nothing to stop them."

"They?" Will asked. "Who are they?"

Orman groaned again, holding his side and stomach and bending over as a wave of pain hit him. Will could see sweat forming on the man's face—he was obviously in a bad way.

"Keren!" Orman gasped finally. "Who the hell do you think?

He's the one behind my father's sickness. He's the one trying to take over the castle!"

"Keren?" Will repeated. "But . . ." He paused and Orman, stronger now that the tide of pain had receded a little, continued angrily.

"Oh, of course. He's taken you in, just like everybody else. I suppose you imagined I was behind the whole plot to get rid of my father?" He looked up at Will for confirmation. Seeing it in the young man's eyes, he nodded resignedly. "Most people do. It's so easy to think that way when a person is unpopular, isn't it?"

There was nothing for Will to say. It was precisely the way he had reacted, now that he thought about it. He disliked Orman and the dislike had led him to the conclusion that the temporary Lord of Macindaw was not to be trusted. By contrast, Sir Keren's open, friendly nature had led him to view the man as a potential ally. But still, there was only Orman's word to go on here. The sallow-faced man continued.

"Look, you may be many things, but I doubt you're really a jongleur." He held up a hand to stop Will's automatic protest. "You're talented enough, I suppose, although your music isn't to my liking. But you gave yourself away the other day when I interviewed you."

"Gave myself away?" Will's mind flashed back to the conversation he had with Orman just before Alyss's arrival.

"I asked about your mandola, remember? I asked if it was a Gilperon."

"Yes," Will said slowly. He wondered where this was going. He remembered a few moments of confusion when Orman had asked the question, moments where he tried to cover up the fact that he hadn't heard of the master luthier, Gilperon. "It was simply that his name escaped me at the time, Lord Orman," he said. "As I said to you, a country musician could never afford a real Gilperon instrument, so the name simply escaped me for a few seconds."

"There is no Gilperon. The name is Gilet," Orman said flatly. "Any true jongleur should have known that."

Will closed his eyes briefly in anger. It was a very old trick that Orman had pulled on him, but it had worked. And now he saw no way out of the trap.

Orman continued. "So then I checked your horse—it's very similar to the breed the Rangers use. And it seems to be very well trained. Even your clothing gives a hint." He gestured to the gaudy black-and-white cloak that Will wore. "It's similar to the camouflage cloaks Rangers wear. Of course, the colors are different, but in a winter-scape such as we have here, black and white would be ideal. I imagine you could disappear into the countryside in moments if you chose to."

"It's a fascinating theory, my lord," Will said. "But unfortunately, it's really no more than a series of coincidences." He saw the anger flare briefly in Orman's eyes and then the other man replied.

"Don't waste my time. I don't have much left. They've managed to poison me the same way they did my father. The pain is becoming worse and worse and in a matter of hours, I'll be unconscious. And then they'll have everything they want. You have to get me out of here."

"You want to get out of here?" Will said, the surprise evident in his voice. That was the last thing he had expected.

"I have to, don't you see?" Orman said desperately. "I've tried to fight them for the past weeks but they've gradually infiltrated the castle. Keren is recruiting his own men and gradually getting rid of the ones who are loyal to me. I have barely a dozen men I can depend on these days, while he must have a score or more of men loyal to him."

Another spasm of pain racked him and he doubled over, groaning in agony. He was unable to speak for some time, then he continued, in a weak voice.

"Keren wants the castle. He's an illegitimate cousin, so there's no way he will ever get his hands on it legally. For some time, I've suspected that he's made an agreement with a Scotti warlord to hand the shire over—as long as Keren keeps the castle. If I'm right, once the snows clear, the Scotti will come through the passes and occupy the entire shire. Without Macindaw to threaten their lines of supply, they'll be able to besiege Norgate and the whole fief will fall before spring is out. Is that what you want?" he added bitterly. He could see Will was wavering and he went on.

"If Keren has me and my father in his power, he won't hesitate to kill us both and take control. Oh, he won't do it obviously. He isn't powerful enough to get away with that—yet. That's why he's dredged up the old legend about the sorcerer. He knows that frightened people will look for strong leadership—which he can provide. He's poisoned my father. He's keeping him unconscious and now he's planning the same for me. If we both die of the so-called sorcerer's curse, he'll have a free hand to take control—and nobody will oppose him. He'll be the only living relative.

"But if I can get away, he can't claim to be Lord of Macindaw. As long as I'm alive, he's stalemated and he gains nothing by killing my father. On the contrary, he'll probably keep him alive as a hostage. Until the Scotti get here, Keren must play his hand carefully. If he's too obvious, the countryside would rise up against him. But once he's established as Lord of Macindaw, it'll be a different story. Then, by the time the Scotti arrive to support him, it'll be too late."

"How did he poison you?" Will asked, and Orman shrugged.

"I have to eat and drink. Who knows? I've tried to be careful and have my food prepared separately. But they may have got to my servants. Or maybe they got their damn poison into the water." He gestured to the books on the Black Art that lay on the work table. "I've felt it coming on for days. They do it slowly, you see. I've been going through those damn books trying to find some clue, some antidote, but so far without any success."

Will looked at the books as the other man pointed to them. "Oh, I see," he said. "I thought . . ." He didn't finish the thought. Orman smiled grimly at him.

"You thought I was a sorcerer? You thought I was behind my father's illness?" he said. Will nodded. There was no point in denying it.

"It seemed a logical theory," he said.

Orman nodded wearily. "As I said, when a person is unpopular, it's so easy to think badly of him." He rose from the chair, moving painfully. "Now my best hope is that you are a Ranger, because I need help getting away from this castle, and I doubt if a simple jongleur would be up to the task." He paused and then added, "I assume that Lady Gwendolyn is also more than she seems?"

"How did you . . ." Will began, then stopped, realizing he had said too much. Orman smiled.

"Don't assume that because a person is unpopular, he's also stupid," he said. "The two of you turned up virtually at the same time, then Lady Gwendolyn had you summoned to her rooms. Very convenient. And then you both just happened to go riding at the same time. I'm not a fool."

Events had moved so fast in the past few minutes that Will had forgotten about the need to warn Alyss to stay out of sight. Making a decision, he apprised Orman of the situation, telling him of the surprising appearance of John Buttle. The castle lord frowned thoughtfully.

"That is a problem," he said. "He's one of Keren's men, of course—a new recruit. Keren seems to find every unattached thief and murderer who drifts through the shire. They gravitate to him. At the same time, he's getting rid of the men who might be loyal to me. I'll send Xander to pass your message to her. Best if you aren't seen by this man Buttle either, I think. Then let's think about how the three of us can get out of here."

He reached for a small silver bell on his table and rang it. There was a pause, then the door opened and Xander entered. Quickly, Orman gave him his instructions while Will dashed off a short note for him to carry to Alyss. The clerk, looking worried, folded the note into the top of his jerkin and left the room. Another thought had been nagging at Will. He voiced it now.

"The Night Warrior—the apparitions in Grimsdell Wood—is Keren behind them as well? What does he gain from them?"

"Oh, you've seen them, have you?" Orman asked. Then he shrugged. "To be honest, I don't know. Perhaps this former healer Malkallam is behind them all. Or maybe it's Keren. Maybe they're even working together. Then again, Keren may have simply taken advantage of the apparitions to use the old legend to his own advantage."

He shuddered in pain again. "In any event, we're going to have to find out what Malkallam is up to," he said. Will looked at him, a question in his eyes, and he elaborated.

"He may well be the only one who can heal me. I need you to take me to him."

27

"ARE YOU MAD?" WILL'S VOICE ROSE IN PITCH AS HE REACTED to Orman's statement. "You think Malkallam will help you? He's a sworn enemy of your entire family!" But Orman merely shook his head, the effort seeming to take a lot out of him.

"Only if you believe in fairy tales," he said. "I don't believe Malkallam is behind all this. I don't believe he's a sorcerer. For years, the man worked as a healer—an herbalist—and a very good one. But then something went wrong and he disappeared from sight. People said he went into the forest and surrounded himself with dark forces and apparitions."

"What went wrong?" Will asked, and Orman shrugged. The minute he did so, he regretted it, giving vent to a little grunt of pain before he answered.

"Who knows? Maybe somewhere along the way, people started confusing his abilities with sorcery. It's happened before, you know—someone develops a skill that's a little out of the ordinary, and before too long, people start believing it's magic." He paused for breath and looked meaningfully at Will. "As a Ranger, you should understand that."

Will was forced to agree. It was exactly the way many people thought of Rangers. And, he realized, he and Alyss had already seen that a lot of Malkallam's so-called sorcery consisted of elaborate mechanical tricks. But still . . .

"Can you afford to risk it?" he asked. "You're assuming an awful lot, after all."

Orman gave him a thin smile. There was not a great deal of amusement in it.

"The question is, can I afford *not* to risk it? Malkallam is the only person within hundreds of kilometers who might have the skill to recognize this drug and find an antidote. Without him, I'll sink into a coma and eventually die."

Will frowned thoughtfully as he digested this statement. The castle lord was right, he realized. Malkallam was a last throw of the dice. There was no other way for Orman to turn.

The door opened to admit Xander. The moment the secretary entered the office, Will saw the look on his face and knew he had bad news.

"My lord, I couldn't reach her. Keren's men are everywhere," he said.

Orman cursed as another seizure struck him. As Xander moved toward his lord, Will stepped to block his way. He felt a cold hand tighten around his heart.

"You mean they stopped you?" he said, then added, with a scathing note of condemnation, "You didn't even try to reach her, did you?"

The little secretary met his gaze unflinchingly.

"I didn't try once I saw them, because I knew they'd see me. And I didn't want to implicate the Lady Gwendolyn," he said.

Will reached out and grabbed the little man's jerkin in both hands, pulling him closer.

"You coward!" he told him. "What do you mean, *implicate her?*"

Xander still met his gaze without any sign of fear. He made no effort to break free from Will's grip.

"Think about it, Ranger. I'm seen hurrying to take some kind of message to Lady Gwendolyn. Then, within an hour, the three of us escape from the castle. Do you think Keren won't put two and two together and realize she's working with you?"

Slowly, Will released his grip and the secretary stepped back, smoothing his crumpled collar. He was right, Will thought. Any attempt to warn Alyss would only endanger her at the moment. Yet if she were to run into Buttle, if Buttle recognized her . . . somehow, he would have to get word to her.

"I've got to help her," he said.

Orman shook his head wearily. "It's too late for that," he said. "If Xander's right and Keren's men are everywhere, he may be about to make his move. We have only a few minutes to get out of here."

Will's anger boiled up and overflowed. "Is that all you can think about?" he demanded. "Your own precious skin? Well, to blazes with you! I don't run out on my friends when they need me."

Orman said nothing. But Will was surprised as Xander took a step toward him and laid a hand on his arm.

"Lord Orman is right," he said. "Your best chance is to get him out of here right away. If you're caught in the castle, there'll be nothing to stop Keren from killing all of you, don't you see?"

Will realized Xander had spoken the truth. His first task, now that he knew Orman was not a rebel, was to get him to safety. But to do that meant leaving Alyss in danger and he hated the idea of that.

"We're wasting time," Orman said quietly. "Look, your friend may be caught. Or she may not. But if they catch us too, there'll be no reason for Keren to keep her alive—particularly once he learns she's a Courier. But if he doesn't have me, he can't claim the castle, and he'll need to hedge his bets. You can even offer to trade me for Gwendolyn if you want. That'll ensure he looks after her." He paused, letting Will think about that. "I assume Gwendolyn isn't her real name?" he added.

"It's Alyss," Will said, distractedly. He was thinking about what Orman had said. It made sense. Once they were all prisoners, Keren would have no reason to let any of them live. But if he and Orman could get away, he could use Orman as a bargaining chip. As he had the thought, he wondered briefly if he would really trade the castle lord for Alyss. He decided that if it came to it, he would.

"All right," he said abruptly. "We'll do it." He paused, gathering his thoughts, then issued orders rapidly.

"Get your things together," he told Orman. "We're traveling light, so keep it to the bare essentials. Warm clothes, a good cloak and boots. We'll be sleeping rough, I should think. I'll go to the stables and saddle two horses." Will paused, glanced at the secretary and amended the statement. "Three horses. Xander, can you get Lord Orman to the keep's eastern entrance without attracting too much attention?"

The eastern entrance was the one that opened onto the courtyard, facing the stables. The little secretary nodded.

"There's a servants' staircase. We'll use that," he said. Will nodded agreement.

"Good. Be there in ten minutes. I'll have the horses ready inside the stable and when I see you, I'll bring them across."

"Then what?" Orman asked.

"Then we ride like hell for the gate," Will said. The other man's face twisted in a sardonic grin, in spite of his pain.

"It's not exactly a classic example of ingenuity, is it?" he said. Will shrugged.

"If you like, we'll dig a secret tunnel, or we could wear clever disguises. But by the time we do it, we'll all be dead. Our best bet is to move quickly and surprise them. I assume some of your men are still on the walls?"

Orman nodded. "Some will be my men. But not many."

"All right." Will glanced at Xander. "Get him out of here now, and use those back stairs. If Keren and his men come calling, I don't want you two trapped in here. But if they can't find you, it might buy us a little time. They might not realize we're on to them yet. Ten minutes," he repeated.

Both of the other men nodded agreement. He hurried to the door, opened it a crack and peered out. There was nobody in the outer room. Xander had apparently dismissed the sergeant major and his men. Will crossed quickly to the exterior door, checked again and went out. The corridor outside was deserted. There were two guards at the far end, but aside from an incurious glance in his direction, they took no notice of him. Forcing himself to walk calmly, he headed for the staircase and started down.

His nerves shrieked at him as he crossed the main hall and then the courtyard outside. Every fiber of his being wanted to run, to get to the stables as quickly as he could. But he forced himself to walk casually, to avoid attracting attention to himself, waiting all the time for some sign that the alarm had been raised.

Once inside the dim stable building, however, all pretense of casualness disappeared. He sprinted to Tug's stall, grabbing his saddle and bridle from the rail alongside. Both Tug and the dog heard him coming and were alerted by his behavior. Tug stood still as Will tossed the saddlecloth and saddle onto his back and fastened the girths. The dog stood guard, sensing that something was out of the ordinary. Once Tug was saddled and ready, Will took the component parts of his bow from the packsaddle and hurriedly clipped them together. His quiver of arrows was hanging nearby and he slung it over his saddle pommel, then led Tug out of the stall.

He hastily checked the adjacent stalls for two suitable mounts. His own packhorse was a sturdy enough animal but it would be too slow if there were any pursuit. There were several battlehorses available, but he ignored them. He didn't think Orman or Xander would be capable of handling the massive beasts. He'd noticed a good-looking bay mare earlier and he led her out now, hurriedly putting saddle and bridle on her. She was calm and docile, but she looked as if she'd have a decent turn of speed. He tethered her beside Tug and hurried down the line of stalls, looking for a third horse.

At the far end of the stable, he found a gray gelding that wasn't too skittish. He saddled it, then checked the girth straps on the bay and the gelding. It wouldn't do to have the saddles slip when Orman and Xander tried to mount. With the horses ready, he moved to the stable entrance and eased one side of the double doors open, peering through the narrow gap toward the keep. He saw a brief movement at the eastern door and realized it was Xander, standing just inside the half-open doorway, in the shadow of the interior. A dark figure was just visible behind him—Orman, he hoped, and then realized it could well be one of Keren's men. He shrugged. There was only one way to find out.

"Fine," he muttered. He glanced at the dog, who was staring expectantly up at him, ears pricked and eyes questioning. "Follow," he said, then added: "Silent." He reinforced the word command with the hand signal he'd taught her. The dog, content now that she knew what was expected of her, dropped to her haunches, ready to move.

Hastily, Will fastened a lead rope to the other two horses, tying the end to Tug's saddle. Then he moved quickly to the door once more, easing one side wide open. He ran back, swung quickly up into Tug's saddle and touched the little horse with his heels.

There was a momentary drag on the lead rope as the mare and the gelding resisted the pull, then they were clattering out onto the cobbles behind Tug, moving already at a brisk trot. The dog slipped along beside Tug, a black-and-white shadow running belly low to the ground.

Xander was already helping Orman down the three steps that led to the keep door. The castle lord looked to be in bad condition, supported by his secretary's arm around his shoulders. There was a moment of confusion as Will hauled on the lead rope to bring the horses to a halt. Tug, sensing what he had in mind, braced his sturdy legs to stop the other horses. They plunged and pulled for a few seconds, then Xander gripped the mare's bridle and held her steady as Orman tried to pull himself up into the saddle. Will heard his quick, painful intake of air and heard also a voice from the battlements as the sudden swirl of movement caught the guards' attention. He slid an arrow from the quiver hanging over the pommel and laid it on the bowstring. Xander would have to help Orman by himself. It would be Will's task to take care of any opposition that might show itself.

As he had the thought, he heard muffled shouting from inside the keep tower, and the sound of running feet. He glanced down at Xander, struggling with the deadweight of his master as the mare stepped skittishly away in a small half-circle. Will urged Tug close beside the mare, held his bow in one hand, reached down with the other and heaved on Orman's belt, hauling him up into the saddle as Xander pushed from below. The castle lord groaned in pain, but he was mounted now and Xander was struggling to get his foot into the stirrup as the gelding danced nervously, affected by the tension and excitement.

Behind him, he heard the keep doorlock rattle, then the heavy door was flung open by someone inside. Twisting in the saddle, barely looking, he shot, slamming an arrow quivering into the wood of the doorjamb at face height. He heard a startled shout and the door slammed shut again.

"Come on!" he yelled. There was no more time to lose. He touched Tug with his heels and the little horse clattered away, dragging the others behind on the lead rope. He glanced over his shoulder, saw Xander half in and half out of the saddle, clinging desperately to the gelding's mane. He couldn't spare the little man any more time or thought. The gatehouse was before them and one of the sentries was running uncertainly toward the giant windlass that operated the portcullis. Will sent an arrow whistling past the man's ear and saw him drop to the cobbles for cover.

There was more shouting behind them now and from the corner of his eye, Will saw movement on the battlements ahead of them, and heard a crossbow bolt strike, skidding, on the stones in front of Tug.

Without conscious thought, seemingly without aiming, he shot again and a figure tumbled from the parapet into the courtyard, his crossbow clattering on the stones beside him.

Then the horses' hooves were thundering on the timber of the drawbridge and the drag on the lead rope was virtually gone as the gelding and mare, drawn by the excitement of the moment, kept pace with Tug. They shot into the darkness under the massive gate tower, then out into the winter sunshine. Within seconds, the hooves were drumming on the hard frozen ground at the end of the bridge and they were clear. He sensed the hiss of crossbow bolts in the air but there were only a few of them. They had taken the sentries by surprise—or they were mainly Orman's men and had refused to fire on their lord. He glanced back and saw that Xander had finally made it into the saddle. He was riding close beside Orman, the taller man hunched painfully in the saddle, but holding firmly to the pommel.

It would be some minutes before any pursuit was launched and Will knew where he wanted to be when they came after him.

28

WILL DREW REIN AS THEY REACHED THE NOW-FAMILIAR EN-
trance to Grimsdell Wood. He allowed the other horses to pull
alongside Tug and studied Orman critically. The castle lord was
swaying in his saddle, his eyes half closed and with a faraway look in
them. His mouth moved but no sound came out.

Xander was watching his lord anxiously. "We have to get him
to Malkallam quickly," he said. "He's nearly unconscious."

Will nodded. He looked away from Orman to the bend in the
road where their pursuers would appear—he had no doubt there
would be pursuers.

"Get him further into the trees," he said. "I'll stay here and discourage anyone from following too closely." He indicated the narrow trail that he and Alyss had followed on their previous exploration
of the wood. "Follow that path for a hundred meters or so and wait
for me there. You'll be well out of sight by then."

Xander hesitated. "What about you?"

Will smiled at him. The little clerk had unexpected courage. He
flicked the cowl of his cloak up over his head and nudged Tug farther into the dappled shadows under a bare-branched oak tree.

"I'm out of sight now," he said. And when Xander still hesitated, he gestured for him to go. "Get going. They'll be up with us any minute."

The secretary saw the good sense of the suggestion. He nodded to Will and, seizing the lead rein for Orman's horse, led the semi-conscious castle lord into the dim shadows of Grimsdell Wood. After fifteen meters, they were lost to Will's sight. He nodded to himself with satisfaction and sat unmoving. The dog was flat on her belly on the ground beside Tug. She emitted a low, rumbling growl.

"Still," he told her, and her tail flicked obediently.

A few seconds later, Tug's ears twitched nervously and he pawed the ground with one hoof. So far, Will had heard nothing. He marveled at the acute senses of his two animals. He soothed Tug, and knowing that his master had heard his warning, the little horse relaxed.

It was another half minute before the band of riders rounded the bend in the road. There were eight of them, all armed and led by a familiar tall figure.

"Buttle," he breathed. The dog allowed herself another almost inaudible growl, then settled again.

The group drew rein about two hundred meters from where Will sat. One of the men was obviously a hunter of some kind and he dropped from the saddle to study the tracks on the road, looking to the snow-covered meadow that separated the road from Grimsdell Wood, where the path taken by the three horses through the snow was all too clear. He pointed toward the wood and moved to re-mount.

Buttle gave the signal for the men to advance, but they didn't move. Will heard raised voices as Buttle turned on them and repeated the order. He smiled to himself. Buttle obviously hadn't heard about the horrors of Grimsdell, he realized. For a moment, he regretted a lost opportunity. If they had come forward, he could have waited till they were in the middle of the open ground and then started shooting. He could probably have reduced Keren's available force by eight men that way. Then he rejected the thought. Some of the men might well be Orman's soldiers, forced to go along against their will. And even if they weren't, he knew he could hardly bring himself to murder eight men in cold blood, no matter how dangerous they might be. That wasn't why Halt had trained him for years to the level of skill he now possessed.

Buttle, however, was a different matter altogether. His total lack of scruples and the basic evil nature of the man would make him a valuable deputy to the scheming usurper. Men like Keren needed men like Buttle, Will knew. They needed men who would obey orders to kill and rob and destroy without any hesitation. Such men made it easier for others to follow suit. He had no doubt that Buttle was already established as one of Keren's key retainers.

And there he sat, just two hundred meters away from Will, who had an arrow nocked to the string already.

It was a long bowshot and there was a slight crosswind. Will could see it stirring the tops of the bare alders that lined the road on the far side. Most archers would have approached such a shot with misgivings, but Will was a Ranger and for a Ranger, a two-hundred-meter shot was bread and butter. And he knew that misgivings were the beginning of a miss. Anxiety over a missed shot all too often rewarded itself with the very result that it sought to avoid. Will raised his bow to the aim position.

The arrow seemed to slide back effortlessly, drawn by the big muscles in his back and shoulders with an ease born of thousands of repetitions. He created his sighting picture, focusing on the target, not on the arrow or the bow. They were simply two parts of the overall picture that culminated in the figure of Buttle sitting his horse two hundred meters away.

He continued raising the bow until he was satisfied that the elevation was correct for the distance. At that moment, had anyone asked him how he *knew* that it was correct, he could not have answered. It was instinctive in him now, another product of those years of practice. He allowed for the wind and held steady a moment. His left hand, holding the bow, was loose and relaxed, so that the shaped grip sat in the gap between thumb and forefinger, supported but not actually gripped. The thumb of his right hand rested against the corner of his mouth, the first three fingers restraining the string at the full draw position, one above and two below the nocking point.

He exhaled half of the last breath he had taken, vaguely aware of his own heartbeat and natural body rhythms, and allowed the string to release itself from his fingers, both hands passive, without a trace of jerking or twisting. The entire process, once he had raised the bow, took less than four seconds.

The bow sang and the arrow leapt away.

Ironically, it was the years of practice that now betrayed him.

The shot was an excellent one. In any other archer, it would have been considered a success. But Will was using the three-piece bow, not the yew longbow that he had practiced with during the last three years of his apprenticeship. Over the two hundred meters it traveled—although it actually covered more distance through the air, moving in a smooth curve—the arrow dropped farther than he had estimated. Instead of striking home into Buttle's upper body, it came out of nowhere and slammed into his thigh, tearing through the fleshy part of the leg and pinning it to the hard leather of the saddle.

Buttle screamed with the sudden burning agony in his thigh. His horse reared in fright, as did several others around him. His men, already wary about venturing toward Grimsdell Wood, took one look at the feathered shaft that had transfixed their leader and turned and rode for the shelter of the bend in the track. Buttle, cursing the pain and his men with equal savagery, wheeled his horse helplessly, then, furious, he gave in to the inevitable and rode after them, reeling in the saddle with the pain.

"Damn," said Will dispassionately, watching him go. He remembered Crowley's words about the bow. A flat trajectory at first, but then it would drop faster than he was accustomed to. "No more long shots," he said to Tug, whose ears flattened back against his head in answer. Will glanced down at the dog, who was looking up at him, her tail moving slowly. It seemed she was quite content to see the arrow hit Buttle anywhere at all, he mused.

He looked back at the road. There was no sign that the men were renewing the pursuit, so he nudged Tug with one knee to turn him and followed the track into the wood.

He caught up to the others a hundred meters down the trail, where he had told Xander to wait. Orman was sinking further and further into the coma that he had predicted, swaying in the saddle, almost totally unconscious, mouthing meaningless words and making little mewling noises.

"How's he doing?" he asked Xander, although the question was clearly unnecessary. The secretary frowned.

"We don't have a lot of time," he said. "Do you have any idea where Malkallam might have his headquarters?"

Will shook his head. "I assume it'll be right in the center of the wood," he said. "But where that might be is anyone's guess."

Xander glanced anxiously at his master. "We'll have to do something," he said, the worry evident in his voice.

Will looked around helplessly, hoping for an idea. He knew that, Ranger skill notwithstanding, they could blunder for days in this thick forest, with its narrow intersecting trails. And they had hours, at best.

His gaze fell on the dog, sitting patiently, head cocked to one side, looking to him for direction. There was a chance, he realized.

"Come on," he said tersely to Xander, and nudged Tug, starting out down the path that he and Alyss had followed only a day ago. So much had happened in that short time, he thought. They skirted the edge of the sinister black mere until they came to the spot where Alyss had found the scorched grass. Will stopped there now and dismounted. Xander, after a moment's hesitation, followed him. He looked at the scorch marks.

"What caused this?" he asked. Will told him of Alyss's theory about a giant magic lantern. Xander's eyebrows went up, but he nodded thoughtfully.

"Yes, she could be right," he said. "Mind you, you'd need a near-perfect lens for the job."

"A lens?" Will asked.

"The focusing device that would create a beam of light. I've never seen one of the standard you'd need for this, but I imagine it would be possible to construct one."

"You'd need one hell of a light source as well," Will told him, but the small man shrugged that objection away.

"Oh, there's plenty of ways you can achieve that," he said. "Whiterock, for example."

"Whiterock?" Will asked. The word was unfamiliar to him. Xander nodded again.

"It's a porous rock that releases a flammable gas when you drip water onto it. The gas burns with an intense white flame. Very hot too . . . just like whatever caused these scorch marks." He nodded to himself several times. "Yes, I'd say whiterock would do the job. But what do you have in mind here?" he added.

Will clicked his fingers and the dog moved closer to him, eyes fixed on him as she waited for instructions.

"I figured if there was some kind of lamp here, there must have been people tending it. And people leave a scent. Maybe the dog can track them. Odds are, if we find them, we'll find this wizard's lair as well."

He ruffled the dog's ears and pointed to the ground around them.

"Find," he said.

The black-and-white head went down and she began quartering the ground by the bank of the mere. After several minutes, she began casting wider and wider. Then she stopped, one forepaw rising into the air as her nose stayed close to the ground. She sniffed several times, then barked once, a sharp, urgent sound.

"Good girl!" Will breathed. Xander looked doubtful.

"How do you know she hasn't scented a deer, or a badger?" he asked. Will looked at him for a few seconds.

"If you've got a better idea, now's the time to mention it."

Xander made an apologetic gesture with his hands. "No, no. Carry on," he said mildly. Will turned back to the dog. As ever, she was watching him and waiting for new orders. He moved to her, pointed to the ground where she had found the scent, and said: "Follow."

The dog barked once and bounded away. She went a few meters, then stopped and turned back, looking at him. She barked again, the message obvious: *Come on if you're coming. We haven't got all day.*

29

The trail wound and twisted and seemed to double back on itself. There were side trails and forks in the path as well, and Will began to wonder if the dog really knew what she was doing or if she was just wandering at random. There seemed to be so many choices, so many different ways they could go. Then, as he realized how focused she was on her task, he knew she was definitely following something. The question remained, though: what was it? He realized that Xander could be right. They could well be hurrying through the wood in pursuit of a badger or some other animal.

Skilled as he was in woodcraft, it wasn't long before Will was totally disoriented, and he knew that he would be hard-pressed to retrace their path if he had to. He realized that Orman's life was now well and truly in the care of the dog and, from the worried glances that Xander kept darting at him, he knew the secretary was aware of the fact as well. They didn't speak. There was no point in voicing their fear and the looming nature of the dark wood discouraged idle conversation. It was as if Grimsdell itself had a presence— a character. Dark, depressing and threatening, it weighed down on them, alleviated only by the occasional clearing and chance view of the sky overhead.

They had been traveling for over an hour, Will estimated, when they came to a three-way fork in the trail. For the first time since they had started out, the dog hesitated. She cast down the right-hand fork for a few meters, then stopped, nose down, forepaw raised uncertainly. Then she snuffled her way back and tried the left fork.

"Oh God," Xander said quietly, "she's lost the scent." He looked fearfully at his master, lolling in the saddle, eyes closed, head sagging, held in place only by a rope they had lashed to his hands and tied to the saddle pommel. If they were to be left blundering through the wood, without any sense of direction or purpose, Xander knew it would spell the end for Orman.

The dog glanced at him, as if in reproach, then uttered a short bark and started down the left fork, all traces of uncertainty now gone. Will and the secretary urged their horses forward to follow. They had gone fifty meters, winding and twisting and perhaps making only twenty meters of progress, when Will heard Xander let out a gasp.

He looked up—his attention had been fixed on the dog, he realized—and saw what had caused the cry of alarm. There was a skull set on a pole to one side of the trail ahead of them. A rough, lichen-covered board below it carried an indecipherable message written in ancient runes. The words might have been enigmatic but the message was clear.

"It's a warning," Xander said.

Will slid an arrow from his quiver and laid it on the bowstring.

"Then consider yourself warned," he said dryly. "Personally, if I'm planning to ambush someone, the last thing I ever do is let them know in advance."

He leaned forward to study the skull more closely. It was yellowed with age. And it was not quite human. The lower jaw seemed to thrust forward more than a man's, and there were fang-like canine teeth on either side.

The dog was waiting impatiently and Will signaled her forward. She started down the trail again, and suddenly she broke into a run, dashing forward and around the next bend, out of sight.

At Will's cue, Tug broke into a canter to follow the dog and they rounded the bend after her . . .

. . . and found themselves in a large clearing, with a substantial one-story building, constructed from dark wood and thatched with straw, on the far side. He heard the other two horses come clattering after him, then slide to a stop beside him.

"Looks like we're here," Will said quietly. Xander looked around the clearing, searching for some sign of human habitation.

"But where's Malkallam?" he said.

Then they saw movement in the trees on the far side of the clearing, and as if the sorcerer's name had summoned them, figures began to step out of the surrounding woods.

There must have been more than thirty of them. And even as he had the thought, Will noticed that there was something unusual about them. They were . . . he searched for the right term, and hesitated. He was not totally sure of what he was seeing. Even in the clearing, the light was dim and uncertain, and the people, if they were people, were staying close to the dark mass of the forest behind them, where the shadows were thick and heavy. He heard Xander's quick intake of breath, then the secretary spoke softly.

"Look at them," he said. "Are they human?"

Then Will realized what it was that had caused him to hesitate. They were certainly human, he thought. But it was as if they were all dreadful caricatures of normal people. They were terribly misshapen—all of them. Some were dwarflike, barely four feet tall; others were tall and painfully thin. One was huge—he must have been two and a half meters tall and massive across the chest and shoulders. His skin was a pallid white, and aside from a few random wisps of yellowish hair, he was bald.

Others were hunched over, their bodies twisted and bowed. There were several who were hunchbacks, their movements awkward and painful as they shuffled forward.

Will's throat went dry as he saw that among the thirty-plus people facing him, there was not one who could be described as normally shaped. Obviously, this was the result of Malkallam's black sorcery, he thought, and as he thought it, he also realized that they had made a mistake bringing the unconscious Orman here. A wizard who would create such painful disfigurement among people was hardly going to help the castle lord recover from the poison that was destroying him.

After their first movement out of the shadow of the trees, the creatures stopped, as if in response to some silent command. Will glanced down as the dog sank slowly to her haunches in front of him. He could feel the low, continuous rumble of warning in Tug's chest. It was an impasse, he realized. There was no sign of the wizard, unless he happened to be one of the misshapen creatures that faced him across the clearing—and somehow, he doubted that.

"Ranger . . ." Xander's voice was low and edged with fear. Will glanced at him and the little man nodded to the far side of the clearing. Following his glance, Will felt his own throat constrict with fear.

The pallid-skinned giant had begun to advance across the clearing toward them, one ponderous step at a time. As he advanced, there was a low, wordless mutter of encouragement from his companions. Will slowly raised the bow, an arrow still nocked and ready, from where it had rested across his pommel.

"That's far enough," he said quietly. The giant was nearly halfway toward them. He took another pace. Now he was in the very middle of the clearing and Will sensed he could not let him get any closer. Those massive hands could tear him, Xander and Orman limb from limb. And probably their horses as well, he thought.

"Stop," he said, a little louder, with more of an edge in his voice. The giant met his gaze. Even though Will was seated astride Tug, their eyes were on the same level. The giant frowned and Will saw his muscles tense as he prepared to take another step. He slid the arrow back to full draw, instinctively sighting on the giant's chest, right where the heart should lie.

"Big as you are, this arrow will go right though you at this range," he said, deliberately keeping his voice calm.

The creature hesitated. He saw the frown deepen on its face. Puzzlement? Anger? Fear? Frustration? He wasn't sure. The grotesque features were so bizarre, it was difficult to read them with any accuracy. The important thing was that the giant had stopped advancing on them. From the silent watchers at the edge of the clearing, he heard a collective sigh. Urging him forward? Advising him to stop? Again, Will had no idea.

What next? he thought. Do we sit here until the next snowfall, facing each other across this clearing? He had no idea what to do. On his own, he would have trusted Tug to get him clear of the situation. But he couldn't desert Xander and Orman.

"Ranger, look!" said Xander in a breathless whisper.

He glanced away from the giant, who had, understandably, been occupying all his attention. Xander was gesturing toward the dog.

She had risen from her crouched position in front of them and was advancing across the clearing toward the giant. Will caught his breath to call her, then stopped and released the tension on his bow as he noticed something.

Her heavy tail was wagging slowly from side to side as she went.

The giant looked down at her as she reached him, stopping just in front of him. Her head was lowered and her tail was still wagging. The frown disappeared from the huge creature's face and he went down on one knee, one massive hand out to the dog.

She moved forward again to sit as his feet and he fondled her ears and scratched under her chin. Her eyes half-closed in pleasure, she turned her head slightly to lick his hand.

And then Xander drew Will's attention to yet another remarkable detail in a wholly remarkable day.

"He's crying!" he said softly. And sure enough, there were tears coursing down the pale white cheeks. "You know, I think he's quite harmless. Thank God you didn't shoot him."

"I must say I agree," said a voice from behind them. "Now would you mind telling me what the devil you're doing in my woods?"

30

WILL SPUN IN THE SADDLE, THE BOW COMING UP, ARROW FULLY drawn. Then for the second time, he hesitated. He had no real idea what he had expected Malkallam to look like. If pressed, he would have surmised that the sorcerer would be somehow larger than life—perhaps extremely tall and thin, or huge and grossly overweight. Certainly, he would be dressed in a voluminous black robe, perhaps marked with obscure, mystical symbols or whirling suns and moons.

And of course he would wear a tall, pointed hat that would take his overall height to nearly three meters.

What he didn't expect was a small, thin person who was a few centimeters shorter than Will himself. He had wispy, thinning gray hair, combed over a balding crown, a rather large nose and ears, and a slightly receding chin. His robe was a simple brown homespun habit, rather like a monk's, and he wore sandals on his feet, in spite of the wintry weather.

But the biggest surprise of all was the eyes. A sorcerer's eyes should be dark and forbidding, full of mystery and arcane danger.

These were hazel and there was an unmistakable light of humor in them.

Confused, Will lowered the bow.

"Who are you?" he asked. The small man shrugged.

"I thought I was the one who should ask that question," he said mildly. "After all, this is my home."

Xander, however, concerned about the rapidly deteriorating state of his master, was in no mood to bandy words.

"Are you Malkallam?" he asked rudely. The small man inclined his head toward the secretary, his lips pursed a little as he considered the question.

"I have been called that," he said, the light of humor disappearing from his eyes.

"Then we need your help," Xander said. "My master has been poisoned."

Malkallam's bushy eyebrows formed into a frown and his voice took on a threatening tone.

"You're begging help from the most feared sorcerer in these parts?" he said. "You enter my realm, ignore my warning signs, risk the anger of the dreadful Night Warrior who protects me, then demand my help?"

"If you're truly Malkallam, yes," Xander replied, uncowed by the threatening tone of the words.

The sorcerer's eyebrows returned to their normal position and he shook his head in some admiration.

"Well, you've certainly got some nerve about you," he said, in a lighter tone. "Perhaps we'd better take a look at Lord Orman in that case."

"You know who this is?" Will said, as the small man stepped

toward Orman, who was swaying unconsciously in his saddle, muttering wordless little sounds. Malkallam laughed briefly.

"Of course I do, Ranger," he said. Will shrugged his shoulders in defeat. So much for his careful disguise. First Orman and now Malkallam had seen through it almost immediately.

"How do you . . . ?" he began, but the sorcerer silenced him with a hand gesture.

"Well, it's not exactly alchemy, is it?" he said crisply. "You've been nosing around my forest for the past couple of days. You ride the sort of horse Rangers ride. You carry a bow and you have that big saxe knife at your side—I'll wager you have a throwing knife somewhere else on your person. Plus that cloak of yours has the most disconcerting habit of blending into the background. What else could you be? A jongleur?"

Will opened his mouth to reply but no words came. Xander, however, was less inclined to silence.

"*Please!*" he said. "My master could be dying while you two prattle on."

Again, Malkallam's eyebrows shot up. "A Ranger and a sorcerer," he said in some wonder, "and he tells us we're prattling on. This *is* a bold fellow indeed."

Yet, even as he said it, his keen eyes were scrutinizing Orman's face. He stretched up to touch the castle lord but couldn't quite reach.

"Trobar!" he called. "Leave the dog for a moment and get Lord Orman down for me."

The giant reluctantly rose from where he had continued to pet the dog and shambled toward Orman's horse. Xander slipped down from the saddle and placed himself between his master and the massive figure. Will, feeling that events were moving a little too quickly for him, dismounted as well. He exchanged a puzzled glance with Tug. The horse seemed to shrug. *How should I know?* the movement said. *I'm just a horse.*

Trobar stopped before the determined figure who barred his way.

"He won't hurt him," Malkallam said, a little impatiently. "If you want my help it will be quicker if you let him carry your master inside."

Reluctantly, Xander stepped to one side. Trobar moved forward, loosened the ropes tying Orman in place and let the unconscious man slide out of the saddle to cradle him in his arms. He looked inquiringly at Orman, who gestured to the house.

"Take him inside, to my study."

Trobar set off, carrying the unconscious man as if he weighed no more than a feather. Xander trotted beside him, and Will and Malkallam followed.

"Interesting, the way he reacted to your dog," the sorcerer said chattily. "Of course, he had a border shepherd as a child, before the villagers drove him out. It was his only friend. I think it broke his poor heart when it died."

"I see," said Will. It seemed the safest reply he could come up with. Malkallam glanced sideways at him. *So young,* he thought, *and so much responsibility.* Unseen by the young Ranger, he grinned to himself. He gestured to a bench on the verandah.

"There's no need for you to come in while I examine Lord Orman," he said. Will nodded and moved to the bench. Xander, however, drew himself up as straight as he could.

"I'm coming in," he said. His tone brooked no argument and Malkallam shrugged.

"As you wish. But you brought him here, after all. It's a little late to start worrying that I might harm him somehow."

"I'm not worried about that," Xander said stiffly. "I'm just . . ." He trailed off.

Malkallam waited expectantly, urging him to finish. When he didn't, the sorcerer finished for him: ". . . worried that I might harm him somehow."

Xander shrugged. It was exactly what he did think, but he realized it wasn't politic to say so when he was asking the sorcerer's help.

"Just remember, I'll be watching you," he said awkwardly. His hand dropped to the dagger at his side but he was all too obviously a man who was unaccustomed to using weapons. Malkallam smiled at him.

"I'm sure your master would be proud of you. If I decide to do anything terrible to him, I'll have to turn you into a newt before I do so."

Xander studied him suspiciously for a few seconds, then decided that he was probably joking. Probably. Without another word, he followed Malkallam inside.

Will sat on the bench and leaned his back gratefully against the rough log walls of the house. The sun was just beginning to sneak under the eaves of the house and it warmed his feet and legs as he stretched out. Suddenly, he was exhausted. The rapidly moving events of the day, the escape from the castle, the search for Malkallam's lair and the subsequent meeting with the sorcerer had kept adrenaline coursing through his system. Now that there was nothing further to do for the moment, he felt absolutely drained.

The other inhabitants of Malkallam's domain continued to

watch him. He tried to ignore them, sensing no threat from them, only curiosity.

He glanced up as he sensed a movement at the door. Trobar, the giant, came out of the house. He looked around the clearing, saw the dog lying watchfully where he had left her and moved to her side. He went down on one knee beside her and fondled her head gently. She closed her eyes blissfully and inclined her head for his touch.

"Dog!" said Will, a little more sharply than he had intended.

The dog's eyes opened and she was instantly alert. Will pointed to the verandah beside him.

"Come here," he said.

She rose and shook herself, then began to lope slowly across the clearing toward him. He looked at Trobar and saw the unmistakable sadness on the disfigured face.

"Oh, all right," he told the dog. "Stay where you are."

He saw the smile break out on the giant's face as the dog allowed herself to be patted once more. He shut his eyes wearily. He wondered what he was going to do about Alyss.

31

ALYSS HAD HEARD THE COMMOTION IN THE COURTYARD BELOW her window in the keep tower: shouts and horses' hoofbeats ringing off the cobbles. She had reached the window in time to see three horsemen galloping full pelt for the portcullis gate.

She recognized Will instantly and, even as she watched, she saw his snap shot that sent a crossbowman tumbling from the castle walls. Behind him rode two other men, one of them swaying in the saddle as if he were barely conscious. With a start of surprise, she recognized Orman.

What on earth was he doing? Obviously, from the way the guards had reacted, he was escaping from his own castle. Yet the very idea was ridiculous!

And Will was with him. She frowned. There was no sign that Will was acting under any duress. He was leading the way, in fact. For a moment she toyed with the possibility that Orman really was a black magician and had placed some kind of spell or compulsion on Will. Then she dismissed the thought. Like most educated people, she didn't really believe in sorcery or magic.

Yet what other explanation could there be?

She remained by the window and a few minutes later, a party of mounted men set out in pursuit. Her first instinct was to dress and hurry downstairs to find out what was going on. Then she stopped and sat down, fingers drumming on the table as she thought. Lady Gwendolyn wouldn't behave in such a fashion. Lady Gwendolyn was an empty-headed, self-obsessed twitterer who wouldn't take the slightest interest in anything that didn't involve new hairstyles, shoes or fashions.

She rose and moved to the door leading to the anteroom of her suite.

Her two maids were chatting quietly as they folded and put away a pile of freshly laundered clothes. Max was sitting in a corner, frowning over a manuscript. All three looked up in surprise at her sudden appearance.

She motioned impatiently for them to relax.

"Sit down, sit down," she said, perching on the arm of a chair. She continued: "Lord Orman and the jongleur Barton just rode out of the castle, pursued by an armed party."

The three looked at her in surprise. They might be servants, but they were privy to her real identity and mission. And they knew Will's real identity as well.

"Max, go down to the main hall and see what you can find out. Don't make it too obvious, just nose around and see what you can hear."

"Very good, my lady." He rose and moved to the door, picking up his soft feathered bonnet from a side table as he went. She could tell that the two maids were aching to ask her more. But she shook her head at them and returned to her chamber to wait for Max's report.

◆ ◆ ◆

Time passed slowly. Painfully slowly. Max returned after an hour or so. His eavesdropping revealed no more than the facts that Alyss already knew. The castle was abuzz with the fact that, for some reason, Lord Orman, his secretary and the jongleur Barton had broken out and ridden away.

"Everyone else seems as puzzled as we are, my lady," Max told her. Alyss began pacing back and forth, deep in thought. Max, uncertain as to whether she wanted him to do anything more, coughed hesitantly.

"Will that be all, my lady?" he prompted, and she turned to him apologetically.

"Of course, Max. Thank you. You can go."

He had barely left her chamber when there was another knock.

"Come in," she called, and was surprised when the door opened to admit Sir Keren.

"Why, Sir Keren," she said, "what a delightful surprise! Won't you come on in!" Then, raising her voice, she called to the outer room, "Max, fetch us some wine, please! The good Gallic white, I think."

Outside, Max hurried to the side table to fetch the wine, while Keren came into the room, looking around, taking in the clutter of gowns, headpieces, makeup and shoes that Lady Gwendolyn surrounded herself with. Alyss indicated a chair by the fire.

"I'm sorry to bother you, Lady Gwendolyn," Keren began, "but I wondered if you heard a bit of a commotion an hour or so ago?"

"Why, as a matter of fact, so I did!" she said. "Horses galloping and men shouting. Who were they? Robbers? Or brigands, perhaps?"

Keren was shaking his head sadly. "Worse than that, my lady. Far worse. I'm afraid they were traitors to the crown."

Alyss sat back, her mouth a perfect O of surprise. For a moment, she considered revealing her true identity and purpose to Keren. After all, he seemed like a solid type and she knew Will had been on the point of taking him into his confidence. But some instinct stopped her.

"Traitors, Sir Keren? Here in Macindaw? How terrifying! Is the castle safe?" she added the last question with a slight look of alarm on her face. Keren hurried to reassure her.

"Quite safe, my lady. We have everything under control. But I am afraid there is serious news. Lord Orman was one of them."

"Lord Orman?" she said.

Keren nodded somberly. "Apparently, he has been scheming to hand over the castle to a Scotti army before spring. And the jongleur Barton was working hand in glove with him."

"No. He's . . ." Alyss began before she could stop herself. But Keren interrupted her.

"I'm afraid so. Apparently he's been passing messages to the Scotti for Lord Orman for the past three weeks—even before he arrived here."

Alyss's mouth snapped shut.

She could believe what he said about Orman. It was quite possible that the strange temporary commander could be in league with the Scotti. But why would Keren lie about Will's role in the treachery? She realized that Keren was waiting for some sort of reaction from her.

"But he has such a nice singing voice," she said. She thought it was the sort of vacuous reply Lady Gwendolyn would make. Keren's eyebrow rose slightly. Doubtless, he thought so too.

"Nevertheless, my lady, he is a spy. I felt it best to keep you informed as I'm sure you were puzzled by the commotion in the courtyard."

"Indeed I was, Sir Keren. And I thank you for your thoughtfulness. I shall be . . ."

Whatever it was that she would be was interrupted by a further knocking at the door.

"Come in," Keren called. That was a little presumptuous of him, she thought, and not quite in keeping with the solicitous knight who had come to reassure her. She was beginning to have doubts about Sir Keren.

The latch rattled and the door was thrown open rather violently. A man entered, limping heavily. She could see his right thigh had been roughly bandaged. He was obviously looking for Sir Keren because, as he entered, he reported immediately.

"They got away, damn them. They went into that blasted forest." He turned toward Alyss and she couldn't suppress a start of surprise.

John Buttle.

32

IT WAS OVER AN HOUR LATER THAT MALKALLAM REAPPEARED. Will had actually dozed off on the bench, as more and more of the sunshine crept in under the eaves and bathed him in its warmth. He started awake when the door latch rattled and the slightly built man stepped out onto the verandah beside him. Malkallam smiled as he saw the question in Will's eyes.

"He'll be all right," he said. "Although if you'd waited any longer, I'm not sure that he would have made it. His servant is still with him, watching over him," he added. Will nodded. He would expect that Xander would remain by his master's side until he recovered.

"He was drugged then?" he asked.

Malkallam nodded. "Poisoned, more accurately. It's a particularly nasty toxin called *corocore*. It's very obscure—not listed in any of the major texts on herbs and poisons. It takes about a week to take effect, so it was probably slipped into Orman's food or drink sometime in the last ten days. One small dose will do the trick. Nothing happens for days, but then, by the time you notice the symptoms, it's often too late."

"How is it that the castle healers didn't know that?" Will asked.

"As I said, it's very obscure. Most healers wouldn't have heard of it and even if they had, they wouldn't know the antidote."

"But you did?" Will said, and Malkallam smiled.

"I'm not like most healers."

"No, you're not. What exactly are you, if I may ask?"

Malkallam studied him for a few seconds before replying. Then he made a shooing gesture for Will to move over on the bench.

"Make a little room there and we'll talk about it," he said. He sat down next to Will and looked around the clearing. Trobar was still playing with the dog, tossing a leather ball for her to fetch. Each time she retrieved it, she would bring it back and then drop her nose onto her front paws, the ball between them, her hindquarters high in the air, challenging him to take it from her. Most of the other inhabitants of Malkallam's little compound had dispersed while Will was asleep. A few of them were engaged in mundane everyday tasks such as drawing water or sawing and stacking firewood.

"So let's begin," Malkallam said. "What do you know about me?"

"Know?" Will repeated. "Very little. I've heard the rumors, of course: that you're a sorcerer—the reincarnation of the black wizard Malkallam who murdered Orman's ancestor over a hundred years ago. I've heard that your home is in Grimsdell Wood and that the wood itself is home to strange apparitions and sights and sounds. I've seen and heard some of them myself."

"Yes," Malkallam mused, "you visited my wood several nights ago, didn't you? And you weren't scared off by the dreadful Night Warrior?"

"I was terrified out of my wits," Will admitted.

"But you came back."

Will allowed himself a wry smile. "Not at night. By daylight. That was when we saw that the apparitions were caused by some kind of gigantic magic lantern show."

Malkallam raised his eyebrows. "Very good," he said. "How did you work that out?"

"Alyss figured it. She found the burned patches on the grass where your lantern had stood."

"I take it Alyss is the young lady who accompanied you the other day?" Malkallam asked. He frowned. "What's become of her?"

"She's still in the castle," Will said.

Malkallam raised his eyebrows. "You left her there?"

Will frowned. "Not for long," he said. It was obviously a sore point with him, but Malkallam made a soothing gesture with his hand.

"Time enough for that. She sounds like a remarkable young lady."

"She is. But we were talking about you," Will pointed out, deciding that he had been sidetracked long enough.

Malkallam smiled at him. "So we were. Well, as you seem to have guessed, I'm no sorcerer. I used to be a healer." His voice became wistful. "I was very good at it, as a matter of fact." He nodded once or twice as he thought about the past. "I really enjoyed life then. I felt I was doing something worthwhile."

"What happened to change it?" Will asked.

Malkallam sighed. "Someone died," he said. "He was a fifteen-year-old boy—a delightful young fellow everyone liked. He had a simple fever and his parents brought him to me. It was the sort of thing I had cured dozens of times —it should have been straightforward. Except he didn't respond to the herbs I gave him. Worse, he reacted to them, and within a day he was dead."

His voice quavered a little and Will looked quickly at him. There was a single tear rolling down his cheek. He noticed Will's glance and looked at him, wiping the tear away with the cuff of his sleeve.

"It happens that way sometimes, you know. People can die for no apparent reason at all," Malkallam said.

"And the villagers blamed you?" Will said.

Malkallam nodded. "Not immediately. It began as a whispering campaign. There was another man who wanted to take my position as healer. I'm sure he started it. He said I just let the boy die. Gradually, I noticed that fewer and fewer people were coming to me. They were going to the new man."

"I assume he was charging them for his services?"

Malkallam nodded. "Of course. I used to charge too. Even a healer has to eat, after all. Gradually the rumors got wilder and wilder, and if a person in the village died after seeing the other healer, he had a convenient excuse: he said I'd cursed them."

"That's ridiculous," Will said. "You don't mean to tell me people believed it?"

Malkallam shrugged. "You'd be surprised what people will believe. Usually, the bigger and the more improbable the lie, the more willing they are to believe it. It's often a case of *that's so outrageous, it must be true*. Anyway, people started muttering whenever I passed them. I was getting black looks from all and sundry and I decided that my own health might be improved if I left the village. I quietly disappeared one day and came into Grimsdell Wood. I lived in a tent for months while I built this house. I knew the locals would hesitate to follow me into the forest. After all, the original Malkallam was supposed to have his lair in here."

"Why did you take the same name?" Will asked, and the healer gave a short scornful laugh.

"I didn't take it. People gave it to me," he said. "My name is Malcolm. After I disappeared, the locals put two and two together and got seven. They decided that Malcolm was merely a disguised form of Malkallam. From there it was easy to make the next step. I was the infamous sorcerer returned from the dead.

"I must say, I took advantage of the fact to protect myself. I set up the apparitions and tricks that you saw. If anyone did get up the nerve to come into Grimsdell, they quickly lost it when they saw my Night Warrior, or heard my voices."

"How do you do the voices?" Will asked. "They seemed to come from all around me when I heard them."

Malcolm smiled. "Yes. It's a rather good effect, isn't it? It's done with a series of hollow tubes set among the trees. You speak into one end and the voice is carried to the other. There's a large trumpet-shaped bell at the end that amplifies the sound. We usually place that in a hollow part of the tree to conceal it. Luka there provides the voice."

He indicated a man who was gathering kindling together at the far side of the clearing. His torso was massive but the legs that supported it were short and malformed so that he hobbled awkwardly when he walked. One shoulder was badly hunched and the features of his face were twisted sideways. The man had grown a bushy beard and long hair in an unsuccessful attempt to conceal the deformity.

"He has the most wonderful voice," Malcolm continued. "That barrel of a chest lets him produce a sound of tremendous force and timber. He can project words with great clarity and volume through the system. Mind you, he isn't used to people answering back. You caused him a considerable deal of fright when you started waving that big knife of yours the other night."

"He caused me a lot more, I can assure you," Will said, studying the misshapen man. "Tell me, where do these people come from? Luka and Trobar and the rest."

"I assume you thought I created them?" Malcolm said, a slightly bitter smile playing around his lips. Will shifted uncomfortably on the bench.

"Well . . . that thought did occur to me, as a matter of fact," he said.

Malcolm's face grew sad. "Yes. People occasionally see them and think the same thing. These are my deformed subjects. My creatures. My monsters . . . The truth is, they're rejects. Ordinary people who aren't wanted in their own villages because they don't look ordinary. They look different or sound different or move differently. Some are born that way, like Trobar and Luka. Others are burned or scalded or disfigured in accidents and people decide they just don't want them around."

"How do they come to you?" Will asked. The healer shrugged.

"I go looking for them. Trobar was the first. I found him by accident when he was eight years old. That's eighteen years ago now. He'd been driven out of his village because he had grown so big. They drove him into the forest to die. He tried to take his dog with him. It was his only friend in the world. It didn't care that he was ugly and deformed. It loved him because he loved it. Dogs are like that. They're very nonjudgmental."

"What happened to the dog?" Will asked. He thought he knew the answer.

"It tried to defend him, of course, and one of the villagers killed it. Trobar carried it into the forest and they finally gave up the chase. He was nursing its body and crying when I found him. We buried the dog together and I brought him back here. Then, over the years, more and more of these people joined us. We'd see them driven out of their villages and we'd collect them and bring them here. Sometimes, they needed the sort of treatment that I could give them with herbs and potions. At other times, they needed a different kind of healing."

"Which you also give them?" Will asked, and Malcolm nodded.

"I try. Often it's enough for them to know they belong somewhere. That there are other people who don't judge them by the way they look. Mind you, it takes time. It's a lot easier to heal an injured body than a damaged soul."

Will shook his head as he considered the story. "So for nearly twenty years, you've been looking after people like this, and you're still regarded as a black magician?"

Malcolm shrugged. "Partly my fault, I suppose. I created the illusion to keep people out. But in the past year, somebody else seems to have realized he could turn the Malkallam fable to his own advantage."

"Keren?"

"It would appear so. The question is, what does he hope to achieve from it all?"

"As soon as I find out," Will said grimly, "I'll be sure to let you know."

33

ALYSS FROZE IN HER CHAIR FOR A SECOND AS BUTTLE'S GAZE passed over her. What on earth was he doing here? How did he get here? Had he recognized her? The questions raced through her mind and it took all her role-playing skill to maintain the outer façade of the air-headed Lady Gwendolyn.

"They got away, blast them!" Buttle said roughly. Noticing Alyss, he grunted in what passed for an apology for interrupting. Then he turned back to Keren, although a slight frown creased his forehead. There was something familiar about the girl. Then he dismissed the thought.

"They said you were here with her." He gestured with a thumb toward Alyss.

"Lady Gwendolyn," Keren corrected him. "The lady is a guest in this castle, the fiancée of Lord Farrell of Gort."

There was an underlying warning tone in his voice. *Don't say too much in front of her.* Alyss sensed it. She assumed a vacuous smile and held out one languid hand to Buttle, palm down.

"I don't believe we've met, sir," she said. Buttle stared at the hand, then shrugged. He grunted again. It seemed to be his favorite method of communication, Alyss thought.

"Lady Gwendolyn, this is John Buttle, one of my new retainers," Keren said, smoothing over Buttle's coarse behavior.

Buttle shrugged and scratched under his armpit. Alyss withdrew her hand.

"So, Mr. Buttle, you were pursuing the traitors? How brave of you!" She fluttered her eyelashes at him.

Buttle frowned for a moment. "Traitors?" he said and hesitated. He glanced uncertainly at Keren. "They weren't tr—"

"I've just been telling Lady Gwendolyn," Keren interrupted quickly, "how Lord Orman and the jongleur were planning to hand the castle over to the Scotti."

Buttle's frown deepened. He paused for a moment, then, just a little too late, comprehension dawned on his face.

"Eh? Oh . . . yeah. Yeah, that's right. Traitors sure enough. Lucky we got onto 'em in time, I say. Why, if we hadn't, they were all set to make . . ."

"Yes, yes, I'm sure Lady Gwendolyn doesn't want hear all the sordid details," Keren said quickly. He had little faith in Buttle's ability to improvise a story without making a hash of it. Best to keep it all simple. Once again, Alyss noticed the hasty intervention and guessed the reason for it. She felt a vast sense of relief that she hadn't taken Keren into her confidence. Apparently, a lot of things about Macindaw Castle were not as they seemed.

"Oh dear, Mr. Buttle, you seem to be injured!" she said now. "You're in danger of dripping blood on the rug here!"

Buttle glanced down at the blood seeping through the rough bandage on his thigh. He cursed, reaching to tighten the binding, swore again as the increased pressure sent a shaft of pain through the wound.

Alyss was breathing a little easier now. After all, she realized, it had been weeks since he saw her and then she had worn her hair down. Today, it was caught up in a tight swirl around her head, and surmounted by a high, pointed hat with a veil attached. It was the latest fashion, Alyss knew, although personally, she found it absurd. But she had been taught the value of a different hairstyle when it came to disguise. In addition, her clothes were vastly different as well. She was wearing a rather ornate gown, festooned with adornments and light lacy attachments, with ridiculously wide, trailing sleeves and pinned with jewelry wherever a space could be found. As a Courier, she had worn a simple white dress.

To complete the effect, she was keeping her naturally deep voice in a higher register, mimicking the slightly querulous upper-class tones that would have come naturally to someone like Lady Gwendolyn.

As a result, Alyss began to feel increasingly confident. But she could see a chance to gather information here.

"Did the traitor Orman strike you with his sword?" she asked, pretending concern for the man. He snorted derisively.

"That gutless bookworm! He couldn't lift a sword to save his miserable life. No, it was that blasted jongleur who did the damage, damn his stinking hide!"

"Language, Buttle," Keren said warningly. Buttle looked at him, uncomprehending, and Keren nodded toward Alyss.

"Eh? Oh . . . yeah. Anyway, the cowardly little swine shot me. Wouldn't face me like a man. Skulked off three or four hundred meters and put an arrow through my leg."

Must have missed what he was aiming at, Alyss thought. What a pity.

"Three hundred meters?" Keren said with a note of disbelief. "That's some kind of shot."

Buttle shrugged. He was the sort of man who would always exaggerate.

"Well, maybe not three hundred. But long enough. He's no jongleur, mark my words. Never saw a jongleur who could shoot like that."

Alyss felt a small thrill of alarm.

"He seemed like an excellent jongleur to me," she said, hoping to head the discussion away from dangerous ground. "After all, he had a most pleasing voice, did he not, Sir Keren?"

Keren nodded thoughtfully. It hadn't occurred to him to doubt Barton's identity or profession. From what he'd seen, the man was a quite adequate jongleur.

"He certainly seemed professional enough," he agreed. "And the dog was definitely well-trained to perform too."

Oh God, Alyss thought. Buttle looked up with mild interest.

"Dog? What dog was that?"

Keren made a disclaiming gesture with one hand. The subject wasn't really important, it seemed to say.

"Oh, he had a black-and-white border shepherd with him. Used to join in the act."

Oh God, Alyss thought again. She had to work to keep her expression from revealing her mounting panic. Buttle's eyebrows had contracted into a deep frown of concentration as he put facts together. An expert bowman, in fact, far more than expert. And a black-and-white border shepherd. Suddenly, he took a pace toward

Alyss and his hand shot out, finger pointing at her. He'd known there was something familiar about her!

"Stand up, you!" he demanded. Keren looked at him in something close to alarm. The man seemed to have taken leave of his senses.

Alyss regarded him with a disdainful smile, as befitting a noble lady who has been ordered around by a commoner.

"I beg your pardon, Mr. Buttle?" she said with great dignity. She turned to Keren. "Really, Sir Keren, my fiancé will hear of th—"

"Stand up, I said!" Buttle demanded, shouting at her now. Keren stood and took a pace toward him, laying a hand on his arm.

"Buttle, what in God's name is wrong with you?"

"I thought I recognized her. I thought there was something about her!" he said. Alyss remained seated, outwardly calm, a look a mild amusement and disdain on her face. She knew all too well why Buttle wanted her to stand. Her height was the one thing she couldn't disguise.

"Sir Keren, would you mind removing this man from my rooms?"

The door to the anteroom opened and Max, alarmed by Buttle's shouting, looked in.

"My lady?" he said. "Is everything all right?"

His hand was hovering close by his dagger. Alyss waved him away. The last thing she wanted was a physical confrontation. Her best chance was to bluff it out.

"Leave us. Sir Keren will deal with this coarse man," she said. Max looked around the room doubtfully. She made eye contact with him and nodded, almost imperceptibly. He shrugged and withdrew, closing the door behind him.

Now Keren stepped between Buttle and Alyss. He was furious with his henchman for this ridiculous confrontation. Lady Gwendolyn was due to move on in a week or so. But if he were forced to detain her, her fiancé might come looking for her—probably with a party of armed men. That was the last thing Keren wanted at the moment, with his plan so close to success.

"Buttle," he said, very quietly, "I'm warning you. Shut up and get out of here. Now!"

But the tall, bearded man was shaking his head before Keren finished his order.

"She's no noblewoman!" he said. "I've seen her before, I know it. Now make her stand!"

Keren turned apologetically to Alyss and shrugged.

"Perhaps if you'll humor the man, Lady Gwendolyn . . . " he began, but she shook her head indignantly.

"I'll do no such thing!" she said angrily. Keren hesitated, a sudden doubt in his eyes. Buttle seized on it as he made the final connection in his mind.

"She's a Courier!" he said triumphantly. "I saw her down south! And she was with a Ranger!"

Now Keren's expression was one of alarm. "A Ranger?" he asked, and Buttle nodded several times.

"Make her stand. You'll see. She's near as tall as I am!"

Keren turned to Alyss. "You are rather tall," he said thoughtfully. "Please do as Buttle asks. Stand up."

Alyss sighed inwardly, knowing she had lost. She could bluff for a few more minutes, but Keren's suspicions were alerted now. Gracefully, she stood, hearing Buttle's quick gasp of triumph.

"That's her!" he said. "I knew it. Knew I'd seen her. Now that she's standing, there's no mistake. And I'll wager that Jongleur

Barton is no more a jongleur than I am. I'll bet he's her Ranger friend!" he searched his memory again, trying to recall the scraps of conversation he'd overheard outside the cabin. "What did you call him? Will! That was it!"

"Will?" Keren was definitely interested in this piece of news. "And isn't that the jongleur's name too? What a coincidence! I think you have a little explaining to do, Lady Gwendolyn."

He smiled at her. But the smile never reached his eyes. They were cold and full of suspicion.

34

ORMAN HAD STIRRED BRIEFLY, CALLING OUT IN HIS SLEEP, AND Malcolm went inside to tend to him. Xander, of course, hovered at his heels, peering anxiously around the healer's small frame to watch his master.

When Malcolm emerged, he found Will tightening the girth straps on Tug's saddle. He'd unsaddled the other horses and placed them in Malcolm's small barn. Malcolm sensed the air of urgency about the young man.

"He's fine now," he said, nodding back toward the room where Orman lay quietly. "Were you planning on leaving us?" he added mildly.

Will tightened one last buckle and put his foot in the stirrup.

"I'm going to get Alyss," he said grimly. Malcolm raised his eyebrows.

"Just like that?" he asked.

"Just like that," Will repeated. Malcolm glanced around, looking at the position of the sun in the sky. There were still four or five hours of daylight left.

"You're going to ride in there in broad daylight and rescue her, is that it?"

Will hesitated awkwardly. He was off balance with his foot in the stirrup, so he removed it and stood beside Tug. Now that Malcolm put it like that, he realized that he could hardly go barging into the castle looking for Alyss. He didn't even know where she might be. If her identity had been discovered, she'd be locked up somewhere—and he had no idea where. But he was seething with anxiety for her, desperate to get her away from the danger that menaced her. He'd done what duty required and helped Orman escape. Now his duty lay to his old friend. And it didn't help to have Malcolm calmly pointing out that he was riding off with no idea as to what he was going to do.

"I'll probably wait till dark," he admitted. Malcolm nodded as if this was a wise idea.

"In that case, you might as well wait here in comfort," he pointed out.

Will shifted his feet irritably. Malcolm was right of course, but he was desperate to do something. Anything. To get moving. Every minute that passed put Alyss in greater danger, as the likelihood grew that Buttle would recognize her. He couldn't bear to just sit here waiting.

"Perhaps we could think it through a little, rather than just go charging off without any plan of action," the healer suggested. Reluctantly, Will acknowledged that the little man was making sense. He patted Tug's neck absentmindedly, then stepped up onto the narrow verandah to join Malcolm.

"I'm sorry," he said. "It's driving me crazy knowing that she's still in there. Knowing I left her there."

"As I understand it, you had no other choice," Malcolm said, and Will sighed as he sat down.

"That doesn't make it any easier to bear. I've been racking my brains trying to figure out where Buttle sprang from," he added.

"He's the one you saw in the castle—just before Orman sent for you?"

Will nodded. "Yes. But by all rights, he should be hundreds of kilometers away from here. I gave him to a boatload of Skandians as a slave."

Malcolm's eyebrows went up slightly. "You *gave* him?" he said, and Will nodded seriously.

"It would have been against the law to sell him," he replied. Malcom nodded sagely, several times.

"Of course. Far more law-abiding to give him, I suppose." He paused to see if there was any reaction, but there was none. This boy does have a lot on his mind, he thought. Then he added: "Perhaps these Skandians of yours came ashore again. I'll ask if there's been any sign of Skandians in the area. My friends here range far and wide through the forest and there's little that escapes their attention. They've become very good at seeing without being seen."

"We're a long way from the sea here," Will said doubtfully. Malcolm nodded agreement.

"Perhaps eighty kilometers. But the River Oosel runs inland from the coast and it's a lot closer. At this time of year, if you were to come ashore, you'd want to get well away from the storms that hit the east coast. Of course," he went on, changing the subject slightly, "the question isn't really *how* he got here, but what he's planning to do."

"It'll be no good, whatever it is," Will said. "What's killing me is the uncertainty of it all. I don't know if she's been recognized. And if she has, I've no idea where they might be holding her."

He turned, hearing the door beside them close gently as Xander returned from checking his lord.

"I take it Lord Orman is comfortable?" Malcolm asked, and Xander nodded.

"He's resting comfortably," he said. Then he had the grace to look a little apologetic. "Thank you for what you've done." Malcolm gave a little self-deprecating shrug. Xander turned his attention to Will.

"If you're planning to go back into the castle," he said, "you might be able to use a little inside information." Will looked at him quickly. The little secretary felt somewhat guilty that he hadn't been able to pass Will's warning on to Alyss.

"I'm assuming that if they've discovered her identity, she'll be in the dungeons," Will said. "There *are* dungeons at Macindaw, I take it?"

"There are," Xander agreed. "But at this time of year, they're often flooded. My bet is that if she's imprisoned, it'll be in the tower cell. It's right at the top of the keep tower—and a lot harder to reach than the dungeons. There's only one staircase leading up to it, so it's easy to guard. And once you're up there, it's easy to keep you up there as well."

Will considered the problem. It made sense, he thought. There were often several ways to get into the dungeons in a castle. But a tower was a different matter altogether.

"Perhaps," said Malcolm, "you might be better to abandon your plan for the moment and hope that your friend hasn't been recognized?"

But Will was shaking his head before the healer had half finished the sentence.

"No. I've wasted enough time," he said firmly. "I'm getting her out. Tonight."

"How?" Malcolm persisted. "Be reasonable. You'd need a force of armed men to fight your way up the stairs to a tower like that."

"I wasn't planning on using the stairs," Will told him.

35

IN THE TOWER CELL, ALYSS WAS FEELING DECIDEDLY UNEASY. Once Buttle had recognized her, there had been little purpose in trying to continue the pretense that she was a dizzy-headed noble-woman on the way to her wedding.

But surprisingly, Keren had made no attempt to extract any further information from her. He had simply frowned, called his guards and had her escorted to this prison. Max, armed only with a belt dagger that was more decorative than functional, had been prepared to defend her, but she'd stopped him. She didn't want to be responsible for his death. He and the two maids were escorted to a locked storeroom. She had no doubt that her men-at-arms would join them before long.

It was Keren's apparent lack of action or interest that had her worried most of all. Obviously, he was the center of the strange happenings that had been going on at Castle Macindaw. To what purpose? she wondered. The most logical one was the intention that he had ascribed to Orman and Will—that he was planning to hand over the castle to Scotti invaders. After all, having usurped the rights of both Syron and Orman, he could hardly expect to gain King

Duncan's endorsement as lord of Macindaw. His only alternative would be to look outside the kingdom for reward.

Whatever he had planned, he was obviously up to no good. It seemed strange that he hadn't tried to question her to find out what she and Will had been planning and how much they knew. Frankly, she would have expected to be questioned most rigorously, even tortured.

Instead, she had been placed in this tower room. And while not luxurious, it was relatively comfortable.

Except for the heat, she thought. The fire in the corner was blazing brightly and the room was hot and stuffy. Her mouth was dry—probably the effect of the adrenaline-charged situation where she had found herself confronting Buttle. She was desperately thirsty but there was nothing to drink in the room.

She turned, startled, as the single door opened to admit Keren.

He looked around, taking in the scant furnishings: a table, two chairs, and a wood-framed bed with a thin straw mattress and two threadbare blankets. A single oil lamp with a polished metal reflector provided light in the room. The window, barred with vertical iron stakes, could be covered by a heavy curtain if the wind became too strong. At the moment, there was no wind and the curtain was drawn back.

"Nice and comfy?" he said cheerfully. Alyss shrugged.

"Things could be worse," she said, and he nodded heartily.

"Oh, yes, indeed they could. And I think you should bear that in mind."

"I assume my people are safe?" she asked. Keren shrugged.

"They're all nice and comfortable, under lock and key. One of your men-at-arms tried to argue. He was slightly injured, but he'll recover."

"I hope you don't expect me to thank you for that," she said. Again, he shrugged as if it was of little interest to him. He dismissed the matter of her bodyguard and gestured toward the table and chairs.

"Let's sit down. I think it's time we had a little chat."

So it's starting, she thought, considering him warily. But there was no point in resisting and she moved to the table, pulled one of the chairs out and sat, straight backed.

"There's nothing to drink. It's very hot in here. I'd like some water," she said. She did it partly to take the momentum of the conversation away from him. And partly, she realized, because she was parched. Instantly, he became concerned for her welfare.

"I'm sorry," he said. "I had no intention of making you uncomfortable." A frown crossed his face and he moved to the door, opening it and calling roughly to one of the guards in the next room.

"You there! Why didn't you give the lady any water? Bring that jug you've got there! You can fetch another for yourself! And a glass . . . a *clean* glass, you idiot!"

He shook his head in mild annoyance as the sentry shambled in, eyes down, with a carafe of water and a glass. He set it on the table and turned to go.

"Pour it for her, you oaf!" Keren's voice cracked at him, and he turned back.

"Sorry, Sir Keren," he mumbled, and he slopped the glass half full of water, spilling some as he did so. Before Keren could rebuke him further, he mopped the spill with his sleeve, then bowed clumsily as he backed away.

"There you are, my lady," he said.

Alyss sipped at the water. Then she realized how parched she was and drank most of the contents of the glass. Her training had taught her that, if you were a prisoner, it was always good technique to make your captors accede to a small demand. Something small at first, then, as they became used to granting requests, the demands could become bigger.

Keren dropped into the chair opposite her and lolled back, one leg crossed over the other. He grinned easily at her.

"Relax," he said. "I just wanted to ask you a few questions."

"It's not the questions that bother me," she said. "It's what will happen when you don't get any answers."

He frowned at her, actually looking a little hurt.

"You surely don't think I'd torture you?" he said. "I'm not a monster, you know. I am a knight, after all."

"You seem to have forgotten some of your duties as a knight," she countered. She yawned. The hot room seemed to be making her sleepy. She blinked several times as Keren continued.

"Well, perhaps it looks that way. But it's easy to take that point of view when you don't know the full picture. For years, I kept this castle strong and well defended. All I asked from Syron was a little consideration, a little gratitude for my efforts. But no. He channeled everything to his son. There was nothing for me. Not even a guarantee that I'd even be employed once Orman took over. I've spent the greater part of my adult life safeguarding the kingdom's border and I've received no more than a free lance's pay for it. I deserved better than that."

"Perhaps you did. But you had no right to look for your rewards from the Scotti," she ventured, waiting to see his reaction. It wasn't long in coming. He looked at her keenly.

"So you figured that out, did you? I wonder how much else you know?"

She smiled. "I'll bet you do," she told him.

He peered closely at her. "You must be feeling tired. It's been quite a day."

She nodded. She did feel tired, now that he mentioned it. She blinked her eyes and rolled her head from side to side to ease the tension in her shoulders.

"That's the way." Keren's voice was deep and soothing. Strangely, she thought, it seemed to be coming from a distance—not from just across the table. "Close your eyes if you want to," he continued. "We can always talk later if you're sleepy now. Are you sleepy now?"

Her eyelids were feeling heavy. They drooped shut. She flickered them open again but the effort was too great to sustain. Slowly, they slid down.

"Those eyelids look heavy," he said in that strange, calming voice. "Aren't you sleepy?"

"Sleepy . . ." she mumbled in reply. In a distant part of her mind, she could feel a faint warning signal stirring. She shouldn't be this sleepy, she thought. But she pushed the thought aside because she was. Incredibly sleepy. Why? Why would she feel so tired all of a sudden?

Keren's voice continued. It was very soothing and it seemed to fill her world.

"Of course you're sleepy. You can sleep. Sleep is good. Your eyes are very tired . . ."

And they were. Then, once again, that little sentient part of her mind was trying to say something. Something about the water she'd drunk. Had he put something in it? Some kind of sleeping potion? She'd been so clever, making him accede to her wishes. But maybe she'd outsmarted herself and the water . . .

But who cared? She was sleepy and he was telling her she could sleep and his voice was so calm and trustworthy. The little warning signal in her brain flickered and died.

"I've brought you something. Something to help you sleep. Look at it."

She forced her heavy eyelids open and looked at what he was holding.

It was a strange blue gemstone, about the size of a quail egg, and he began to roll it back and forth in his hands. It was very beautiful, she thought, and she marveled at the way it seemed to draw her in so that she felt she could dive into the stone as if it were a deep pool of clear blue water. She leaned forward, looking more closely, smiling. It was a beautiful stone.

"Look into the blue," he said gently. "It's beautiful."

He was right, she thought. It was perfectly round and the blue seemed to grow deeper as you looked into it. She had the fascinating impression that, if she looked hard enough, she could see beneath the surface of the stone, and into the depths beneath.

"It's very beautiful, isn't it?" he said. His voice was quiet and relaxing and very soothing. "I often wonder how there can be so many layers in such a small object. Look at it as it turns . . . "

He slowly rotated the stone and she saw that he was right. The blue seemed to drop away from the light, in ever deepening layers. It seemed impossible that they could all be in such a tiny gem. And so beautiful. So blue. She loved blue. She had never before realized that blue was her favorite color.

"You never told me your real name," he said gently.

"It's Alyss. Alyss Mainwaring." There seemed no harm in telling him that. After all, he knew Lady Gwendolyn was a false identity.

Strange, she thought, how that little blue stone seemed to be growing bigger with every second.

"You don't really have a fiancé, do you?" he said, and she could hear the genuine amusement in his voice. She laughed in reply.

"No. I'm afraid not," she admitted. "I think I'm doomed to be an old maid." It was a shame that they were enemies, she thought. He was actually quite a nice person. She went to look up and tell him so.

"Keep looking at the blue." His voice was very gentle and she nodded agreement.

"Of course."

He was silent for a while, letting her study those shifting blue tones. It was very relaxing, she thought.

"What about your friend Will?" he asked softly. "No romance there?"

She smiled quietly at the question, didn't answer for a few seconds. "We've known each other forever," she said. "We were very close before he began his training."

"As a jongleur, you mean?" he said. She was on the brink of shaking her head when some instinct stopped her.

"Will's a . . ." she began, but the same instinct stopped her from saying any more. The warning light in her mind was back, flaring brightly now. She blinked, realizing that she had been on the point of saying *Will's a Ranger*. She lurched back in her chair, as if rearing back from the edge of a cliff. In a way, she was.

She tore her eyes from the blue stone on the table, amazed at how much effort it took to do so.

"What are you doing?" she demanded, horrified that she had been about to betray Will. She racked her brain now, trying to think what she had told him, how much she had revealed to him. Her name, she thought. But that didn't matter too much. So long as she hadn't told him Will was a . . .

She stopped herself. Best not even to think of it, she thought. That damned blue stone obviously had some very strange properties. Keren was smiling at her. It was a surprisingly friendly smile, considering.

"You're a strong one," he told her admiringly. "Once a person gets in that deep, it's very unusual for them to come back. Well done."

"The water . . . it was drugged, wasn't it?" she said. She knew now that it was no accident that the room had been so hot. The fire had been deliberately stoked. Keren had known she would want water. He smiled.

"Just a harmless drink to help you relax—so my little blue stone could do its work."

"What is that thing?" She pointed at the stone, loathing it. He picked it up from the table, tossed it in the air and caught it, then placed it back in his inner pocket.

"Oh, just a little bauble I amuse my friends with," he said, rising and turning toward the door. He paused with the door open, then his smile faded.

"We'll do this again," he said. "And the next time, it will go a lot quicker. It always does after you've given in once. After that, it gets easier and easier every time. I'll see you in an hour or so."

The door closed behind him. Alyss heard the key turn in the lock and she dropped her head onto her forearms on the table. She felt totally exhausted.

36

"THIS IS AS FAR AS YOU COME." WILL SAID, DROPPING INTO A crouch and signaling for Xander and Malcolm to do likewise.

They had left the horses back behind a crest and now the dark bulk of Castle Macindaw loomed less than one hundred and fifty meters away.

"You'll get no argument from me," Xander said. He crouched beside Will, studying the castle and its tall central tower. "There. See the light at the top of the tower? I'll wager that's where your friend is. That's the tower cell and it's occupied. There was nobody in there this morning."

"The windows are barred, of course?" Malcom said and as Xander nodded in connfirmation, he continued. "Have you thought how you'll deal with them?"

Will frowned. "I have a file," he said and Malcolm shook his head, then passed across a small leather-bound flask.

"Too slow and too noisy. This will do a much better job."

Will studied the flask. "What's in it?" he asked.

"It's a very powerful acid. It will eat through the iron bars in a few minutes." He smiled as Will handled the flask gingerly. "There's a glass bottle inside, but it's padded with straw and protected by the leather covering. It's quite safe. Just be careful how you handle it."

Will decided not to point out that those last two statements seemed strangely at odds with each other. He slid the flask into his waistband in the middle of his back. It would be secure there, he thought.

"Moon's almost set." Malcolm pointed out. Will nodded.

"I'll be off then."

But he didn't move immediately. He spent a few minutes studying the landscape and absorbing the natural rhythms of hte night. Then he simply melted away into the darkness.

Will paused in the deep shadow at the base of the wall. This was where he would climb, in the angle between wall and tower. Neither the tower sentry nor the guards on the wall above could see him here. The only possible danger was from the other tower sentry, thirty meters away. But the man was still hunched over the wall, staring fixedly out into the night.

He explored the wall's surface with his hands, discarding his gloves and tucking them through his belt to do so. The stonework, which appeared smooth and sleek from a distance, was actually rough and uneven, with plenty of cracks, crevices and protrusions to provide hand- and footholds for a climber of Will's experience. In addition, the right angle formed by the wall and the tower would give extra purchase if he needed it. He smiled. He would have been able to climb this wall by the time he was eleven years old.

He had a long rope coiled around his shoulders under his cloak, but that was intended to help Alyss down, not for him to climb up. With the sentries on duty, he could hardly risk throwing a rope up to catch between the crenellations at the top of the wall. Flexing his fingers, he reached high above his head, found two secure handholds in the cold stone and hauled himself upward.

He moved slowly and smoothly up the wall. At times, he had to move to the left or right of his original starting position as he sought the best purchase. His fingers ached with the strain and the cold but they were hardened and strengthened by years of practice.

As he neared the top of his climb, he heard the sentry's approaching footsteps and paused, hanging like a giant spider on the wall, fingers and toes aching with the strain. The sentry stopped at the end of his beat and stamped his feet once or twice. Then he moved off again, heading back the way he had come. Will waited a few more seconds, then swarmed up and over the battlements. Moving like a shadow in a night full of shadows, he crossed the walkway and slipped quietly down the stairs leading to the courtyard below.

He paused at the base of the stairs. There were no sentries here but there was always the chance that someone might emerge from one of the doors leading into the keep or the gate tower. He studied the situation for long minutes. The open space leading to the keep tower was well lit by burning torches set into the walls. He would be better served by walking directly, without any attempt at concealment. A figure seen walking toward the door would be less likely to raise suspicion than someone who was obviously skulking. He threw back the cowl on his cloak, took a soft, feathered cap from underneath his tunic, straightened it and placed it on his head. Then, walking confidently and without any attempt at concealment, he walked to the stairs leading to the keep's main door.

As he reached the stairs, he slid smartly to his left and merged into the shadows formed by the stairway itself. He discarded the cap and pulled the cowl up over his head once more. Crouched by the stairs, he surveyed the walls opposite to see if anyone had noticed him. But the sentries' attention was focused outward, not inward, and there were no casual observers around.

Satisfied that he had gone unseen, he moved around the base of the tower to a point midway between two of the flaring torches. At the extreme edge of the light cast by each, the lighting was uncertain and shifting. He took a deep breath, felt to make sure that Malcolm's leather-clad flask was securely and safely stowed in the small of his back, and began to climb once more.

As he had expected, the keep tower was built from the same rough stone as the wall and there were plenty of foot- and hand-holds for him. He climbed steadily. Even with his excellent head for heights, he avoided the temptation to look down. You never knew when vertigo might seize you. The outer wall had been a mere eight meters high. This tower was over three times that height, soaring up to thirty meters above ground level. As he rose higher, the wind picked up, whistling around him, attempting to pluck him from his precarious handholds.

Three out of four, he repeated to himself—the old dictum he had practiced when climbing since he was a boy. It meant that he never moved a hand or a foot to a new vantage point unless the other three were securely positioned. There were several lit windows in his path and he skirted around them. He was tempted to look in but he realized this could be a fatal error. If an inhabitant just happened to be looking at the window, the sight of a strange face peering in would be sure to raise the alarm.

The wind grew stronger the higher he went, making the freezing air even colder. His hands were growing numb, which worried him. He needed feeling in his hands to seek out only the most secure cracks and protrusions in the stone. If he couldn't feel them properly, there was always the chance that he'd seize hold of a loose stone and have it give way when he transferred his weight to it. Mentally, he shrugged. There was nothing he could do about it now and he was already three-quarters of the way up the tower anyway. He glanced out to one side, where the snow-covered land lay far below. Several kilometers away, he could see the dark mass of Grimsdell Wood itself, the tops of the trees dusted with white where snow had collected. If he'd been climbing for the sheer fun of it, he might have stopped to admire the superb vista. He smiled sadly. It had been a long time since he had climbed solely for the fun of it.

He glanced up and saw that the narrow ledge around the top of the tower was only a few meters away. He covered the distance and reached up carefully. One never knew what might be found on ledges. Some castle designers liked to set iron spikes in them to discourage climbers.

There were no spikes, but he frowned as he touched the freezing surface. Ice, he thought. Rainwater had collected on the ledge and frozen as the temperature dropped. That would make it tricky. Most climbers would have reached eagerly for the ledge, transferring all their weight to their hands as they did so. With slippery ice all over the ledge, that could be fatal. Will kept some weight on his feet as he searched for a clear spot to grip. His toes curled with the effort and he could feel the beginnings of a cramp in the arch of his left foot. He found a clear spot with his right hand and heaved himself a little higher, his left foot searching for a new foothold. Three out of four, he repeated. He moved his left hand to the ledge, sliding it back and forth till he found a spot clear of ice. Then his right foot came up and he was able to haul himself up to the ledge, turning carefully to sit upon it, his back pressed to the wall behind him. As he leaned back, a little more forcefully than he'd intended, he was aware of something pressing into the small of his back. His heart leapt to his mouth as he remembered the flask of acid. Encumbered as he was by his cloak, if it broke now, there was no way he could get rid of it in time. He leaned a little away from the wall and counted seconds. Ten. Fifteen. Twenty. A full minute went by and there was no burning sensation of acid eating into his flesh. He heaved a sigh of relief.

"Now where's Alyss?" he asked himself.

As he had done when climbing the outer wall, he had zigzagged up the wall from his original start point, searching for the best handholds. He looked to his right now and saw that the window he assumed to mark Alyss's cell was some three meters away. He shuffled sideways along the ledge to it, his legs dangling over the drop. He frowned as he moved toward the window. There was a lot of ice on the narrow ledge and that was going to make it difficult for him to stand and turn around to look in the window.

At least, he thought, he'd have the bars to give him a secure handhold. He stopped moving when the window was on his right, the bottom sill a little above the height of his head. He reached up with his right hand, felt along the sill, then found one of the iron bars.

If the room was occupied by someone other than Alyss, he

thought, this could be dangerous. His hand would be in full sight of anyone looking at the window, and as he turned and stood he would be totally exposed as well. He would have to commit himself before he could check the room's occupant. But, given the icy state of the ledge, he had no alternative.

He swiveled to the right on his buttocks, bringing his left foot up onto the ledge. His weight was supported almost fully by his right hand now and since there had been no outcry from the room, he assumed that whoever was in there wasn't looking at the window. The footing on the ledge was definitely unstable, he decided, as he put more weight on his left leg, slowly turning to his right and straightening the bent knee to lift him higher.

His heart leapt as he felt the foot begin to slip sideways in the ice, and he turned more quickly, throwing up his left arm to get a good grip on another bar in the window. He was just in time. His left foot slid out over the edge of the icy ledge and he found himself hanging by his two hands. With a soft groan of effort, he heaved himself upward. His right foot found the ledge and took some of the strain—not too much, as he didn't trust the footing.

He blessed the years spent practicing with his bow and the development of his arm and back muscles that had resulted. Now his left foot was back on the ledge and took a little of his weight as well.

Slowly, his eyes came level with the bottom windowsill and he could see into the room, to where Alyss sat, slumped at a rough table, her back to the window, her head in her hands.

37

EIGHTY KILOMETERS TO THE SOUTH, AN ARMORED KNIGHT WAS riding into the biting north wind.

The sun had long since sunk below the horizon and darkness had flooded quickly over the land. Any sensible person would have stopped to camp and shelter from the wind-driven sleet and snow long ago. Yet the knight continued to force his way northward.

His surcoat was white and his shield was marked with a blue fist, the symbol of a free lance—a knight looking for employment wherever he could find it. The knight's equipment was standard—a heavy lance was couched in a receptacle on his right stirrup and a long cavalry sword could be seen beneath his cloak. Only the shield was unusual. In an age where most knights preferred kite-shaped shields, this one was a round buckler.

The battlehorse beneath him danced a few steps sideways, trying to edge away from the bitter wind and the stinging sleet that it carried. Gently, he urged it back onto its northern course.

"Just a little farther, Kicker," he said, the words coming thick and slurred from his half-frozen lips.

The horse was right, he thought. It was madness to continue

traveling in this weather. But he knew there was a small hamlet a few kilometers farther along the road, and the protection of a barn's walls would be more comfortable than any shelter he could rig among the trees. He half regretted that he hadn't stopped in the late afternoon, when he'd ridden through a village with a comfortable-looking inn. That would be a nice place to be right now, he thought.

Then he thought of his friends and the possible danger they were in and he didn't begrudge his decision to keep forging on through the dark cold night.

Although he doubted if Kicker agreed. He tried to grin at the thought but his lips were too stiff and ice-rimmed now.

He shifted uncomfortably in the saddle, feeling an icy runnel of water slide down his back, and thought back to his meeting with Halt and Crowley, a few days previously.

"So you want me to go to Macindaw?" he'd said thoughtfully. "What do you think I can do that Will and Alyss can't?"

They were in Crowley's office in one of the soaring towers of Castle Araluen. It was a small room but comfortably furnished and kept warm by an open fire in one corner. Halt and Crowley exchanged glances and the Ranger Commandant gestured for Halt to answer.

"We'd feel better if Will and Alyss had a little more force at their disposal," Halt said.

Horace smiled. "I'm just one man."

Halt regarded him keenly. "You're a lot more than that, Horace," he said. "I've seen you at work, remember? I'd feel reassured to know that you're covering Will's back. And we need to send someone they'll both recognize and trust."

Horace grinned at the prospect. "It'll be nice to see them again," he said. Life at Castle Araluen in winter tended to become a little boring. The idea of being sent on a solo mission like this had definite appeal. He and Alyss had been friends since childhood and he hadn't seen Will, his best friend, in several months.

Halt stood and paced to the window, looking out over the gray winter landscape that surrounded the castle. This far south, there was no snow but the cold bare trees had a desolate look to them that matched his mood.

"It's the uncertainty that's worrying us, Horace," he said. "By now we should have had a routine message from Alyss's man. Or a reply to the pigeon we sent yesterday. After all, they didn't have to wait for the bird to recover. He had another half dozen ready to send."

"Of course, a hawk might have taken the pigeon we sent," Crowley put in. "That does happen."

Halt showed a flash of annoyance and Horace sensed that the two old friends had already been through this conversation— possibly more than once.

"I *know* that, Crowley!" he said crisply. He looked at Horace again. "It may all be nothing. Crowley may be right. But I don't want to take chances. I'd like to know that you're on your way. If we hear from them in the meantime, we can always send a messenger to recall you."

Horace regarded the small gray-haired Ranger with some warmth. Halt was more worried than he might otherwise have been because it was Will who was up there in the snow-covered northern fief, Horace realized. No matter how many years passed, a part of Halt would always see Will as his young apprentice. He moved toward the Ranger.

"Don't worry, Halt," he said quietly. "I'll see that he's all right."

Halt's eyes showed his gratitude. "Thanks, Horace."

"That's Hawken," Crowley put in, deciding it was time to get on with the business at hand. "Better get used to it."

Horace frowned at him, not understanding.

"That's your new identity," Crowley told him. "It's a secret mission and we can hardly have the most famous young knight in Araluen turning up in Norgate Fief. You'll go as Sir Hawken and you'll be a free lance. Better get your shield painted accordingly."

Horace nodded. "So I'll provide the muscle and let Will and Alyss do all the thinking?" he said cheerfully.

Halt regarded him seriously, with a slight shake of his head. "Don't sell yourself short, Horace," he said. "You're a good thinker. You're steady and you're practical. Sometimes we devious Rangers and Couriers need that sort of thinking to keep us on track."

Horace was surprised by the statement. Nobody had ever called him a good thinker before.

"Thanks for that, Halt," he said. Then his smile broke out again. "I can't convince you to come with me? Be like old times in Gallica."

This time, Halt smiled as he shook his head again. "There's already one Ranger in Macindaw," he said. "For anything short of a full-scale invasion, one is usually enough."

The wind had picked up and the sleet was blowing harder into their faces. Kicker grumbled a complaint, tossing his head, and Horace leaned forward to pat the battlehorse's neck.

"Not much farther to go, Kicker," he said. "Just give me a few more kilometers. Will needs us."

38

"ALYSS!" THE BLOND GIRL SAT UP, STARTLED, AT THE WHISPERED sound of her name. She swung around in the chair to see Will's face at the barred window, the familiar, irrepressible grin lighting up his features.

She rose quickly. The chair toppled backward as she did so and she only just caught it in time and stopped it from clattering to the floor. Then she crossed quickly to the window.

"Will? My God! How did you get here?"

She looked out at the dizzying drop below him and realized he was perched on the narrow, ice-covered ledge with no other sign of support. She recoiled a half step, her head swimming. Alyss would face most dangers without flinching but she had a terrible head for heights. The sight of the dark drop below the window filled her with dread. Will was fumbling beneath his cloak now and beginning to thread the end of a long rope through the bars.

"I'm here to get you out," he told her. "Just hold tight for a few minutes."

She looked anxiously over her shoulder at the door as he continued to feed the rope through into the room, uncoiling it from beneath his cloak. Her mouth went dry as she realized what Will had in mind.

"You want me to climb down there?" she said, pointing fearfully at the drop below him. He grinned reassuringly.

"It's easy," he told her. "And I'll be here to help you."

"Will, I can't!" she said, her voice breaking. "I can't bear heights. I'll fall. I'll freeze up. I can't do it!"

Will stopped for a moment, contemplating. He knew that there were people who were terrified of heights. Personally, he couldn't understand it. All his life he had been totally at ease scaling trees, cliffs, castle walls. But he realized that such a fear could be totally debilitating. He frowned briefly, then smiled.

"No problem," he said. "I'll tie the rope around your waist and lower you down from here."

The last coil of the rope was free now and it fell onto the pile beneath the window.

Then Alyss realized that her fear of heights was immaterial. There was no way out through those bars—unless Will planned to file through them, a task that would take far too long. She looked fearfully at the door again. Keren said he would be back in an hour or so. How long had she been slumped at the table? Did "an hour or so" mean half an hour? Forty minutes? He could be on his way now.

"You have to get out of here," she said, a new purpose in her voice. "Keren could come back at any minute."

"Then he'll wish he hadn't," Will said, his grin fading. "Have you figured out what he's up to?" he asked. He figured that the best way to stop her from worrying about the climb was to distract her. Alyss shook her head impatiently as he fumbled about behind his back, producing a small leather-covered bottle from beneath his cloak. He handled it very gingerly as he laid it on the windowsill, she noticed.

"You have to go!" she told him. "We don't have time. He's coming back to question me again."

Will stopped what he was doing. "Again?" he said. "Has he hurt you?" His voice was cold. If Keren had harmed her, he was a dead man. But she shook her head once more.

"No. He hasn't hurt me. But he has this strange stone . . ." Her voice trailed off. She didn't want to tell him how close she had come to betraying his real identity.

"A stone?" he repeated, puzzled.

She nodded. "A blue gemstone. It . . . somehow . . . makes me say whatever he wants me to. Will, I nearly told him you're a Ranger!" she blurted out. "I couldn't stop myself. It just . . . makes you answer questions. It's uncanny."

Will frowned thoughtfully. A memory stirred of his first night in the castle dining hall, when Keren's followers reacted so enthusiastically to his suggestion that Will should perform another song. Perhaps the usurper had been dabbling in mind control for some time.

He pushed the thought aside. Drawing his saxe knife, he began to chip away the mortar at the base of the middle bar to form a well for the acid. There were four bars in all and he thought if he removed the middle two it would create a large enough space for his purposes. He could climb into the room and tie the rope around Alyss's waist, using one of the remaining bars to give him purchase as he lowered her to the ground. Once that was done, he'd tie the rope off and go down it himself.

"Well," he said, "no harm done there. If Buttle's here he's probably guessed who I am anyway." He smiled to try to lighten her mood, but he could see she was upset by what she saw as her own weakness.

"He could only suspect it," she said miserably. "He couldn't be sure. But somehow he nearly got me to tell him."

"It sounds as if Keren has been our sorcerer all along," Will said thoughtfully. Alyss looked at him, puzzled.

"What do you mean?" she asked.

"He's the one behind Lord Syron's mystery illness. And he's managed to poison Orman as well. That's why I had to get him out of here. Now you tell me he has some mysterious way of making you answer his questions. Keren has used the old legend, and the stories about Malkallam, as a smokescreen for his own treachery. He wants to take over the castle—although how he plans to keep it once word gets out is beyond me."

"He's done a deal with the Scotti," she said. Earlier, she had made the accusation against Keren as a wild stab in the dark. His answer had confirmed her suspicions.

"The Scotti?" he said. He thought for a moment. If the Scotti had control of Castle Macindaw, their path into Araluen would be secure. They could raid the surrounding countryside with impunity, even stage a full-scale invasion. Small as it was, Macindaw was a vital key to Araluen's northern security. "Then we've really got to stop him!"

"That's right!" Alyss said, a new sense of urgency in her tone. "That's why you've got to get out of here now! Go to Norgate and raise the alarm. Bring back an army to stop him!"

Will was concentrating on the strange leather flask, the tip of his tongue poked out between his front teeth as he carefully removed the stopper. He looked up at her briefly and shook his head.

"Not without you," he said. Very carefully, he poured a small amount of the liquid from the bottle into the depression he had gouged around the base of the iron bar. The liquid fumed as it hit the stone and iron, melting some of the ice around the depression as it did so. The cloud of pungent fumes that rose set Will coughing. He tried to smother the sound, with limited success. Alyss moved back a pace or two, covering her nostrils with a corner of her sleeve.

"What is that stuff?" she said.

"It's acid. Very nasty stuff indeed. Malcolm said it would burn through these bars in a few seconds." He frowned. The bar still seemed solid. "Or maybe he said minutes," he amended. He re-stoppered the bottle and moved to the next bar, using his saxe once more to dig a retaining well at the base.

"We'll leave that for now and do the next one. While I'm doing that, you might tie that rope off to one of the other bars."

She did as he asked. But she was still thinking over something he had said.

"Who's Malcolm?" she asked. He looked up at her and smiled.

"That's Malkallam's real name. He's actually quite a nice fellow when you get to know him."

"Which you have, of course," she said dryly. It was so like the Alyss of old that his smile widened.

"I'll tell you all about it later. Just give me a minute, this is the tricky part."

He had the acid bottle again and was pouring liquid into the shallow well he had dug in the stone and mortar. Again, a cloud of bitter fumes billowed up, followed by a smell like burning rust. He paused, lips pursed in concentration, and watched the result. As before, the acid seemed to be taking longer than it should. He tested the first bar and felt a little movement. It was working then—but nowhere near as quickly as he had been led to expect. He considered pouring more acid in, then discarded the idea. It would only spill across the windowsill and that was something he felt they should avoid.

There was nothing they could do but wait. He replaced the stopper and handed the leather bottle through the bars to her.

"Here. Put this somewhere," he told her. He had no wish to do another climb with that stuff in his pocket. Absently, she placed the bottle on its side on top of the deep stone lintel above the window.

"What beats me," he continued, trying to keep her mind off the climb ahead of her, "is where that damned John Buttle sprang from? By now he should be with the wolfship on Skorghijl."

"The wolfship got into trouble," Alyss answered. Buttle had boasted about it when he had first recognized her, before Keren had her brought to this tower room. "They were caught in a storm. It drove them west and they hit a reef off the coast. She was badly holed and they barely made it to shore. They ran up the River Oosel to hide out for the winter—but when they thought the ship was sinking, they untied Buttle, so he'd have a chance."

"I take it he repaid that act of kindness in his usual form?" Will said, and she nodded.

"They were exhausted when they made it to the Oosel. He killed two of the guards and escaped. He came here purely by chance."

"And found he fit in perfectly," Will said. She nodded.

"It's funny," Will continued, "how people like Buttle and Keren seem to find one anoth—"

He stopped in mid-sentence as she held up a hand. He looked at her curiously, seeing the blood drain from her face. She had heard the door to the outer room open and close, and the sound of voices as Keren spoke to the guards outside.

"It's Keren!" she whispered urgently. "Will, you've got to get out of here! Go now!"

She bundled up the rope and shoved it through the bars, letting it fall to the flagstones far below. Will tugged desperately at the first bar. It moved farther now but it was still too solid to remove.

"Go!" Alyss repeated desperately. "If he finds you out there, he'll kill us both."

Reluctantly, Will conceded that she was right. Trapped on this narrow ledge, he couldn't hope to fight Keren and the guards. And at least if he were free, he'd have another chance to rescue Alyss.

There was a burst of laughter from the anteroom outside. Alyss's eyes widened as she heard the key turn in the lock. Will knew he would have to leave, but there was one thing more he had to tell her.

"Alyss," he said, and she looked at him in a fever of agitation. "If he questions you, tell him anything he wants to know. It can't do us any harm now. Just answer his questions."

She couldn't reveal his plans, he thought bitterly, because he didn't have a plan. But there was no sense in her suffering to conceal facts that Keren had probably guessed already.

"All right!" she said.

"Promise me," he insisted. "Nothing you can tell him will harm me."

Alyss was on the verge of panic but she knew he wouldn't go until she had promised.

"I promise! I'll tell him everything! But go! Now!"

He was busy looping the rope between his legs, up his back and over his right shoulder.

He tugged on his gloves and seized the tied-off end of the rope with his left hand about half a meter above his head, using his right to belay the loose end against his hip.

Alyss's stomach heaved as Will let himself plunge backward into space, controlling his fall with the loop of rope running around his body, fending off from the wall with his feet.

"I'll come back for you," he called softly. He began moving slowly down the wall. The temptation was to get to the bottom as quickly as possible, but he knew that rapid movement was more likely to attract the attention of the sentries on the ramparts.

Hurriedly, she moved away from the window, pulling the curtain across it before she did. She had to stop Keren from noticing the rope for as long as possible. If Will were caught halfway down that drop, he was as good as dead.

39

Alyss had barely made it to the table when the door opened and Keren entered. As he locked the door behind him, she took a deep breath and forced herself to calm down, using all her willpower to face him with a look of utter contempt.

"Well, I'm back again," Keren said. He smiled cheerfully at her, ignoring the icy stare she turned on him. Then he frowned, his nose wrinkling as he sniffed the air.

"Good God, what's that dreadful smell? Have you been burning something?"

Alyss thought quickly. She had grown accustomed to the pungent fumes from the acid but they were obviously still in evidence. Keren's question gave her an idea, however. She drew herself up to her full height and looked at him disdainfully.

"Some documents of mine," she said. "I thought it best if you didn't learn what was in them."

Keren regarded her thoughtfully. "Is that right?" he said, a little less cheerfully than before. "I suppose I should have searched you earlier. That's what I get for being a gentleman—you try to deceive me." He reached into the pouch at his belt. "But you seem to forget that my little blue friend here can make you tell me everything that was in them."

Alyss's heart beat faster as he produced the blue stone. In spite of all she knew about it, she felt an almost overpowering compulsion to look at it. She wrenched her eyes away from it with a supreme effort.

"You seem to forget," she said, mimicking his sardonic tone, "that the last time, I managed to break its hold on me."

Keren sat in one of chairs, crossing one leg over the other while he tossed the blue stone casually in his hand. He smiled in genuine amusement.

"True," he told her, "but I did tell you that the second time would be much easier?"

Alyss turned her back on him and walked toward the door, ensuring that his gaze was directed well away from the curtained window. She wasn't sure, but she thought she could hear an occasional creak from the rope tied there.

"Your cheap sorcery doesn't impress me," she said. "It's all tricks and delusions and I know how to counter them."

Keren nodded indulgently at her. "I'm sure you could," he said, "if it was, in fact, sorcery. But this is something altogether different. This is mesmerism—a form of mind domination. The stone is merely a focus point for your mind. It relaxes you and helps me control you."

Alyss laughed scornfully, although she was deeply worried by what he had just told her. She was way out of her depth here, she realized. But she had to play the game out to give Will more time.

"And now that you've told me, I'll make sure I resist the temptation to relax," she said. Keren shook his head.

"Normally, you could do that. If you know the purpose of the stone, you can resist it. But you've already been entrapped. And that initial control creates something called 'post-hypnotic suggestion.' "

Alyss rolled her eyes in derision. "How absolutely terrifying," she said. But a worm of fear was eating away inside her. Keren was altogether too confident, and the one thing she had learned about him was that he didn't make empty boasts.

"Not terrifying. Just useful," he said, in an eminently reasonable tone. "You see, while you're hypnotized, I can plant a suggestion in your inner mind that will allow me to bring you instantly under my control again. All I have to do is go back to the subject we were last discussing."

"I'm sure it was quite boring," she said sarcastically. But the fear was growing with each word he spoke. He continued to smile at her. He admired her courage and her fighting spirit. But then, he thought, he could afford to admire it because he could mesmerize her again in an instant. He held the stone up before her. She quickly turned her face away.

"No, no, no," he said smoothly. "You have to look at the stone." She kept her eyes averted and a threatening edge crept into his voice. "I can have my men force you to do it if you refuse. But you *will* do it."

Reluctantly, she allowed her gaze to return to the stone. So blue. So deep. So beautiful.

Keren's voice seemed to come from a long way away. It was deep and soothing now. There was no threat in it.

"Just relax, Alyss. Relax and breathe deeply. That's the way. Good girl. Isn't this a much more pleasant way to behave?"

"Yes," she said dreamily. "Much more pleasant."

"Now, as I recall," his voice went on, seeming to fill her consciousness. "We were talking about your friend Will the last time."

"Will is a Ranger," she said. Deep within her mind there was a sense that she had said something wrong. Something she should have kept secret. For a moment, she felt a vague sense of revulsion at her craven behavior.

"Of course he is. We knew that anyway," said the soothing voice, and she felt a little better. If he knew, there was no harm in her telling. "But now I'm interested in those documents you burned. Tell me about them."

"There were no documents," she said. Again, on another level, her mind struggled to regain control. Her words were flat and unemotional and she couldn't stop herself as she realized she was revealing the most dangerous secret of all. "It was the acid you could smell."

His smile disappeared and a small frown took its place. He didn't understand . . .

"Acid? What acid?" he asked her quickly.

"Will put acid on the bars," Alyss said. Inside, her mind was screaming: Shut up! For God's sake, shut up! Will needs time to get away, you weak coward! Then, horrified, she heard herself saying the last few words.

"Will needs time to get away."

Comprehension dawned on Keren's face as she said it. He hurled himself out of the chair. All signs of the relaxed, casual attitude he had assumed were now dispelled as the chair crashed to the floor behind him. He reached the window in two long paces and tore the heavy curtain to one side.

The fumes were much stronger now as the acid continued to eat through the iron of the bars. Thin spirals of smoke rose from the bases of the two center bars, which he could see were surrounded by small pools of liquid. The acid, formerly clear, was now a rusty brown color as it destroyed the iron. Keren grasped the right-hand bar and tugged at it, breaking through the last threads of iron that held it in place. His eyes narrowed and he turned back toward Alyss.

"Where has he gone?" he demanded. Logic told him that Barton could not have escaped out of the window, although how he had made it into the room in the first place puzzled him.

It didn't occur to him that Will had never been inside the room itself. And, his eyes drawn by the fuming pools of acid around the two middle bars, he hadn't noticed the rope tied around the extreme left-hand bar.

There was no answer from Alyss. Overcome by the conflicting strain in her mind, she had collapsed in a faint as he erupted from his chair. She lay crumpled on the floor beside his overturned chair. Cursing quietly, he started toward her. He'd get the answer, he promised himself, if he had to beat it out of her. Then he stopped as he heard a slight creaking sound from the window. He spun back and this time he saw the loop of rope around the bottom of the bar. He dashed forward, cursing again as he leaned on the windowsill and burned his hand on a splash of acid. The rope was taut, the fibers creaking as it moved slightly with the weight of something—or someone—on the end.

In a second, Keren had his dagger out, reaching through the bars to saw at the taut rope, feeling the strands give way under the knife. He thought of summoning the guards outside Alyss's cell, then realized there were others closer to hand. He shouted at the top of his lungs to the sentries on the wall.

"Guards! Guards! Intruder in the castle! Intruder in the keep! Stop him!"

Far below, Will heard the shouts, felt the faint vibration on the rope as Keren sawed away with his knife. Knowing he had only seconds, he released his feet, letting them drop below him so that he swung in against the wall. Desperately, he scrabbled with his right hand for a handhold, finally finding a deep crevice between two of the granite blocks. Then he released his grip with the left hand and sought another vantage point. He had no sooner done so than the severed rope came tumbling down past him, coiling on the flagstones below like a giant serpent.

He was still seven meters from the bottom of the tower and he could hear the confused cries of the sentries on the ramparts behind him as they tried to make sense of Keren's words. He scrambled recklessly down, tearing skin and nails as he went, ripping the thick hose over his knees against the rough stone of the wall. With three meters to go, he let himself drop, landing like a cat, letting ankles and knees flex to take the shock. All around him, confused shouts were echoing as the sentries called to one another, trying to make out what was happening.

Four meters away, the door into the keep tower flew open and a sergeant, armed with a halberd—a combined ax and spear set on a long handle—dashed out, looking from left to right to see what was going on. Before the man noticed him, Will dashed the cowl back on his hood and stepped out into the half-light, pointing at the tangled pile of rope.

"He came this way!" he shouted. "After him! He's heading for the stables!"

It was only natural for the sergeant to react to the peremptory tone of command. In the confusion of the moment, the last thing he considered was that the person barking orders at him might be the very intruder he was looking for. He moved in the direction Will had indicated. As he came closer, he lost the advantage of his long-handled weapon, as Will intended.

Too late, he recognized the young face of the jongleur who had escaped the day before.

"Just a minute," he said, "you're—" Even before he finished the sentence, he lunged clumsily with the halberd. Will's saxe knife was in his hand and he deflected the heavy ax head to one side. Grabbing the sergeant's arm, turning and crouching in one movement, he threw him over his shoulder to the flagstones of the courtyard. The sergeant's head slammed into the hard stone. His helmet rolled to one side and he lay stunned.

Will grabbed the helmet and the long, heavy weapon. Then he paused to cut a length of rope from the pile before heading for the stairs. Far above in the tower, he could hear Keren shouting as he saw him running. Will started shouting too, partly to drown him out and partly to add to the confusion.

"They're in the keep!" he yelled. "Hundreds of them! All guards assemble at the gatehouse!"

He pounded up the stairs to the battlements, continuing to shout a string of contradictory orders, directing men to the gate-house, the keep and the north tower, clapping the sergeant's heavy iron helmet onto his own head as he went. Confusion was his best ally, he knew. That and the fact that he knew everyone he saw was an enemy, whereas the castle guards would have to identify each new person as they saw them.

He emerged onto the rampart of the south wall, by the battle-ments. There were three sentries running toward him, the western tower door behind him. The men paused as they saw him. He ges-tured wildly toward the wall behind them.

"Get down, you fools! They've got archers!" he yelled. Since they didn't expect an enemy to warn them of imminent danger, the three men obeyed instantly, dropping flat to the ground, expecting the hiss and thud of arrows any second.

Will turned and dashed into the tower, slamming the door behind him. There was a large barrel nearby and he rolled it against the door before exiting through the other side to the west battlements. There were more men running and shouting at the far end, but here it was relatively quiet, although he could hear footsteps pounding down the internal stairs from the tower battlements. Deftly, he looped the rope over the halberd staff in a series of half hitches, then wedged the halberd between two of the crenellations, letting the free end of the rope fall outside the wall.

Holding the rope, he dropped over the edge, walking backward down the rough stone. He came to the end of the rope before he reached the ground. Looking around, he saw that he had less than two meters to fall and dropped the rest of the way. This time, he didn't land so easily, hitting the uneven ground and toppling onto his side, cracking his knee against a sharp rock.

"I'm going to have to use longer ropes," he muttered. Then, reasoning that any pursuit would come to this side of the tower, he backtracked, limping around the base of the tower to the southern wall, staying close to the rough stone and remaining in the deep shadow of the tower and the wall itself. Once there, he let go a piercing whistle—a short, high-pitched sound that ascended one tone.

Above him, there was the sound of shouting and running feet. Orders and counterorders were being yelled. He could no longer hear Keren's voice, and he guessed that the renegade knight was pounding down the stairway from the top of the keep to take control of the hunt. Let him pound, he thought grimly. He whistled again. Nobody in the castle seemed to notice the sound in all the confusion. But one hundred and fifty meters away, just beyond a slight rise, keener ears were listening.

Will was about to whistle again when he heard the faint drumming of hoofbeats. It was a gait he recognized easily—Tug's short-legged, churning gallop.

He saw the little horse top the rise and start toward the castle, heading slightly to the right of where Will was concealed. He whistled again and Tug corrected, swinging to run down straight to him.

Abandoning any attempt at concealment, Will now sprinted away from the castle. He heard more shouts behind him, but whether he had been discovered or whether it was just part of the ongoing confusion he had no idea. Nor did he have any desire to stop and find out.

Tug slid to a stiff-legged halt beside him, ears back, teeth bared as he neighed a greeting. Will didn't bother to mount. He grabbed hold of the pommel with both hands as the little horse spun about in his tracks.

"Go!" he urged. "Go! Go! Go!"

Now he could hear shouts from the ramparts and he knew he had been sighted. But unless anybody had a crossbow ready and was capable of hitting a fast-moving target in the half-light, he knew he was safe. Tug gathered and launched himself away from the castle, reaching a full gallop within half a dozen strides. Knees drawn up to clear the ground, Will hung from the saddle for a few meters, then, judging his moment and his horse's speed and gait, he let his feet touch the ground, using the impact and the momentum to swing up into the saddle. Tug shook his head in approval.

"Good boy," Will told him, leaning low over his neck to pat him.

Without breaking stride, Tug neighed briefly. There was a note of condemnation in the sound.

I thought I told you to stay out of trouble.

"Don't be a nag," Will said. Tug very rightly ignored him. They crested the rise and Will saw the dim figures of Xander and Malcolm waiting for him. He checked Tug with a twitch of the reins.

"What happened?" Xander asked. Will shook his head.

"I saw her. Spoke to her. But Keren arrived before I could get her out, damn him."

"So what do you plan to do now?" said Malcolm.

"Now, we head back to the forest," Will said, giving in to the inevitable.

Xander looked at him curiously. The young Ranger seemed to be admitting defeat, but there was a note of grim determination in his voice. Xander knew that this matter was a long way from finished.

"What then?" he asked.

Will turned to face him. The deep cowl of his cloak hid the top part of his face in shadow. Xander could see only the mouth and the determined set of his jaw.

"Then," he said, "I'm getting Alyss out of your damned castle— if I have to take it apart stone by stone to do it."